'An affecting and humane tale of atonement in a troubled society'
Guardian

'A complex and exciting work of fiction which moves to a terrific climax . . . The scenes have a devastating accuracy, with a tender depiction of love among the disregarded and abused' *Independent*

'A deeply impressive novel . . . at once surprising, thematically rich and often very moving. Wilson's unshowy but always precise and often lyrical prose adds to the impression of accomplishment'
Observer

'Wilson's powerfully compassionate novel is a moving book that weaves its tale of everyday transcendence with an understanding of the profound damage that humans can be forced to suffer, and the astonishing capacity of the human spirit to overcome it' *Metro*

'Paul Wilson's stunning, shattering, and ultimately moving tale is not for the faint-hearted' *Daily Mirror*

'A joy to read . . . wonderful writing by a very talented author'
New Books

'Wilson is one of a number of writers who really should be making the Booker shortlist on a regular basis . . . He is serious without being obscure or difficult. He is that golden-egg of publishing at the moment; a potential literary-bestseller; who deserves his place on the top table with McEwan, Barnes, and the like' *Book Munch*

'A great writer' Catherine O'Flynn

'Wilson takes th   ld considers failures and
portray   th a sense of
each in   e'
                                                        Carol Birch

Also by Paul Wilson

The Fall from Grace of Harry Angel

Days of Good Hope

Do White Whales Sing at the Edge of the World?

Noah, Noah

Someone to Watch Over Me

The Visiting Angel

Paul Wilson

**Tindal
Street
Press**

This edition published in 2012
by Tindal Street Press Ltd
First published in 2011
by Tindal Street Press Ltd
217 The Custard Factory, Gibb Street,
Birmingham, B9 4AA
www.tindalstreet.co.uk

2 4 6 8 10 9 7 5 3 1

A CIP catalogue reference for this book is available
from the British Library

ISBN: 978 1 906994 29 7

Typeset by Alma Books Ltd
Printed and bound in Great Britain by
CPI Mackays, Chatham ME5 8TD

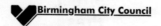

To Shirley, a love story

Chapter 1 – The King of Providence   11

Chapter 2 – The Grace of Swimmers   41

Chapter 3 – The Memory of Objects   68

Chapter 4 – The Naming of Parts   94

Chapter 5 – The Rules of Flight   117

Chapter 6 – The Faith of Angels   146

Chapter 7 – The Weight of Dreams   178

Chapter 8 – The Theory of Everything   213

Chapter 9 – Switzerland   248

Chapter 10 – One Quiet Night   276

'Each of us is meant to rescue the world.'
Confucius

I

THE KING OF PROVIDENCE

His brother, as a boy, was unafraid of heights.

'He's from the angels,' Patrick's mother used to whisper to him, as if in explanation of the fact that Liam seemed to be gifted in ways that he was not. He would be sat on her knee, playing with the band on her finger, turning it curiously so that it caught the light in the room. She would say it in fun, but Patrick was only seven when she told him for the last time and so a part of him was prepared to believe that it was true. Their mother, after all, was familiar with these things. She always dreamed of angels the night before a baby was born to someone she knew. She smelled violets in the night when someone had died.

She carried such hope for her two boys. 'Pass here, you princes of hope,' she would say as she rounded them up for the tea table, or for the Sunday evening bath they shared together in front of the fire in the back room, leaning with the palm of her ringed left hand flat against the doorframe so that her good arm, her strong arm in which she could pick them up, formed an arch for them to pass beneath.

Liam had been the most successful scaler of trees in the neighbourhood. He was not the best climber but he was the least daunted. It was a kind of wilfulness that permeated everything he did. Each winter, when the boating lake in the corporation park froze over, Liam beseeched their mother to take him there, and while she glided sedately from bank to bank on skates that had once been her mother's, Liam would propel himself furiously across the ice, his arms outstretched, his legs stiff, his face beatified by the cold and the concentration required to stay upright. Patrick meanwhile, eleven months younger than his brother, less knowing about the world, stoically asthmatic and wary of the ice, would stand and watch from the little wooden jetty by the boat hut, imagining all the while that the business of growing up – the accrual of secret knowledge and simple bravery – meant nothing more or less than the act of becoming Liam.

As a boy, Patrick had difficulty learning to read. The letters would not lie still and hold their meaning for him, sliding like snakes in his head. He couldn't grasp how, to other people, written words could be joined on the page into sentences, and the sentences woven into stories. As a consequence, he didn't always understand the difference between his brother reporting tales he had read in books, and at other times entertaining him with imagined accounts of his own. He thought that Liam was making them all up himself. In his adult life, he would learn to recognize his symptoms as dyslexia and a few good people would do much to remedy things, but growing up on the outskirts of Manchester in the sixties there was no one to make such a diagnosis and so he was considered to be a slow child. In contrast, Liam had made it clear from an early age that when he grew up he was going to be a writer – in London, or New York. That was where all writers lived – on the tops of skyscrapers, Liam said, so they could watch like sentries as people lived their lives down below.

To bring stories to life like his brother did, Patrick came to realize that an author walked a fine line between what to reveal and what to withhold.

'There's a trick to telling stories,' Liam used to say to him.

Although for years Patrick was unable to read the printed words of stories himself, he was an attentive listener. The stories Liam made up came alive in Patrick's head. They were so good that Patrick was convinced throughout much of his childhood that his brother *knew* all the people in the stories he told. He thought that all Liam's tales were his own, that everything was true, that somehow – skating out across the rooftops and ledges of the world whenever he was out of Patrick's sight – he bore witness to these stories unfolding beneath him and then came back to report them, honed and beautifully balanced, to his brother. Patrick grasped instinctively how, just like the skill required to traverse high places, storytelling was all about balance. He saw how the endings of Liam's stories always drew everything together. He understood how *that* was the trick. When Patrick asked his brother where the stories came from, Liam shrugged as if he hadn't ever paused to wonder about it before and said vaguely, 'I dream them.'

Patrick waited for his own dreams to come, but they never did.

When news of Liam's death reached him, Patrick had not seen his brother for many years. It was a friend of Liam's who wrote to tell him. The letter was unspecific about how he had died. Patrick wondered whether it was possible for someone to have been so hungry for new things that he could simply have used up his full life early. It struck him at the time that Liam would have reached forty in the week of his death. Perhaps half a life. It occurred to him that even here, in the timing of his brother's death, there was a storyteller's symmetry.

For some reason, perhaps because of that sense of timing, or through some ambiguity in the letter, it had crossed Patrick's mind that his brother's death may not have been an accident. He had no evidence to support this. Liam's brief notes over the years – written on anything from the backs of postcards to restaurant napkins, sent latterly from America and running generally to no more than two or three lines – had shown no hint of trouble or distress, but nevertheless the thought had entered Patrick's head.

As a consequence, Patrick would sometimes find himself speculating about the manner of his brother's death. He was drawn to imagining Liam on some high place – a roof, a bridge. Liam would be standing quite still. He was calm and almost smiling each time Patrick pictured him. Patrick would sense the air currents at that sickening height flowing past his brother in waves. He could visualize Liam closing his eyes, raising his arms out wide. He would see Liam stepping off into the universe's high and empty spaces and floating, falling, star-shaped, unperturbed.

The letter Patrick received explained that a non-denominational cremation had taken place some weeks before in Brooklyn, and only subsequently had it come to the attention of those who knew Liam in New York that he had a brother who lived in England. The letter-writer was sorry that Patrick had missed the funeral, and enclosed some small personal mementos which he felt Liam might have liked him to have: a photograph of Liam in a diner as a young man holding a copy of his first novel, and a rosewood jewellery box that had once been their mother's. Patrick used the box to store all Liam's letters, taking them out randomly to read now and then. He pinned the photograph to the notice-board in his office at the Limes, beneath two pictures he had torn years before from magazine articles about high-wire walkers. The wire walkers' art, their bravura, had reminded him of Liam. They had consoled Patrick in his own earthbound state.

There had seemed no point in Patrick organizing any sort of memorial service. There was no one else he knew who might have known Liam when they were growing up. But he often found himself wondering, afterwards, what he would have said at such a service. What kind of eulogy would he have delivered?

Patrick had no doubt he would have found the task traumatic. This was not purely because of the emotion of the event. He was an uncomfortable public speaker and he would have felt the need to prepare by writing down his speech word for word. In the days beforehand he would have forced himself into repeated rehearsals. At the event itself, he would have tried to avoid looking out at the congregation from the lectern of the church, to concentrate solely on what he was reading out loud, to trace each word as he approached it with the tip of his finger. He knew, as well, that somewhere high above him as he imagined it – amongst the rafters of the nave – Liam would be smiling in wry amusement at Patrick's decision to use a Catholic church to mark his death. His brother would have been puzzled by Patrick's decision to stage the kind of service that reflected so little of him. He would have perceived it as the legacy of a simple-minded childhood credulity that Liam himself was never really given to.

Patrick often wondered what he might have said at the service. He supposed he would have talked about how we all get gathered up in the wool of life. He would have conceded that we all get distracted by things that turn out to be irrelevant. He would have confessed that he had spent most of his own adult life weighed down by unnecessary boyish fears (waking suddenly in the night with his heart pounding, speaking to strangers on the telephone), constricted by pet loathings (wooden dominoes, the colour yellow, the country Switzerland), and the sense that his brother was, in his own mind, the only person he knew who had somehow managed to rise clear of this sort of junk. Perhaps Patrick would simply have admitted that, even as boys, Liam had already seemed more prepared than him for the lives that lay ahead of them.

But in amongst all these misgivings, Patrick knew for certain how he would have begun his eulogy.

'My brother, as a boy,' he would have started out, 'was unafraid of heights.'

The gasp of Patrick's breathing, the smack of his shoes on the pavement, made people momentarily wary. He was dressed in corduroys, and a collared shirt that had worked free and was flapping from his waist. The pedestrians around him, sluggish, solitary, shuffled along in coats through the streets that were softened by Manchester's evening drizzle. Their journeys were unremarkable except for the small drama of the anxious man running past them in a flapping shirt. They were making for the train station and the outlying car parks; they were done for another day, heading home to make tea and put the telly on, curious to see if 'Little Lucy' was still missing in the city.

There was a lack of grace to Patrick's movements as he ran. His shoulders were too tight, his feet splayed. Then his mobile phone started to ring. Reluctant to slow down, he grappled to pull it free from his trouser pocket. Without stopping, he held the mobile up close to his face, squinting to see if he recognized the number of the caller, panting all the while. A pair of youths walking towards him smirked at the sight of his middle-aged foolishness.

'Knees up.'

'Missed your fucking bus, mate.'

Patrick was oblivious. He let the mobile continue to ring until it tripped to the message function, clutching it in one hand as if it were a baton he was intending to hand over in some urgent and inexplicable street relay. He ran on, dodging between the lines of people, slapping through small puddles. Further along the road, before the lights stopped the traffic at the T-junction, he turned into the wide courtyard entrance of the police station.

Inside the reception area, Patrick could feel his chest tensing in the sudden stale warmth. He felt for his salbutamol, held it to his mouth and inhaled a shot of the spray. Already, the sweat was rising on him. It made his shirt stick to him between his shoulder blades. He felt gobbets of sweat swelling on the dome of his head from where his hair was receding. He told the duty officer who he was and gave him the name of the detective.

While he waited for the detective to come through, he checked the message on his mobile. It was a referral request. He could deal with it later. He switched the mobile off. He was still breathing hard when the detective appeared.

'Patrick Shepherd?'

Patrick nodded. 'What's happened to Edward?'

'We need to go and talk for a minute before we interview him.'

Patrick was led through several sets of double doors to a vacant interview room.

'I want to check a couple of things,' the detective said.

'What's he done?' Patrick said. 'Is he all right?'

'You run the residential place where Edward Lyle used to live, is that right?'

Patrick nodded.

'Are you still responsible for him?'

'Am I responsible?'

'Are you in charge?'

'I visit him. I keep an eye on him.'

'How long have you known him?'

'About a year.'

'What sort of place is it?'

'Hobart Trust? It's mental health rehabilitation.'

'What do you call them – patients?'

'Residents. Edward moved out about three months ago when he and Lillian got married. Lillian was another of the residents. They met while they were there.'

'So what exactly is wrong with him?'

'With Edward? How do you mean?'

'The police surgeon advised us to have an appropriate adult present during questioning, which is why you're here.

I'm trying to work out whether he's mostly mental health or if he's backward.'

'If he's been arrested for something, he's probably mostly frightened.'

The detective looked at him.

'It takes him a while to get used to new things,' Patrick said. 'He struggles with reading and writing. He goes to an adult literacy class at the college. Will you tell me what's happened?'

'Any problems with him? That you're aware of?'

'He and Lillian have had a bit of bother with some of the local kids.'

'What sort of bother?'

'I'm not sure. General harassment, baiting them in the street, that kind of thing. They look different. They're easy targets if you get your kicks like that. Will you tell me what you're holding him for?'

'He got picked up in the park near the Gallowfield estate in the night by a patrol car.'

'They live on the Gallowfield estate. Edward doesn't sleep well. He'll often go out walking at night.'

'At the time the officers stopped him, he told them he was looking for Lucy.'

'The missing girl?'

The detective nodded.

'He can get obsessive when he's worried. It's the kind of thing – the missing child – that would affect him. There's something else. I was round at Edward's flat yesterday. He told me Lillian has gone back to her sister's. I'm not sure why. That's bound to be distressing him. I'm trying to contact Lillian's sister to find out what's happening.'

'Do you think that might be enough to send him off the rails?'

'I don't think it's enough to make him abduct a little girl. I thought there was another incident. A man with a car trying to coax a child into it. Edward doesn't drive.'

'We don't think the two are linked. You know what Gallowfield is like. It could have been anyone who tried to take the other kid. Neighbour, kids, joyriders, anyone.'

'Listen, it wasn't Edward. I know it wasn't. I've worked with him for the last twelve months. He wasn't even speaking when the hospital first referred him. He went from that to being married.'

'Has he got a temper, your man?'

'We've all got a temper if we're pushed enough. It doesn't mean we're gonna go snatching little girls off the street.'

'I just thought – maybe if the big lads on the estate are having a go at him and he can't hit back at them, he gets even by taking it out on one of the little ones.'

'It's not Edward who took the girl.'

'You can account for all his movements in the last eight days?'

'I don't mean that. I mean –'

'We did some digging on your man. You'll know what we found.'

'You looked at his file?'

The detective shrugged an acknowledgement.

'That was twenty years ago,' Patrick said.

'It's a schedule one offence. He was convicted.'

'It was a misunderstanding. He knew nothing. It was some girl in a pub who shouldn't have been there who'd been teasing him with her mates all night. He pushed her up against a wall in an alley outside and grabbed her breast.'

'She was fifteen.'

'She knew more than he did. He was stupid. He learned. It's a million miles from abducting a six-year-old.'

'When the officers picked him up he was carrying a child's anorak in a carrier bag.'

'You think he stole an anorak?'

'Not exactly.'

'What then?'

'They asked him whose anorak it was. He wouldn't say. He got agitated, started walking away. The thing is, we know who the anorak belongs to.'

'So can't you just return it? You think Edward stole an anorak?'

'It belongs to the missing child.'

'The little girl? Lucy?'

The detective let Patrick's question hang in the air between them.

'Are you sure?' Patrick said.

'It's the girl's coat. It's got her name in it. It's been ID'd. One theory is that he was out in the middle of the night trying to ditch it when the patrol car came across him. He won't say himself why he had the coat.'

Patrick said nothing. He brushed the flat of his hand slowly over his head. He left it braced at the back of his neck. He felt a creeping breath escape from him slowly. He closed his eyes.

'He won't see a solicitor,' the detective said.

Patrick nodded.

'We told him legal aid would pay, but he was adamant.'

'He's frightened of anyone in a suit,' Patrick said. 'Especially lawyers. What happens if he carries on not speaking?'

'You need to hope he does say something. For his sake.'

'Haven't you got to charge him after twenty-four hours?'

'The Super can agree another seventy-two hours on extended detention. And we'd go for a warrant to search the flat.'

'What happens after that?'

'We'd go to court to get an order if we still needed one.'

But when they went next door for the interview, Edward wouldn't talk about the missing girl. When the detective asked him about the coat, he shrugged. When Patrick asked him again about Lillian, he just looked steadily away into the corner of the room.

Afterwards, Patrick sat outside in the courtyard. It was raining more steadily now. His back was pushed against the wall of the police station. A marked patrol car rolled slowly past in search of a parking space. Patrick's shirt was saturated with rain, and with cooled sweat. His car was parked up half a mile way away. He closed his eyes, listening to the sighing of his breaths. He was knocking the back of his head steadily against the brickwork to the slow rhythm of his voice.

'Fuck. Fuck. Fuck.'

Patrick had worked at the Limes for seventeen years. These days there were eleven residents living there and, at any one time, between twenty and thirty former residents whom he continued to support in the community. Patrick thought of them as people who had lost their way. They had turned up shipwrecked at GP surgeries, in casualty, on ledges, the threads of their lives having slowly unravelled.

Whenever he started working with someone new, Patrick asked them about the future. It was something Benedict had taught him. If you close your eyes, he would say, and imagine a better life ahead of you in the distance, what image do you see? What small thing do you picture as part of it? He did it to show them that it was possible, even for lives that had gone badly awry, to envisage something better. It was easier to start small, he said to them – with a single detail. And so they told him what they saw. He kept a record of each one. Clean washing pegged out on a clothes line. Preparing vegetables in a sunny kitchen. The settled feeling that came from listening to someone playing Bach on a cello. A vase filled with cut flowers. A freshly painted blue front door. That was what Edward had imagined when he arrived at the Limes – a blue front door.

Those who came to the Limes shared with Patrick their stories of defeat and disillusionment. They gathered themselves. They looked for ways of starting out again.

Then Patrick moved them out into the community as they took up their independent lives again. That was always the plan. He had come recently to believe that it did not work. Every now and then, usually late at night and out in the long narrow garden at the back of the Limes, Patrick would find himself reflecting on the small dreams that the residents had arrived with – the blue front door, the clean washing on the line, the cut flowers. He would lie there on the grass looking up at the stars, measuring the distance between those fragile symbols of hope and the reality that had subsequently unfolded, calculating in an unselfconscious and arbitrary way the extent of his failure.

When people asked Patrick what kind of work he did, he told them that he listened. People sometimes shrugged, believing they had been taught a lesson not to ask, or they smiled knowingly, believing there was a kind of code in there just waiting to be cracked, seeing it as shorthand for a myriad of other things that they and he secretly understood – recovery, rehabilitation, deliverance. But the truth was that it was harder to believe in those things as the years went by, especially after Benedict had finally been ousted.

Patrick was no longer sure if it was any of those things. He wasn't sure *what* it was he offered other than a general hopefulness, a reverence for the mystery of the thing. Maybe it was the case, he had come to think, that all he really did do was listen. Maybe nothing came of it. Maybe he was nothing more than a bystander. When he had started out with the trust as Benedict's apprentice, things had seemed clearer. Simpler. Back then, all things, including the possibility of his own redemption, had seemed possible.

The Limes was part of the Hobart Trust. The organization ran projects across the north of England and more recently, as its expansion gathered pace, as far south as Oxford and as far west as Bristol. When Patrick had started, the Limes had been classed as a halfway house, staffed by a team of four people who worked closely with the residents for anything up to two years. In recent years, the trust had re-designated projects like his as 'independence units'. As part of the change, there had been a series of staffing culls. The workers who were left had become coordinators working either in pairs or, like Patrick, alone. In the latest change, the residents' stays had been capped at twenty-six weeks. As part of the contract, a fee for 'progressing' the client was then levied on whichever social services department was footing the bill. After that, the trust charged for the cost of community support over a further ten weeks before charging a final completion fee.

The operational director of the trust, Jeff Piggot, had himself once worked under Benedict. These days, Patrick saw little of him or of anyone else from head office. On a regular basis, however, people in curious new parts of the organization under Jeff Piggot's control with names like Quality Services and Systems Review dispatched reports and brochures which arrived unannounced at the Limes in the post. These confirmed that the Hobart Trust was improving year on year. They outlined performance-management systems. They concluded that the organization's continued growth was proof of its success. They argued that the trust was now a national player in the independent social care sector. Yet when Patrick rang up to see if he could have the money to mend the residents' shower, he was told the maintenance budget for the year was spent. When he asked for cover while he was away on leave, he was told it wasn't policy any more. He received emails telling him he was accepting too many unsuitable cases as referrals, meaning the ones that didn't yield quick enough results. The monthly reviews posted out from the Performance Management Unit said he was jeopardizing the unit's income stream by not ticking all the boxes on the progression documentation to confirm that a full set of personal achievement outputs had been positively met. But they weren't, Patrick explained, and the response he got back indicated that he wasn't looking at it in the right way at a time when turnaround and progressions were key words in the organization's expanding business lexicon.

Patrick wasn't clear how things had come to this. In the most recent brochure to arrive, aimed primarily at impressing primary care trusts and social services commissioning managers who contracted with the independent sector, Jeff Piggot and some of the other senior staff at head office were pictured on the front cover in dinner jackets and bow ties at a charity dinner held to mark the fortieth anniversary of the founding of the Hobart Trust. After he saw the photograph, Patrick started to think of the trust as a big ship on the move – a kind of glamorous passenger liner full of shiny people in evening wear typing documents at keyboards and sipping cocktails while someone played piano. He imagined the ship setting sail from port. He pictured himself on the dockside, waving to the liner as it sailed away, left behind in a city filled with people whose lives, he knew, would continue to fall steadily apart around him and who were destined to be referred back to the Limes over and over by the local hospitals or the community mental health team, broken and bowed once more. If he had trouble sleeping, he would sometimes take to the garden at the back of the Limes and describe repeatedly with his outstretched arms the perfect circles of their lives – and his – which led back each time to the same point, and he would wonder out loud to anyone who might be listening at three a.m. just who he had been kidding.

The referral request had come through from the emergency duty team. The woman had tried to ring the hospital social work office, but they had all finished for the weekend.

'There's no one left on site?'

'There's no one to do an assessment until Monday. Sorry, Patrick. Not unless we're talking about sectioning him.'

'And are you?'

'I don't think so – not from what they've said so far. It sounds like there's some evidence of mental distress, but not enough for an admission.'

There was a concern about an out-patient at the hospital's GUM department. There had been no threat of violence, but there was enough unease for hospital security to have been called. Someone in the department had rung social services to ask them to get involved, but the call had tripped through to the emergency duty team who operated the out-of-hours service. It was EDT who had rung Patrick.

'There's no one in his family who'll take responsibility for him?'

'There isn't anyone he knows round here. That's what he's saying – that he's not local.'

'Why's he turned up here?'

'Not sure. Might be work, but it doesn't sound like it. Maybe he does know people locally and he's not saying. But I think I'd want to avoid sticking him in a B&B for the weekend, at least until there was a proper mental health assessment done on him. Will you take him until Monday? Do we still pay a retainer for an emergency bed at your place?'

'It doesn't mean I have to take anyone who gets thrown at me. It's meant to be for locals in crisis. What do you know about him?'

'Nothing yet. The thing is, I haven't even got a surname for him. He's called Saul. That's the name he's given.'

'You're kidding me.'

'And it might be Monday before anyone admits to knowing him, so will you at least have a look at him before you say no?'

'I'm not taking someone I know *nothing* about. It's too big a risk.'

'Patrick, this one's bound to have been in contact with mental health services somewhere in the city. You might be able to get the information out of him yourself if you see him. That way, at least the problem's sorted for the weekend.'

'*If* his story stacks up; and *if* someone at the other end will vouch for him.'

'Come on, Patrick; don't force me to have him sectioned or have to stick him in some crappy B&B.'

'Where is he now?'

'He's still in the clinic at the hospital. He's, er, sat out on a ledge.'

'Oh, for crying out loud! You didn't tell me that before.'

'It's not a suicide, Patrick. They're adamant. He's talking to them. They're trying to coax him back inside for you.'

'Does he know you're talking to me?'

'They've told him they're trying to find him a place to stay. Are you okay with that?'

'I've told you, I'm not making a decision about whether I'll take him until I've seen him. Even then, I'd want a guarantee that there'll be an assessment done on Monday. I don't want him any longer than that if there's a risk he's going to blow.'

'I'll chase them first thing on Monday. I promise.'

'Anything else I should know?'

'Something the nurse in the clinic said – the one who's been talking to him. She's adamant she doesn't think he's dangerous, but she says he's been saying some odd things.'

'How odd?'

'Some delusional stuff. That's when she tried to ring the hospital social work team.'

'Schizo?'

'Maybe. You might want to check him out about medication. It's possible he's missing doses if he's travelling around or sleeping rough.'

'Okay. I'll ring you back later if he'll admit to knowing anyone who might agree to take him in.'

'Or if he blows while you're out there and you need a section?'

'Fine.'

'Patrick . . .'

'Yes?'

'Thanks.'

When Patrick left Providence House at fifteen, he had worked his way through a series of jobs. Carpet factory; auto spare deliveries; refrigeration wholesale; mutual assurance; industrial cleaning products. All the while, it seemed, there was a gulf between his own amateur fumbling self and the crafty world he had been cast adrift in. The point was, he hadn't expected much. He went to night school to try to improve his literacy in his diligent, plodding way, and a succession of unkempt, wearily patient souls in dusty, high-ceilinged classrooms confirmed his idiocy.

'I tell everyone who starts here,' the manager at Barry Brothers Refrigeration said to him, 'if you're going to make it in this business, you've got to show you want it more than the man standing either side of you in the queue for your pay cheque. You've got to make sure it's you who comes out on top. You've got to want to be the best.'

Patrick's colleagues in sales and marketing at Barry Brothers took up the challenge. They understood that, by chance, they hadn't been granted privileged lives by birth, and they resented it. They wanted the keys to a secret garden of weekday golf and patio'd villas and slim-hipped blondes anxious to do their bidding. They wanted to discover the password and join the club – to become real men and displace the big-bellied Rotarians who seemed to have made it ahead of them in easier times and gone soft.

It was a time when, suddenly, everyone had money or the expectation of it, and the sales team at Barry Brothers wanted some too, but they wanted something more; they aspired to wielding their own casual authority. They delivered one-liners against people whose hands they had just shaken warmly. They kept scores. They were unworried about the collateral damage. That was the point. Patrick had to steel himself each day to take part. He lacked guile. He had no talent for intrigue. He couldn't always divine the rules of the subtle games being played around him.

Barry Brothers was his fourth or fifth job. By this time, his marriage had already been and gone. He had not been prepared for it. Barbara had been employed as a typist in the office of the discount carpet factory. His upbringing in a council orphanage made him seem vaguely exotic, an interesting catch. Patrick had no sense of himself as a lover. Barbara, three years younger, skipped ahead of him always, and he came clumping after her. She set the pace, the rules. He drew no sense of comfort or safety from their alliance. It left him feeling outside of something, forever trying to fathom his way in. He was sick with the passion and the ecstasy and the not knowing what to do. He was a landed fish.

'Do you love me?' she teased. He couldn't begin to understand the question. The thing that stayed, the scorch of memory, the shame, was the moment at the very start of it when Barbara, sat with two other girls from the office, had caught his eye in the canteen that day and not withdrawn her gaze. He had rolled the incident around deliciously in his head for days. It was a revelation. It set off gun blasts in his head. It lit a fire between his legs. By the time the frenzy had burned away ten months later, Barbara had cleared their account and left him for a rival with a footballer's perm and a Ford Capri with spoilers mounted on the sides.

'It's like a piece of you is missing,' she'd scream at him. 'You're a fucking ghost.'

He felt only relief that there were parts of him she hadn't uncovered, that he had not betrayed everything. He slipped back naturally into his single man's routines. He continued to drift from job to job. He learned to hide the distress. He welcomed failure each time it came. It was years before circumstances finally rescued him.

There was a bridge he used to drive under in his beaten-up Anglia. It carried the railway line over the arterial road. A single line of graffiti appeared one day, spray-painted on the underside of the bridge.

Pass here, you princes of hope, the graffiti said.

It was then that Patrick realized that his mother's words must not have been her own. The graffiti sprayed on the railway bridge seemed proof that her evening benediction to Patrick and his brother was part of a more widely known quotation. It didn't upset him that their mother had apparently borrowed the phrase, that it wasn't really hers. Nor did he mind, after that, having to keep driving under the daubed message. It was comforting.

Patrick was by then selling buffer pads for floor polishers and boxes of two dozen cream cleansers to factory supervisors. Each time he drove past and the graffiti was still there he felt a kind of relief. He found he was starting to organize his journeys so that the routes carried him past the bridge. He would look up and read it and smile. It offered hope that there were others out there like him who were lost, unknown to each other, but linked by the quotation and the message it conveyed – other princes of hope going surreptitiously about their troublesome business.

He made sporadic efforts to find the source of the quotation. He wanted to piece together the larger maxim. When Liam's occasional redirected correspondence arrived in the post, Patrick would make a note of any authors his better-read brother was quoting to see if he could trace their mother's sentence to any one of them. He bought a book of quotations in an Oxfam shop and worked his way laboriously through it. He found William Hazlitt, Samuel Johnson, Robert Burns and a score of others musing on hope or deliverance, but none of them was the one he was looking for.

A few weeks after the graffiti went up, Patrick saw a job advertised. The council's homeless shelter wanted a temporary worker. It was for three months, to cover sickness absence. The graffiti gave him the courage to apply. He got the job, mainly (it became apparent to him afterwards) because no one else had been interested in applying for a three-month job in a dosshouse with no rules and little prospect of being kept on. Patrick was desperate enough for the shortness of the contract not to matter. By chance, at the end of the three months, he got a month's extension, then a further two-month contract. He looked around to see where he could move on to next, and so he fell under Benedict's tutelage at the Limes.

'Sometimes,' Benedict told him when Patrick went for the interview, 'I find that people who come to work in places like this need a sanctuary of their own. Do you need a sanctuary?'

Under Benedict, he made stubborn, incremental progress.

It occurred to him from time to time that perhaps he had done no more than retreat back inside those same circles of social care he and Liam had entered on the day Aunty Maureen had delivered them to the welfare office behind the fish market. Yet this new work didn't send him home raw with humiliation. It seemed to expose fewer of his limitations. It wasn't easy work – it took its toll in other ways – but it required a different kind of courage to the sort he had needed to keep returning each day to refrigeration and mutual assurance and buffer pads.

He liked the fact that the work alongside Benedict and the others could sometimes take so long for the smallest of breakthroughs. It was satisfying that he was always at the foot of a mountain. The point was that it was the same slog for everyone passing this way. At least he could see the mountain, and his stubbornness could translate into stamina. Besides, he felt an affinity with people who were lost. Vulnerable people felt safe around him, and he was happy to enter their worlds no matter how lopsided or crazed their lives appeared from the outside. The faith of such people in Patrick made him braver. Here was a kind of redemption. He realized with relief that he didn't want to be the best, he wanted to console the weakest.

One evening, Patrick and Benedict had been slumped in armchairs, the rest of the house long since gone quiet. Benedict's Scotch was standing on the window sill and the late-night snooker coverage was running on the telly in the corner. Benedict loved watching the snooker. He said it had the honesty of the working classes about it. Out of some rambling conversation that had touched on the prospects for recovery of a couple of the longer-term residents Benedict said lazily, as if he hadn't quite realized that he was voicing the thought out loud, 'So what do you think people are, by nature?'

There was a twitch of recognition on Patrick's face. Benedict saw it and demanded to know the answer.

'We are part of God's creation, made in the image of God,' Patrick said.

They both laughed out loud at Patrick's retrieval of the catechism from some distant recess of his mind, and Benedict smacked the arm of his chair with the flat of his hand in delight.

Each evening, Benedict would pour two fingers of Scotch. It was a nightly ritual. After they had locked the ground-floor office for the night and hung the 'On Call' notice on the door, they retired to the cramped staff quarters on the top floor that the two of them shared because the other two staff lived out. There, Benedict would retrieve the bottle from the wooden cabinet on which the portable TV was balanced. He would pour out the measure and put the fat-bottomed glass on the window sill. Now and then Patrick would catch him regarding the glass – not longingly, not with a drunk's calculating slyness, but in defiance. It put Patrick in mind of a boxer eyeing a dangerous opponent in the ring. At the end of each evening, Benedict would pour the Scotch away down the sink.

'Addiction is a decision,' he had told Patrick. 'People will tell you it's an illness, they'll tell you it's in your genes and so you're powerless; they'll say the only way off is to admit you're helpless and to surrender to a higher power – but they're wrong.'

Benedict believed that everyone who came to the Limes could be saved – could turn their lives around – but not by God, and not by believing that stuff wasn't their fault when it was. He grew angry with those social workers who saw everyone as blameless victims. He didn't want people to surrender. He wanted them to see how what they did affected others. He wanted them to take responsibility for who they were, and who they wanted to be. He didn't think meditation and a twelve-point plan was enough.

In his later years with them, when the trust was busy realigning itself to match the latest government funding streams, Benedict's approach hadn't fitted in with the organization's, but then he didn't care much about that. He had been there from the start – he had been Dick Baird's right-hand man when Dick had founded the original community as a halfway house for alcoholics and set it up as a charitable trust. He and Dick Baird had been in rehab together. That made Benedict more or less untouchable. Benedict had been Dick's choice to work alongside him at a time when there were just two houses up and running and when Dick wanted to expand into mental health. By the time Patrick started working there, the organization consisted of a dozen houses in Merseyside, Lancashire and Yorkshire. Dick Baird had by then been eased out and was back on the drink, but Benedict – unyielding and didactic, and untrusted by the new corporate leadership – was still untouchable thanks to friends he had among the board's trustees.

Jeff Piggot thought addiction was an illness. He'd been Benedict's deputy for a brief and troubled period, until Benedict had thrown him out for being too full of theories and too short on people skills. He'd sent him back to head office in Sheffield where Piggot skilfully rode the tide of new thinking that was around, took up some kind of training brief and emerged two years later with a neatly trimmed goatee and an MBA from a nearby higher education college as Benedict's senior in a newly created regional manager role. Benedict called him the Thought Police, and the two of them would continue to fight a guerrilla war against each other until Piggot, still on his inexorable rise, would finally prevail.

Patrick knew none of this when he responded to the summons from Benedict. He had expected some kind of formal interview, with a panel firing questions at him. Instead, Benedict sat him down alone in an armchair in the staff quarters – a low-ceilinged attic room with a galley kitchen at one end.

'What is it that you believe in?' Benedict had asked him, sitting back and waiting for an answer, and apparently in no hurry for one as he fussed with the lighting of his pipe.

Patrick didn't know what he believed in – only what he didn't – so he told Benedict about that. He talked about Providence House, and about Liam. He reported to Benedict about the graffiti – *Pass here, you princes of hope*. He told him about the book his brother had written and which had been published in America. Liam had written the title down for him on the back of a restaurant menu he had posted from a place called Rossetti's. There was a coffee ring imprinted over the restaurant's address – Henry Street, Brooklyn Heights, New York.

'I like that,' Benedict said. '*The King of Providence*. Why do you suppose he called it that?'

Patrick shrugged. 'I just thought it was because of where we lived. Providence House.'

Benedict went across to the bookcase and pulled down an ancient, leather-bound dictionary from one of the shelves. 'Let's see what it says,' he said, and he stood thumbing happily through the pages. Finally he looked up.

'"Providence",' he read, puffing on the pipe clamped between his teeth. '"The foreseeing protection offered by God or by some other force." It's from the Latin *providentia* – to have foresight.' He pushed the book back onto the shelf and grinned.

'Good title,' Benedict said. 'Make sure to let me know what the next one's called.' He returned to his chair and began talking about the work that went on at the Limes, and Patrick listened. Eventually, Benedict rose to show him out. At the door, Patrick asked when there would be a decision about the job. Benedict, who seemed to have forgotten that the meeting was meant to have been an interview, asked if Patrick could start the following week.

In response to the call from the emergency duty team, Patrick returned to his car and drove across the city, past the stern grandeur of Victorian municipal buildings; past the elaborate glass and steel frontages of the Arndale development erected since the IRA bomb had shattered that part of the city centre in 1996; past the line of takeaways and bargain furniture shops and tyre fitters a mile further out; on to the arterial road; underneath the railways bridge: *Pass here, you princes of hope*; past the industrial estate, skirting the outpost that was the Gallowfield district.

Gallowfield was famous, at least for the moment. Patrick found it impossible not to stare as he drove by. Until recently it was nothing more than a sixties overspill housing estate. It was the place where Edward and Lillian had been housed three months ago. It was just Gallowfield. It used to belong to the city council, but then it had been sold off to a happier-sounding housing association with a green and yellow logo. Now, temporarily, it was famous beyond the city because of what had happened. It was a name denoting not a place or a community but an event. The little girl had been missing for eight days. For now, the estate was in the news. Until the girl came back. Or until she didn't.

The kiosk inside the hospital's reception area was selling copies of the *Evening News*. There was no mention yet of Edward's arrest. The headline said: 'Little Lucy: New Sighting Discounted'.

After eight days it was hard for Patrick not to feel that he somehow knew the girl. The constant reporting of her absence had made her part of people's daily domestic lives. Like everyone else, Patrick knew her age, her history, the school she attended, her movements on the day she disappeared, the way the alarm was raised by her step-father thirty minutes after she failed to return from the local Spar.

The papers were all calling her Little Lucy. The television kept showing the same image of the child. The snapshot showed her balancing on one leg in the kitchen doorway of the family home. She was almost smiling, self-conscious in the camera's gaze. For eight days the six-year-old Lucy had been gazing into the lens of the camera, not quite smiling. Most nights, the television showed the photograph as part of an item about the abduction. Each day, when people tuned in, she was still there – a constant, unsurprising presence in the same way that people's husbands or wives or children remained unexceptionally present. She was balancing on one leg in the doorway, listless, silent, still as a corpse.

Each time Patrick drove past the estate as he went to and from the Limes he found himself looking for the girl. He couldn't help it. At thirty miles an hour coming off the arterial road he would scour the ginnels and grassy banks of the estate for a sighting, believing in the possibility of suddenly spying her. Then the narrative of the story would start to run again in his head – the things that were known and the things that were conjecture; the question of whether she had been snatched by a car driver or had been lured away by someone she knew; the puzzle of what had happened to her after that, what was still happening; the absence of clues; the question of whether she was still alive. Except that now the police had decided that there were some answers – that Edward was responsible for Lucy's disappearance.

Patrick stood in front of the kiosk reading the first couple of paragraphs of the day's Lucy story on the front page of the *Evening News*. He was reminded of Benedict's instruction to him when he had first started working with him at the Limes. This is a *sanctuary*. A place of safety. That's how I want it run. You want to know why? Because that's what people need most. A sanctuary. Do you believe that?

He did.

Lucy's disappearance, her likely fate, had dumbfounded most local people. But it wouldn't have surprised Benedict. Even with a houseful of residents with psychiatric labels, Benedict had always taught him that the more sinister madness wasn't in the halfway house; it lay out there in the stridency of the larger world, in the malevolence from which his clients often came seeking protection.

Patrick had worked with Edward at the Limes for as long as the system had allowed him, coaxing him out of the shell into which he had retreated after his breakdown. He had watched Edward grow stronger bit by bit, seen him befriend Lillian when she had arrived, been a witness at their wedding at the register office three months ago, just before the couple had moved out of the Limes and into their own flat on the Gallowfield estate.

And now?

Now the police had found Edward in possession of the little girl's anorak and had arrested him, and Edward was in the cells, and Lillian was God knows where, and all the work of those months was being dismantled piece by piece in a police interview room two miles away, and Edward was hiding in the rubble.

The real truth was that these days Patrick felt a daily dread of failing. He woke sometimes in the night overwhelmed by dark fears he could not name. He would turn a sudden corner during the day and momentarily perceive his own helplessness with startling clarity. His GP had recently prescribed for him a course of anti-depressants. For now, at least, some of the trapdoors in his head had been wedged shut.

It seemed to Patrick that whatever knowledge of the world he had truly gained was negligible. So many of the things in it still lay stubbornly beyond his grasp. Simple, stupid things. He didn't understand why airplanes stayed in the air. Why yeast made dough rise into bread. What made people dream. What electricity actually was. How politicians and lawyers, presented with only the same base materials as him, unplagued by doubt, knew the answers to everything. How voices travelled between mobile phones. Why people prayed. Why they ate fast-food burgers, or kept caged birds, or took out endowment mortgages, or mugged old ladies, or injected themselves intravenously every other night, or snatched a six-year-old from the end of her street. Why some men seemed so bent on bringing other men down. Why women sometimes knew things secretly that men did not. Why vandals never tired of the challenge of glass. Why so many people fell apart. Why people died before their time. Why, when someone you loved died, the world didn't pause in shock, even for a moment. It kept on rolling, a never-ending, oblivious flow of other lives, as if nothing was sacred or meaningful; as if no loss deserved to be marked with reverence; as if, in the end, there was nothing that mattered.

There was so much about his brother's life he hadn't known. The notes that arrived sporadically in the post from Liam over the years had contained only limited biographical information. Patrick had always taken it as his brother's way of saying that those things weren't really of concern. What came, instead, were brief postcard scribbles – exhortations, trivia, admonishments, quotations from William Blake or Marcus Aurelius or John Donne, which Liam seemed to suppose were useful or which, perhaps, he had simply taken a fancy to. As for Patrick, he was left to fill in the gaps as best he could.

His notes had always been addressed to *Patrick Shepherd, care of Providence House*. They were forwarded by a series of sympathetic secretaries to the superintendent, then after 1984 by staff working for the specialist behavioural unit into which Providence House had been converted. Patrick left messages there in return for Liam in the hope that it might occur to his brother to contact the place himself, but there was never any indication that he ever did.

From the notes that Liam sent to Providence House Patrick learned that his brother had lived first in London, then Spain, before finally at the age of twenty-one moving to America. In these same notes Liam promised intermittently that he would come back to Manchester to visit Patrick, but somehow circumstances always intervened. In 1997, the former Providence House was converted into a curriculum centre for the education authority. Patrick didn't know what that meant or what they did there now, but by then the letters had ceased.

He knew Liam had settled in New York, and was a published novelist at twenty-four. He was gratified that his brother had become remarkable. He knew that the publisher of *The King of Providence* had its offices in the Flatiron Building. '23 skidoo!' Liam wrote in the margin of a note, and Patrick had to research the Flatiron Building's history to make sense of the obscene doodle he had scrawled beneath it.

Patrick had never read the book. It hadn't been published in England. The bookshop he had gone into twenty years ago to ask about it said he would have to find a specialist importer to order it for him from the States. But what was the point? Patrick couldn't have read it anyway. The discipline of three hundred pages, line by line, inch by inch through a forest of words would have been beyond him. Its meanings and nuances would have danced their way out of reach. The book would only have gathered dust on a shelf, and so he had waited instead for Liam to turn up with a copy of the book in person, as one day he surely would, and make the story truly come alive. For now, Patrick reasoned, at least he had the magazine cutting with the brief review Liam had sent him. Every now and then Patrick lifted the cutting out from amongst his other treasures in the rosewood jewellery box and read its four-sentence summary through in his over-cautious fashion and he understood instinctively that the book was about Liam himself, that it was his brother – the author in New York – who was the King of Providence.

He used to wonder if it was a woman who had coaxed his brother finally to put down roots, though Liam never said and Patrick was never sure even of this fundamental point. Instead, Patrick knew ridiculous things about him. He knew that Liam had gone climbing in the hills outside the city, somewhere in the Catskills. He knew the beers Liam liked. He knew the name of the man who ran the stall who sold him his lunchtime bagel; the betting scams of the Costa Rican concierge in his apartment block; the Chinese woman in the neighbourhood grocery store he had befriended who could tell, simply by looking at another woman – often before the woman herself was aware of it – that she was pregnant.

'Do you remember Mam's dreams?' he said in the sentence that followed the revelations about the grocery store woman. 'Do you remember the violets?' And Patrick did. He remembered his mother smelling violets the night before the death of someone that she knew. Then his signature in a flourish, *Liam*, with a swift double line beneath, and he was gone for perhaps another three or four months. No address; no meaningful exchange of information; no chance for Patrick to remonstrate about never seeing his starlit brother as a grown man.

It didn't strike Patrick as odd, simply as unfortunate. It had always been his brother's way to pursue things wholeheartedly. Patrick simply supposed that Liam was making up for lost time. Liam knew how to get in touch with him, and Patrick was content to be patient and let his brother rocket across his distant, more remarkable trajectory. There would be time enough for reunions. It had always been comforting that he was out there, somewhere high above Patrick's own small orbit, and it was cruelty beyond imagination that now he was not.

And all the while, Patrick – who had travelled barely ten miles across the Manchester conurbation from where he had set off – was working with his own lost causes. It wasn't the Catskills. It wasn't the Flatiron Building. In the years after Benedict had departed and the grey suits had taken over the running of the Hobart Trust he would close his eyes and listen for his brother, more often than not when he lay on the grass at the back of the Limes with his arms outstretched in despair and defeat, and with the big black night asleep around him like a settled cat, and he could hear Liam saying:

'*Little Frog, those things aren't what's important.*'

But by then Liam was dead.

2

THE GRACE OF SWIMMERS

When Sarah emerged from her office, the man had disappeared. She had been aware of him each time she had come out into the waiting area. He had seemed unperturbed, unworldly. Not anxious. Not obviously troubled. If anything, some stillness in him seemed to set him apart from the others, some disconnection or some small things on his mind. He had been making notes, or perhaps writing reminders for himself, apparently oblivious to the clinic's general discord around him. He had been interviewed by Dr Vass for the tests more than an hour and a half ago. Since then he had been waiting for her to call him in. Each time she came out of her office he had been there, but she was running late and when she did finally come out to call him in he was gone. She checked his name again on the sheet provided by the reception nurse. Saul. First visit. Self-referral. The GUM department used only first names at its clinics when calling people from the waiting area or addressing them in the treatment bays. He should have followed Tusa. He would have been her final client of the day. She went back inside her room to finish writing up Tusa's notes.

Sarah averaged eighteen appointments, plus emergencies, in a four-hour clinic, and wrote her notes up in batches through the session as and when she could. She kept the notes brief, arranging them in bullet points. On the file she had open on her desk she wrote:

- *Unclear whether Tusa is taking the medication consistently. Baby due on 20th. Talking to me more about whether the baby will be positive, and what that will mean for her. Still won't consent, though, for her daughter to be tested.*
- *She's adamant that Grace 'doesn't need it'. Still hoping to persuade her but there's a strategy conference been called next week to push for legal proceedings to compel her to allow Grace to be tested before the new baby is born, so it may be taken out of my hands.*
- *Housing is still a concern. Welfare rights still haven't got back to me. Social services won't say whether they believe they have a responsibility to help until there's a human rights assessment, but I can't find anyone who knows how to do one and they don't seem in any hurry. What sort of system is that?*

She filed the notes and went back out into the waiting area. It was still empty. On the floor around the chair where the missing man had been sitting was a scattering of peanut shells. She supposed he had grown fed up of waiting and had gone home. She had about a dozen no-shows a week. She followed each one up with a letter to the address the person had given (if they had given one). The follow-ups were part of her own attempt to try to keep the local incidence of chlamydia at bay by tracking the transmission routes.

The television attached to the wall facing the four lines of plastic chairs was still on. A game show was playing. Sarah walked between the rows of chairs and turned it off. The sound ceased with a smack, then a crack of static as the TV closed down. She felt a rush of physical relief unfurling in her chest. She closed her eyes and let out a slow breath into the silence. It occurred to her that the pain at the side of her head she had been conscious of in mid-afternoon was still there. The only noise she could hear now was from a trolley being pushed somewhere down a corridor beyond reception. She looked at her watch. It was a quarter to six. She had been there since eight o'clock, even though on a Friday she was meant to finish early to compensate for the evening shifts she did.

She went through to the office behind reception to see if she could beg paracetamol from someone, but both the reception staff had gone. She leafed through the day's set of index sheets in the tray on the desk. She was looking to see if there was an address for the last no-show. She found the sheet for Saul. The receptionist had written down 'Saul Montague St'. It wasn't compulsory for clients to give an address. The minimum information the department required was a first name and a date of birth. The receptionist entered whatever was on the sheet into the computer database. Some people, she knew, filled in the boxes with made-up names and addresses. She stood still for a while, deliberately savouring the absence of movement and noise.

For a moment she had read his name as *Saul Montague*. Then she realized it was a first name and a street name he had given. It heightened her curiosity. She was Sarah Montague. It wasn't a common surname. Usually there was a sense of relief when she was running late and the last client was a no-show, but she found herself feeling disappointed that *Saul Montague St* had disappeared from his corner chair. It made the coincidence of her almost-namesake more pointed. Her misapprehension hinted at some kind of quiet alliance with the missing man, and she was curious about whether he would come back. There was another reason she was disappointed, but as yet she was struggling to frame the thought in her head.

She liked to believe that, in a way, there was no such thing as coincidence. She had read a lot about chance. *Those bloody books*, Gary called them. She rummaged through tomes on popular science whose authors trawled biology and physics and DNA research to speculate on bigger notions. She wanted to know what coincidences might mean. She liked the idea that everything in the universe was connected by some invisible web. She wanted to know how. She didn't talk to Gary about it any more. He thought it was bollocks.

Montague was her married name. She liked it. Looking back, it was the one classy thing her husband had brought to the relationship. If ever she had elected to make a fresh start she would have chosen to remain Sarah Montague.

She wondered whether to head straight home from the hospital. Often she went back a longer way, safe in the knowledge that her sat nav would guide her home. Sometimes she would drive for as much as an hour, picking up roads where she could drift along without having to concentrate too much on the driving, even though she lived only ten minutes from the hospital. She would play Miles Davis laments or Frank Sinatra ballads to keep her company. She had always liked Sinatra's voice, the early vulnerability before it broadened into swagger sometime in late middle age. It didn't bother Gary what time she got in as long as he thought she had come straight from the hospital. More often than not he wasn't there anyway when she arrived home. He'd be out doing some deal. If ever she questioned him she received a lecture on the perils of running your own business. Work didn't just come to you, he'd say – you had to go out and get it. She would arrive home and there would be no sign of him, and she would assume that Gary would be out somewhere *getting it*.

Sometimes when she was driving he would ring her mobile to see where she was. She never said that she was driving. She would pull the car over and say she had someone with her in the office, or that she had been in a meeting, or the clinic was running late. If he was at home she would say that she was in the car park, or that she had just pulled into the traffic outside the hospital, and then she would set the sat nav and swing the car around at the next turn-off and head for home. Her favourite evenings were when he didn't ring and she knew he was out, and she could drive and drive, and listen to the radio or the Sinatra tapes, and work out what she would make herself for supper.

There had been a time when it was different. There were moments that had promised something better than this. Gary, six years older and already 'in business' when Sarah was a callow student nurse fresh from grammar school and netball fixtures, had seemed ready to take on the world. He had a steel about him that she liked. There was nothing that was going to stand in his way. It was so different to her parents' own sober lives, their cautiousness about rules and risk. It was, looking back, some small rebellion. Gary taught her to drive. He would take over the wheel and thrash the little sports car around the lanes over the moors and make her scream on fast bends. He flattered her. She was going to be his partner in this great adventure. There were surely good times ahead. For the time being, he was going to work hard to provide for both of them. He was working on the dream.

The flexibility of being a nurse had worked well for her when Katy was a baby. She'd been able to organize her shifts to minimize how much nursery time they had to pay for. At the outset, they had calculated that when Katy reached school age Sarah would switch to nights. Three nights, thirty hours, rotas built around weekends – with Gary confined to the house on Saturday mornings while Sarah caught up on her sleep. Her job in general nursing allowed them to plan like that.

The switch to genito-urinary medicine came later. Gary was still working on the dream, but so much else had changed. A new specialism and the promise of a little operational independence as the GUM's health advisor offered a new challenge in Sarah's career. Her job involved some evening work, and the commitment to getting through the daily backlog of clients without cover or anyone to double up with. In her new role she could never be absolutely sure when her shift would be over, but by then it didn't matter.

She still liked the work itself, but the job hadn't turned out as she first imagined it five years ago. The consultant she had gone to work for had moved on. Whenever the inspection teams were in, all the hospital's systems were re-invented overnight to avoid the appearance of blockages. The workload was ludicrous and the agencies used by the hospital to supply the extra staff couldn't cover her specialism. She was a nurse and yet she wasn't, and so there was no obvious manager to report to. The sister attached to the department who managed the nurses and reception staff was envious of Sarah's advancement and keen to maintain her own claims to authority. And Vass, the new consultant, was a clown. He had few skills as a communicator and no interest in responding to the issues about the service that Sarah brought to his attention. Early on, he had closed the door to her office and stroked her leg vaguely as he spoke of the pressures of the job. When she asked him to move his hand he had smiled and made a point of letting her know that he was playing squash that evening with the chairman of the acute trust which managed the hospital, and she had understood the message he was giving her.

For the last eighteen months she had been telling Vass that the local level of chlamydia was rising fiercely and the clinic should be working with other departments to test more systematically, but to no avail. Sarah supposed that either she was good at her job but that no one had noticed, or that she wasn't and her seniors were waiting to pounce as soon as she dropped the ball, but she had no way of knowing which scenario was true.

When she looked up he was there again. He must have returned while she was looking for his address, but she hadn't heard him and she couldn't work out which direction he had come from.

'Saul?'

He was dressed entirely in black – black trousers, black shirt, black coat almost to his knees – even though it was a warm day. He had nothing on his feet. Sarah supposed he might have taken his shoes off in the waiting area. She had come across worse eccentricities in the clinic. He was perhaps in his fifties, though it was difficult to tell, and somewhere between lean and gaunt. His face, scraped clean with a razor in the last hour or two, had a translucent quality to it. He acknowledged her without seeming to do very much. He was idly shelling a peanut. He let the shell fall to the floor and slipped the nut into the pocket of his overcoat.

'I'm sorry we kept you waiting so long,' she said across the empty room. 'We've been running late all afternoon.' She gave him the brief smile she offered to everyone as she summoned them from the waiting room. She came out from behind the reception desk and walked towards her office. He stood up and followed her.

For her consultations Sarah used two low chairs either side of a coffee table. Part of her job involved giving people the results of their tests for a range of sexually transmitted infections, and two armchairs seemed a better arrangement than sheltering behind a desk. She had told a sceptical Vass that it seemed fairer to look someone in the eye without a barrier between you when you were letting them know they were HIV positive. She lifted her notes from the desk and took the armchair nearer to the door. She had been on a risk management course where the hospital's health and safety officer had insisted this was a mandatory precaution. She had pointed out in response that the only time she had ever felt threatened in her office was when Dr Vass was in the room levelling accusations about things he himself had forgotten to do.

Sarah indicated for Saul to sit in the other chair. She realized he was still barefoot.

'What do we do now?' he said. He was curious, amused, unhurried.

'You haven't been to a GUM before?'

'First timer,' he said.

'Okay – I'll run through what happens next, some information about the tests. And if you're okay with it, we should talk a little about your own situation.'

'My situation?'

'Some background information. Part of my job is to help you manage your own sexual heath.'

'You want to ask me questions?'

'Just a few.'

'Fine.'

'Are we okay to start with that?'

'If you want.'

'All right. Are you in an ongoing relationship?'

'I have a cat.'

'With a person.'

'No.'

'How many sexual partners in the last three months?'

'A couple.'

'What sort of sex?'

'Well, we tried to do it together.'

'I'm sorry?'

'You get out of practice, don't you?'

'Vaginal? Oral? Anal? That was the question.'

'Ah, I see. Ah, vaginal.'

'Did you use any sort of contraception?'

He thought. 'I don't think so.'

'You can't remember?'

'I think I was drunk.'

'Every time?'

'Just once with each. I couldn't tell you their names.'

'And you were drunk both times?'

Saul seemed to be trawling for information to respond with. 'It's possible,' he said eventually, 'to reach a stage in your life when it's safest to be drunk in certain situations. Don't you think?'

Sarah didn't respond.

'Have you had any sexually transmitted infections before?'

'I haven't been to a clap clinic before.'

'And no STIs?'

He shrugged. 'Not that I know of. I like the picture.'

'The picture?'

He indicated the large framed print on the wall behind Sarah's desk.

'You like whales?' he asked.

'Yes, I do,' she said without looking around. She took out her pen. 'Is "Saul" okay? People sometimes use different names in the clinic. We don't mind.'

She watched as he took out another peanut shell.

'Saul,' he said as he cracked the nut. He seemed to be trying out the name. 'No, that's okay.'

'Do you want me to get you something for those?'

He looked at her.

'For the shells. A plate or something?'

He glanced at the peanuts in his hand, then back at her, weighing up the options. 'Thank you.'

She found a plastic dish on one of the shelves and passed it to him. He took it and dropped the pieces of shell from two recently split nuts into it. He slipped the two peanuts into his pocket.

'You're saving them for later?' she asked.

'They're for my cat,' he said.

'I didn't know cats ate peanuts.'

'It's odd, isn't it?' he said.

'Is there a surname you want to give me? Again, you don't have to.'

'Saul's just fine,' he said. 'It's a nice room in here. The waiting room is a difficult place, but this feels good.'

'It can get quite hassled in the waiting room. People getting aggravated, couples bickering. Is that why you went out for a while?'

He shook his head. 'I can cut myself off from things when I need to. Do you mind if I ask – do you like this room?'

'I do like it, yes.'

It was a response designed to bring him back on track, but it wasn't a lie. She did like it. Her room was a sanctuary, away from the human traffic and the politics of the hospital at large. In some ways it was more of a refuge than home was. At least here she didn't have Gary on the prowl, and even Dr Vass had finally been trained to knock before he entered.

'I've got some details of the tests Dr Vass has done,' she said. 'He's checked for the standard range of conditions. The NSU slide showed positive, but it takes a while for the other results to come through.'

'NSU is . . .?'

'Non-specific urethritis. That's probably what was responsible for the soreness. Has the doctor given you some tablets for that?'

He dug into his overcoat pocket. From amongst a small handful of shelled peanuts he retrieved a phial of tablets to show her.

'And he's advised you not to have sex for six weeks while you're taking the course?'

'He said that.'

'Good.'

'How long for the other results?'

'Well, gonorrhoea's usually seven to ten days, syphilis and HIV about a week. Chlamydia's two weeks.'

'It's a blue whale, isn't it?'

'What is?'

'In the photograph on your wall.'

'Yes, it is.'

The photograph showed a single blue whale. She found herself turning around and examining it briefly herself. Beyond the foaming whitecaps, caused by the animal surfacing, was an otherwise endless ocean.

'Did you choose the picture?'

'I did, yes. Did you book an appointment at the desk for your results?'

'In two weeks,' he said. 'Is it your picture?'

She nodded. 'We should have everything back by then. If you want, though, I can arrange to see you before then to give you the result of your HIV test – if you feel you'd like to know that one sooner rather than wait. People are usually anxious to know about it if there's any kind of concern.'

'Sure. That would be okay.'

'Have you any reason to think you might be HIV positive?'

He smiled. 'I just had some unwise sex and I've got an itchy dick.'

'And some discharge, it says here on the notes.'

'That's what you call it? Yeah, that. Will the tablets clear that up?'

'Maybe. Let's see how the other tests come back first.'

'Isn't it a worry, if you think I might have HIV, that I could just not turn up again?' he said, running the thought idly around in his head. 'You don't know where I live or anything. You don't even know who I am.'

'It's a risk we take. But it's not like TB or something – it's not a notifiable disease. It's not like you can be sectioned for treatment. If people want to collect their results and get treatment, they come back. If not, they don't.'

'It's a free country?'

'Kind of.'

'Is that a problem?'

'Only to me. It makes a mess of tracking the transmission routes for stuff like HIV and hep C if we're missing information.'

'Are you good at this stuff?'

Sarah shrugged. 'I don't know. I do what I can. So do you want me to make you an appointment for the HIV result?'

'Yeah, why not. I get the feeling you're good at this stuff.'

'It's possible we might have some of the other test results

back in a week, so I'll give you what we have when you come in.' She stood up to retrieve her appointments diary from the top drawer of her desk.

'The thing about a blue whale,' he said, 'is that it spends most of its life travelling alone. It moves from the Arctic to the equator and back on its own every year of its life.'

She picked up the diary and then stood examining the framed picture. It had been up on the wall so long that she had stopped noticing it, but she had loved it when she had first seen it in the gallery and bought it and then brought it into work to hang in her office.

'It doesn't swim with other whales?' she asked.

'Sometimes. But mostly each one swims on its own. I think that's why they grow so big.'

'How do you work that one out?' She sat back down with the diary on her lap.

'The hum that it makes – because the whale is so big – is so loud and so low that it travels for hundreds of miles in the water. Only a really low hum can travel so far. Only a really big animal could make a hum so low. I think they're that size so they can sing to each other, so they don't go out of their minds with the loneliness when they're crossing the ocean alone.'

Sarah thought about the blue whale swimming alone in the ocean. She imagined its song being sent on a thousand-mile journey in search of a fellow traveller to hear it.

'Do you swim?' he said.

She seemed not to hear him. 'What do you suppose it says when it's singing?' she asked.

'I don't know,' he said. '*Is anyone out there?* That's what I'd sing. Maybe that would be enough.'

Sarah turned the pages of her diary, heading towards the right week to write in the appointment.

'Do you swim?' he repeated.

'I do,' she said. 'What about Wednesday – for the appointment?'

'Do you swim often?'

'Yes. Every week.'

'It must be good. A good thing to do.'

'It is. I like to swim.'

Sarah found herself momentarily visualizing herself swimming, stroking the quiet lengths she did one evening a week when the local pool was closed to the kids, swimming alone in the way that the whale swam. Swimming was the time when she was most herself, when she was closest to the core of who she was. She had long recognized this about herself. Out of the water she felt rushed and ungainly. She had large knees. She felt big-boned. She never knew what to do with her hands. Her hair was cut short for want of any bright ideas. In the water it was different. She loved the solitary, diligent lengths that she did. She liked the feeling of weightlessness, the rhythm, the grace of her body, the separateness of everything else. She had never before connected it to the photograph of the blue whale. She liked the way she was in control when she swam, and the sense of her own otherwise imperfect and troublesome and no longer size-ten body as sleek and responsive.

'Next Wednesday,' she repeated.

'Okay.'

'Three o'clock?'

'Sure.'

'You want an appointment card?'

'I'll remember.'

'You have a good memory?'

'I don't have too much else on.'

'You're not working at the moment, then?'

'I'll be free on Wednesday afternoon.'

She recognized his response as a gentle conversational steer. It was the kind of thing she did herself with inappropriate patients, and with doctors on the pull like Vass.

'I didn't mean to pry,' she said.

He shrugged. 'We all have secrets.'

She nodded.

'You, me, everybody.'

'Yes.'

'I'll trade you one if you want,' he said.

'You'll *trade* me?'

'I'll trade you one of yours for one of mine. Secrets.'

She allowed herself a smile. 'What sort of secrets do you want to trade?'

She was remembering her counselling training. Keeping a sense of the boundaries in the session; calculating whether he might be edging towards some kind of small disclosure about his condition. Or maybe, it occurred to her, she was just interested in him. She had another reason to be curious, and the thought still kept plucking at her. She didn't, after all, want to believe in coincidence.

'It doesn't matter what. Anything. A small one of yours for anything you want to know about me. You first. Anything. A silly thing.'

Perhaps he was ready to confide something. That possibility on its own made it seem worth going along with him. She pondered what she might reasonably be able to trade, and something occurred to her.

'You just thought of something, didn't you?' he said.

His easy awareness of it bothered her.

'It showed in your face.'

'I was thinking about the houses,' she said.

'What about them?'

'I was just thinking,' she said. 'I get a copy of the *Evening News* for the property section. I go through it looking at the houses.'

'So?'

'So, I'm not moving. I don't have any intention of moving. But every week I always get the paper. I have this thing that every week I have to choose the house I like the most – the one I would choose to live in.'

'Do you ever go to look at them?'

'You mean the houses? No, never. It's just a game. It's silly, really. It's just something I do. That's my secret.'

He nodded acknowledgement. 'Okay.'

'So do I get to ask you something now?'

'That was the deal.'

She thought about it. 'I wanted to ask you what you do.'

'You mean apart from queuing up in your waiting room?'

'I mean, do you work? Did you work? What job was it?'

He pulled a face, as if weighing up what the answer should be.

'You don't have to answer,' she said. 'Not if you don't want.'

'I've done different things, but my situation's changed.'

'So just tell me how it's changed. What do you do now?'

'Do you really want to know?'

'Only if you want to tell me.'

'You won't believe me. That's the hard part.'

She shrugged. 'Okay.'

'Now I have more of a calling than a job,' he said.

'So what's your calling?'

'You're sure you want to know?'

'I was just interested.'

'I'm an angel.'

'You're an angel?'

'You're smiling.'

'Of course I'm smiling.'

'You don't believe me?'

'Should I believe you?'

'It doesn't matter whether you do.' He sounded like it didn't matter.

'Shouldn't you have wings?'

'That's just a misconception,' he said. 'I know what you're thinking.'

'What am I thinking?'

'You're thinking, what's an angel doing in a clap clinic? Right?'

'That's part of it.'

'That's a reasonable thought. It's occurred to me, too.'

'Why don't you tell me what you think an angel is?' she said.

'An angel is a messenger. You're still smiling.'

'Yes.'

'It's not so odd. Count up how many people believe heaven is real. More than half the people in this hospital know for certain that there is life after death. And if there are two worlds, surely it makes sense that there are messengers travelling between them.'

'You're a messenger?'

'The thing is, angels are just like people while they're here. In what they feel, what they eat.'

'Just like ordinary people?'

'Pretty much.'

'So, is there a difference – between angels and other people? Apart from the fact that angels appear not to wear shoes.'

Saul looked down quizzically at his bare feet. 'Well, there is a technical difference.'

'How technical? Not the wings thing?'

'No, not the wings thing.'

'Then what?'

'They only have so long.'

'I don't understand.'

'They have a job to do. A task, an errand – for someone who died, or a message to convey. Something specific. Something that was left undone when the person died. And as the messenger, you only have so long to complete it.'

'And what's your task?'

'I have to save someone.'

'Who?'

'I'm not sure yet.'

'And then you go back to where you came from?'

'Yes, if I complete what I came here to do.'

'So how long have you got left?'

'Eight days.'

Sarah worked it out.

'Next Saturday,' Saul prompted.

'So you were a person, and you died?' she said. 'That's what you're telling me.'

'No, I'm an angel. I got *sent* because somebody died.'

'How did they die?'

'I don't know,' he said. 'I don't think it matters. Do you think I should know?'

'You tell me,' she said, 'you're the expert.'

He shook his head. 'I'm not an expert. I just found myself here. This is as strange for me as it is for you.'

'So who gave you this task?'

'I don't know that,' he said. 'The first thing I can remember is this astonishing white light all around me, and then I find myself at the side of the road and it's night-time and I'm dressed like this, and when I felt in the pocket of the coat I found this.'

He produced a crumpled brown envelope from his pocket. He unfurled it and pulled out a fistful of small white business cards. He put them down on the table in a heap.

'There are forty-seven,' he said. 'I counted them.'

Sarah picked one up. The single word *Saul* was printed in the top left-hand quadrant of the card. On the right-hand side of each card was a design that looked to Sarah like a copy of Leonardo da Vinci's *Vitruvian Man*, with his arms and legs stretched out into a star shape. She turned the card over. On the back was a name.

'Who is Hughie Gallagher?'

Saul shrugged. 'I don't know.'

'Perhaps he's the person you have to save?' Sarah said.

Saul shook his head. 'Every card has a different name on it.'

Sarah flipped over several more of the cards. As he had said, each of them had a different name printed on it.

'Maybe you're meant to save them all?'

'No – only one person. I'm sure of that.'

'How do you know?'

'I just am. I think that must be a piece of information I've been given.'

'So what are the cards for? What do they mean?'

He shrugged again. 'I don't know. I'm trying to work it out.'

Sarah remembered something. 'What are you doing with a cat if you're supposed to be an angel?'

'I don't know. It just kind of adopted me. You know how cats get when they find someone they feel comfortable around.'

'Saul, can I ask you something? Are you on any medication at the moment?'

'Yes, I am – the doctor just gave me these.' He reached for the phial again and held it up.

'Those are for your urethritis.'

'Yes they are.'

'Nothing else?'

'I don't think so. Depending on what today's tests come back like, I suppose.'

'So you're an angel and you're in a GUM clinic at the hospital being tested for sexually transmitted infections?'

'Who'd have thought it, eh?'

'Don't you think that sounds a little strange?'

'It does to me.'

'I thought angels were supposed to be sexless. I read that somewhere.'

'Well, I'm only guessing because I'm new to all this, but I figure you probably have to take the *form* of a man or woman for this kind of job. So while we're here I suppose we have the same appetites, the same weaknesses, as people when we're in this form. The same distractions.'

'The same STIs?'

'It looks like it.'

'Saul, do you have a social worker? Someone I can ring?'

'I don't have a social worker, no. I have an errand.'

'Whereabouts are you living? Have you got somewhere to stay? I saw what you wrote on the index card and I haven't come across a Montague Street in this part of Manchester before. Did you make that up?'

'I guess I could do with somewhere better to stay.'

'You look like you haven't had too much sleep lately.'

'That's the thing about angels. We don't sleep.'

'And shoes. What about shoes?'

'I don't know,' he said. 'I'm not sure what happened to them.'

'What size are you?'

'I don't know.'

'Stand up,' she said. Saul stood up. 'Maybe an eight. Wait there a minute.'

She went out of the office and across to the reception area. She came back holding a pair of white plimsolls.

'Try these on,' she said. 'They're tens, but they might do you for the time being, until you can sort yourself out.'

'Who do they belong to?'

'Dr Vass. He leaves a spare set of kit here in case he gets a call from the chief exec to play squash at lunch time.'

'Won't he mind?'

'Not if he doesn't know who stole them.'

Saul smiled at her. He tried the plimsolls on. 'They're nice and roomy,' he said, wiggling his toes. 'Thank you. I'll return them when I'm done.'

'Keep them,' she said. 'Think of them as a gift from the NHS. It's not like we need the money. The PFI people are practically giving away the new wing they're building.'

'Is that right?'

'Saul, would it be okay if I got the hospital to ring round to find you somewhere to stay?'

'You don't believe me, do you?'

'I don't believe you're an angel, no. I think you might need somewhere to sleep for the night. Does it matter that I don't believe you?'

'No, it doesn't. It doesn't change anything.'

'Do you believe there's anything different about you? What is it that makes you an angel?'

'Apart from having an errand?'

'Sure. Apart from that.'

'You have a different perspective on things.'

'Like what?'

'We know things.'

'What sort of things?'

He looked around the room. 'You want me to try something?'

'I don't know.'

'What about if you think about something in your desk?' He was starting to shell another peanut.

'You want me to think about something?'

'Something that's in your desk – that's out of sight in one of the drawers. Just imagine it. Just picture what it looks like. Will you do that?'

Saul dropped the shell into the container and slipped the peanut into his pocket.

'And then can I try to get you somewhere to stay for the night?'

'All right, yes. Are you ready?'

'Yes.'

'And you're picturing what it is now?'

'Yes.'

Nothing happened. He didn't say anything. She was starting to feel foolish for getting involved in the exercise. She was about to call a halt to the charade.

'It's not a useful thing, is it?' he said.

'What do you mean?'

'It's not practical. It's decorative. It's a photograph. Is it a photograph?'

'Yes, it was. It was a photograph I was thinking of. How did you know that? Is that a guess or something? That's a good guess.' She was trying to work out whether he might have been in the room at some point in order to look. She wondered whether he'd planted some small verbal cue to encourage her to think of a photograph.

She stood up. 'Look, I'm going to make that call now,' she said. 'I'm going to see if the hospital social work team can find you somewhere to stay.'

'Keep holding it in your head,' he said. 'The photograph.' He was leaning forward in his chair, watching her.

'There's one person,' he said. 'It's a photograph of one person. It's a little girl.'

She didn't say anything.

'It's a photograph of a little girl.'

His face was registering something close to surprise.

'It's your daughter.'

She waited. She wasn't sure at first whether he had finished, but he was silent. She stood up and went over to the desk. She opened the drawer. Under assorted bits of paper she found the photograph. She stood looking at him, trying to work out what had just happened.

'My daughter's dead,' she said softly.

He looked at her for a long time.

'I know,' he said eventually. 'I'm sorry.'

The security guard had his back settled against the GUM reception counter. He had a boy's vacant face. His brown uniform was designed to fit someone half a size bigger. His arms were folded in repose.

'She told you I was coming?' Patrick said.

'She said she'd rung social services, yeah.'

'He's climbed out of a window?'

'She came out here to make the phone call – presumably that's where you got involved? – and when she went back in' – he gestured towards her office door – 'the window was open and there was no sign of him. Then she realized he'd climbed out of the window. You'll have seen the scaffolding everywhere for the new hospital wing. It runs right the way along this side of the building for the re-cladding. He's gone out on that.'

'What's happening now?' Patrick asked.

'There's two coppers turned up. One's in the nurse's office trying to talk him back in. The other's down in the car park trying to break up the circus. You know what it's like if they think someone's gonna jump.'

'Where's the woman – the nurse?'

'Gone across to the canteen. Apparently she hasn't eaten since she came to work this morning and they said it might be a long haul getting him back in.'

'Where's the man?'

'He's out on the scaffolding with his legs dangling over the drop. Turns out he thinks he's a sodding angel.'

'She told you that?'

'No, I heard her telling one of the cops.'

'Do they think he might jump?' Patrick asked.

The security guard pulled a face, calculating the odds. 'Nah, don't think so. Me neither. The thing is with these people, you end up sometimes wishing some of them would just get on with it. If he's after throwing himself off, why'd he hang around all afternoon for his Friday bloody appointment? God knows, there's enough places for him to take his pick in the middle of the night and do it quietly – and then we'd all have been none the wiser until we had to scrape him up in the morning.'

'How long's he been out there?'

'Couple of hours now. Centre of attention, I suppose. That's how they like it. In my experience they don't hang around this long if they're really going to jump.'

'You have a lot of experience?'

'You see things in this job. We get three or four a year jumping from the hospital buildings. Last summer we had some kid go through a glass roof – not a proper suicide, just some kid pratting about on the roof. Hit a steel beam on the way down and then the floor forty feet below. The top part of his head was sliced off like a boiled egg. His brain . . . we found the biggest part of it twenty feet away from the body, just lying there.'

Patrick nodded.

'What about you?' the guard said. 'You work with these people. You ever get anyone jumping?'

Patrick shook his head. 'No.'

'Do you get them talking to you about it, though? About wanting to?'

'Sometimes.'

'Do you think it's brave?'

'Do I think what's brave?'

'Jumping. Ending it like that. Do you think it takes guts?'

'I don't know,' Patrick said.

'I nearly did it once,' the guard said. 'Before I got this job.'

'Did what?'

'Not like this. Not jumping. We'd been playing cards all night. Gone through a bottle of Johnnie Walker. My father-in-law had gone to bed and I tried to blow my head off with one of his guns.'

He said it as if he didn't quite believe it had happened, as if he had only just remembered the incident. Only Patrick's job, and the strangeness of the situation, made it possible for him to tell the story.

'The hammer jammed,' the man said. 'Turns out the thing hadn't been fired for twenty years. Can you believe that?' He grinned, as if he didn't quite believe it himself.

'So were you brave,' Patrick asked, 'when you tried it?'

'I was too pissed to remember.'

They stood in silence for a moment. 'Do you mind if I go through to see what's happening?' Patrick said.

'I suppose it's okay with it being you,' the guard said. 'I'm meant to keep everyone away, but with it being you.'

The sign on the office door said 'GUM Health Advisor'. When Patrick pushed it open he could see that the policeman was standing at the open window on the far side of the room, hands resting on the sill, leaning out. When he heard Patrick he pulled his head in and turned around. Patrick held up his palms to indicate that he wasn't going to come any nearer for the moment. He pushed the door closed behind him and sat down on one of the chairs placed either side of the coffee table.

The policeman leaned out of the window again to speak to the man.

'Saul,' he said loudly, projecting his voice so that it would reach several yards away across the scaffolding. 'The man's arrived – the one who runs the hostel place. Is it all right if I go back inside the office for a few minutes to talk to him?'

Patrick couldn't hear the reply. After a moment, the policeman pulled back slowly from the window.

'So you're the cavalry, are you?' he said.

'I'm the nearest the emergency duty team could find,' Patrick said. 'What's he doing now – Saul? That's his name?'

'He's smoking a cigarette. He's not in any rush to come in. He was talking quite a bit to the nurse earlier, by all accounts, but he doesn't want much to do with me. Can I tell him you're going to take him back with you?'

'Maybe,' Patrick said. 'It depends.'

'On what?'

'Is he distressed?'

'Not distressed. Distracted, maybe.'

'It's not exactly usual to be climbing out of a fifth-storey window onto scaffolding for a smoke.'

'He's settled down a bit now – he's sat down – but the nurse said he was walking around out there for a while. She said he wasn't even watching where his feet were going. It was like he thought he couldn't fall off, she said.'

Patrick picked up a coaster from the coffee table in front of him. Something had been written on it in felt-tip pen.

'What's this?' he said.

'The nurse found it. She went to phone social services out in reception so she could speak privately without him hearing, and when she came back she realized that he'd gone out through the window onto the scaffolding, and then she saw that.' He indicated the coaster.

Patrick read what had been written over the top of the printed logo of the hospital trust.

'*Waste no more time arguing what a good man should be. Be one.*'

'She said when she first saw it – when she saw that the window was open and realized he must have gone out – she thought it might have been a suicide note. She thought he'd gone over the edge.'

While Patrick was still looking at the coaster, the policeman moved back over to the window.

'Tell him he can have a bed at the unit for the weekend if he comes back inside,' Patrick said.

The policeman leaned out of the window, and then Patrick heard him talking to the man before drawing back inside the room.

'He says he'll talk to you. But he wants you to go out there. Not the whole way along – just on to the ledge outside the window. He says he'll talk to you there.'

'Why won't he come back inside?'

'He says it's not time for him to come back inside yet, but he will talk to you out there. You're honoured. The bugger hasn't wanted me anywhere near him.'

Patrick walked across the office and leaned out of the window. He could see the back of the man's head several yards away. Patrick looked down. He could see all the way to the ground through the gaps in the scaffolding walkway that was laid three planks wide. He felt a bubble of apprehension like air in his bowels. It rose through his chest and burst a moment later just behind his eyes. The jolt in his head made him giddy.

'*Jesus!*'

'Are you all right?' the policeman asked.

'I'm not good with heights,' Patrick said.

Slowly he levered one leg out of the window until he was straddling the window sill. He tried to judge how much further he needed to shift his balance before he could place his foot on the walkway of the scaffolding.

'Oh, fuck.' He closed his eyes.

When he opened them again the man was still sitting in the same position facing away from him. Patrick leaned a little further out, then a little more. Just as he felt himself toppling forward he made a clumsy grab for the metal cord of the sash window. The window slammed up another two inches into the top of its wooden frame. Patrick made an involuntary sound. His chest was instantly squeezed of air.

Half out of the window, gripping the cord, he watched the traffic on the road rumbling past the hospital and the vast side of the new extension being added on to it. The voices of people far below on the ground lapped against the building in a distant tide. He couldn't decide whether to close his eyes or open them. Each time he opened them his gaze was drawn to the easy, casual fall that beckoned him.

'I can't go any further,' he said out loud in the man's direction.

He tried to organize another breath before he spoke again.

'I don't like heights.'

Another breath.

'You'll have to come back in for us to talk.'

And then he remembered the quotation scribbled on the coaster. He realized that he knew where it came from.

He fought for concentration. He gathered a rhythm to his erratic breathing so that he could speak.

'*Waste no more time arguing,*' he said out loud, '*what a good man should be.*' I know it. It's Marcus Aurelius. It's from his *Meditations.*'

Patrick wasn't sure at first whether the man had heard what he had said. He watched as Saul's hand reached for something from the pocket of his overcoat. Patrick closed his eyes again as another swell of sickness ran over him. He opened his eyes again. It looked like a peanut in Saul's hand. He must have broken open the shell because a moment later Patrick saw him hold the pieces of shell out to the side of him. He watched them being released, then saw them fall to the ground. He felt his stomach roll again. Saul had shifted position to watch the fall of the peanut shell. Patrick saw his face for the first time.

The man's expression didn't alter.

For a moment, Patrick lost all sense of fear. He forgot that there was nothing between himself and the treacherous fall.

Patrick saw his face.

And he said –

He saw his face.

It was his face.

He said –

'Liam?'

Patrick watched the man glance around, registering him, measuring him curiously across the distance that separated them on the scaffold.

Patrick waited for him to speak.

It was his face.

'Liam's dead,' the man said finally. 'My name is Saul.'

3

THE MEMORY OF OBJECTS

When Sarah typed the word 'angels' into the computer the search engine came up with more than four million websites. Some of them were simply product sites; others were the names of organizations which, by chance, included the word angel in their title, or in the titles of bulletins posted on the internet. But some of them – many more than she had imagined – were the kind she was looking for. They were about angels as she had understood them from childhood. Several of them confirmed that 'angel' came from the Greek *angelos*. It meant messenger.

Some of the websites were maintained by religious organizations – Catholic, or Christian evangelical sites giving theological definitions and official church histories of angels. She read that American surveys (no one seemed to ask British people) suggested that sixty per cent of the population in the US believed angels were real beings. The sites that interested Sarah most, though, were the encounter sites. As far as she could tell, these were non-denominational. In some cases they weren't even official religious sites. They contained the claims that people had made about their encounters with angels.

Sarah read how, in the winter of 2001, one man had been driving at night in snow. He was badly injured in an accident when his car skidded on a patch of ice on a quiet road and hit a tree. His eventual rescuer had pulled over in his own car and rung the emergency services on his mobile phone. The passer-by had given the injured man advice about the best way to lie until help came so that his punctured lung wasn't in danger of flooding. The two of them had passed the time by talking about the injured man's family and the things he had done in his life, not all of which he was proud of and some of which he wished he could put right. When the emergency services arrived, the injured man asked them where his rescuer was. The medics told him he was on his own and that, apart from those of the ambulance, his were the only car tracks in the snow on the road.

There was the woman bringing up two children alone on three cleaning jobs and welfare benefits who was handed an envelope by a man she had somehow been drawn into conversation with while she was looking in a toy shop window in the city. When he had gone, she had opened the envelope and inside found precisely the amount of money in cash that she was in debt to the money lenders for.

There was the pregnant woman in a hospital in Wisconsin who had started haemorrhaging over a holiday weekend. During the three-hour wait that she and her husband endured in a side ward while a technician was being summoned from another hospital to carry out an ultrasound scan, a man came into the room and told her not to panic and that the babies would be fine. She had asked her husband afterwards what kind of doctor he thought the man was. Her husband said he hadn't seen anybody in the room, but that he had suddenly felt much calmer and more assured that things would be all right. The woman had finished reporting her story by saying that she wasn't particularly religious but that she now believed that maybe everyone had angels in their lives looking out for them.

The more Sarah read on the websites, the more she saw how the encounters people claimed fell into certain types.

There were the rescuers, intervening actively, sometimes physically, to save people in life-threatening moments, or to warn them of impending danger and steer them towards a safer course of action. Then there were the messengers – those who provided a link between people and their deceased friends or family members, like the man who made the long journey home from another city after attending the funeral of his son with whom he had been out of contact for several years, and on his home-security camera found an image of his son knocking at his front door recorded at the moment of the funeral service a thousand miles away.

The third sort of encounter was the advisor or counsellor offering hope at a time of crisis. Usually this meant illness or bereavement, or where difficult choices had to be made, and involved a male figure (the angel was almost always male) offering insights based on knowledge about the person that no one else but an angel could have known.

What Sarah found disconcerting wasn't the number of claims, or the range of them. It was their matter-of-factness. It was the straightforward acceptance of the events by the people who described them. The incidents were reported in much the same way that these people might have reported catching a train or buying a bag of groceries. It was as if these two wholly separate universes – the domestic world of supermarkets and TV and catching colds and paying rent, and this other world she was reading about on the websites she had found – lived unremarkably side by side, one set of realities imprinted on top of the other.

Did you have to be a simpleton to believe that? Did you have to live in a backwater community in Alabama, or be one of the happy clappies in a born-again congregation? It was much harder to accept it all when you spent your days plotting the transmission routes of chlamydial infection across north Manchester, and counselling people about the anti-retrovirals that would help combat their newly diagnosed status as HIV positive. It was an irony not lost on her that Saul himself had urethritis and gonorrhoea and whatever else was going to show when the rest of the test results came back and he turned up to hear them – if he turned up. Could angels be so much a part of this world that, even as celestial messengers, they could catch gonorrhoea? Did they weep pus? Certainly, inside Saul's head they did. She could imagine Saul shaking his head in apparent puzzlement and saying, 'It's crazy, isn't it?'

Some time after Katy died, Sarah had found herself talking to her daughter as if Katy were still alive – as if she were there with her in the room. She didn't *see* Katy. She wasn't, in any sense that the staff on the psychiatric ward on the floor below her would comprehend, insane. These were conversations that Sarah held in the privacy of her own head. She was lonely, and it made talking to herself somehow more acceptable, and so it was Katy she addressed in trying to frame her grief, in seeking answers, in working out how she might find a new life. But after a while she had started to imagine Katy's disembodied voice answering her. It happened frequently enough for her to become wary of the place she was retreating to in her head. She had been reminded of all this again in the last few days. She wondered what the man who had been called out from his hostel in order to take responsibility for Saul might have made of her mild and private lunacy. She wondered if Patrick Whatever-he-was-called would have calculated that she had been going mad. Anyway, for better or worse, she had stopped it.

In place of talking to her daughter, Sarah had taken up talking to herself. It was a reflex which, over a number of weeks became, in her mind, a dialogue with a disembodied spirit she imagined was part of her but not her. She held these conversations in the car while she was driving through the city.

She came to imagine him (she always thought of the entity as a him rather than a her) sitting in the back seat, which allowed her to talk unselfconsciously as she looked ahead at the road. After a while, she decided to give the entity a name. In quiet moments sitting in her office she practised writing alternatives down on a sheet of paper she kept in her desk drawer, adding new ones as they came to her, discarding others by putting a line through them, all the time whittling them down. She left him messages, bulletins on her state of mind. She kept them in the drawer, too. In the end she chose a name for him and stuck with it. She underlined it twice and put it back in the drawer. She called him Saul.

She told herself in the days after her visitor had turned up at the GUM department that she didn't need to believe or not believe. She could simply let the idea roll pleasingly around in her head for a few days. It made her happy to think that she had not completely crushed the thought. It accounted for some things. It made sense if you chose to look at the world in a certain, squinting way. It made more sense, for example, than the benefit rules around asylum seekers, or Vass's ineptness in running the department. It made more sense than the way the hospital tried to rig the star rating it got from the auditors. It made more sense than things like that. It made more sense than Katy dying.

Even as Aunty Maureen loads Liam and Patrick on to the bus with their two duffle bags and a small cardboard suitcase she declines to say exactly where they are going.

'We're seeing a man about the situation,' is all she will say. The situation – whatever it is – has required a bath for both of the boys and her best coat with the fur collar, the one that Eric says is made of hamster fur.

'What situation?' Liam says.

'Never you mind,' is all Aunty Maureen will counter.

When they climb off the bus Eric seems to guess at last where they are heading. As they walk along he keeps turning around to grin at them. Eric is their cousin. He is older than both of them and he has been brought along to help carry one of the bags, and because he wanted to come. Eric can fart on cue after counting down from ten, usually as he is leaving the box room at the back of their big house in which Liam and Patrick have been staying for the last six weeks since their mother's death. He is also an exponent of the catapult, never leaving the house without a small supply of stone pellets in the pockets of his shorts and as happy to ambush passing pedestrians as to startle the neighbourhood cats.

Aunty Maureen leads the way. Eric, alongside her, is trailing one of the duffle bags along the pavement. The two brothers in blue anoraks, shorts and knitted blue balaclava helmets trudge behind them on their unspecified journey, Liam hauling the suitcase. Patrick, with the second duffle bag over his shoulder, is now half a dozen steps behind. Eric taps his mother's arm conspiratorially. She glances behind her.

'Patrick, get hold of my hand. We'll never get there at this rate.'

She holds out her hand. Patrick eyes her, then feels Liam slip his own free hand into his. Aunty Maureen shrugs.

'Well, keep up then,' she says. This is business, it seems, that is best resolved without a fuss.

Eric looks around. 'You want to know where you're going to?'

'Where?' Liam says.

'An orphanage,' Eric says with satisfaction.

'*Eric!*' Aunty Maureen says. 'I *told* you!'

The Welfare Department is a red-brick building behind the fish market. Aunty Maureen leads them up four stone steps and through a door into a waiting room. She tells the woman behind the high counter that Mr Briffet is expecting her. The woman disappears into a back office. Liam puts the suitcase down and sits down on a wooden bench. The room is empty except for a two-bar electric fire and a table pushed against a wall on which a pile of *Woman's Realm* magazines and *Reveille*s are decaying neatly. Patrick stands tracing a line with his shoe around the pattern of the black and white linoleum squares. Eric starts to whistle. From the counter, Aunty Maureen flings an arm vaguely towards him in warning, and he stops.

'When's our dadda coming for us?' Liam asks.

No one says anything.

Eventually a man appears. He is shuffling through a sheaf of unruly papers. One of the buttons of his shirt is undone beneath his jacket. Patrick can see the hairs on his large belly.

'Mrs Mellor?' he says finally, looking up momentarily from the papers.

Aunty Maureen nods.

'Two boys?' he says. His voice fills the waiting room. He seems familiar with situations like this.

'Liam and Patrick,' Aunty Maureen says. She points them out, but the man is looking down at his pile of papers again.

'How old?'

'Eight and seven.'

'What about the father?'

Aunty Maureen roots around in her handbag and produces an envelope. 'He sent this last week.' She holds it out. Reluctantly, Mr Briffet dumps the papers he is holding on to the table, submerging the copies of *Woman's Realm*. He takes the envelope from Aunty Maureen.

'He cleared off down south when the second boy was a baby,' she says as he starts reading the letter. 'She always reckoned it was for the work, but we knew the real reason. He wasn't ever going to stop around. We knew he only married her in the first place because she was expecting. She was never going to land a good catch, not with her arm and everything.' She mouths the next word silently for him. 'Polio.' Then she adds, 'It was when she was a child. Held her back, really. Shame for her.'

'Was he wanting to take custody?'

'He was supposed to. I was meant to be just seeing to them while he was making his arrangements.'

Behind her, Eric has levered himself off the ground by grabbing hold of the back-rest of the wooden bench. He is swinging his legs free of the ground.

'And then it turns out he's going to do no such thing. He says in the letter he couldn't cope with it, and will I have them for now. Well, what am I supposed to do? I've got one of my own, and a husband with a responsible job, comes in and wants his tea on the table. Having two more while we've been sitting around waiting for miladdo in Bethnal Green to make his mind up has been plenty, thank you.'

'How long have they been with you?'

'A month and a half. She was in the hospital at Christmas. Christmas Eve was when they saw her last.'

'I'm sorry.'

'So am I, but it doesn't mean . . . I never said I was here to be taken advantage of. Anyway, that's water under the bridge now. I'm just passing on what he's written in his letter now that you're responsible for them.'

Eric is still swinging in the space between the wooden bench and the wall. Aunty Maureen glances towards him. 'Eric, will you stop that!' she hisses.

He stops momentarily. When her attention has gone Patrick watches him slowly resume the momentum of his swinging, inch by inch.

'There is no other family?' Mr Briffet asks.

'Not on his side, that I know of. They were an odd lot. Never even came to the wedding, most of them.'

'Will you be wanting to go and visit them?'

'Of course I'd like to – they're family – but I have one of my own to see to. And it's not like they're affectionate boys. They're not like Eric.'

'If you do want to see them, make sure you let them know in advance so they can tell you about visiting times.'

Behind them, Eric falls from the bench, hitting the linoleum floor with a clatter. Aunty Maureen spins around.

'Will you stop messing around and stand still? We're nearly done.'

Eric picks himself up, rubbing the back of his head ruefully. Aunty Maureen turns back to the man. 'Is there something I'm supposed to sign? The letter said I'd have to sign something.'

'There is – somewhere. I can't lay my hands on it at the moment. It's in the pile.'

While he searches, Aunty Maureen proffers a second piece of paper taken from her handbag.

'This is the note I told you about – the one they found in the hospital after she . . .' Her voice trails off.

The man looks at the three paragraphs written on the piece of paper. Then, to Aunty Maureen's surprise, he begins to read the note out loud, causing her to investigate the contents of her handbag intently as he reads through each one in turn.

'*1. Tell them I've written to their father asking if he'll come back for them.*'

Patrick cannot remember their dadda. He doesn't know what the man looks like. Like God and the angels, their dadda exerts a pull on them without having a face or a voice or a smell of his own. Their lives have been shaped by their mother alone. Each time Patrick pictures her now he sees her taking them to mass on Sunday mornings, her tiny headscarf framing her plain and beautiful face. Patrick remembers her chanting the solemn, satisfying Latin liturgy and singing the hymns in what Liam will refer to afterwards as her honey and sunshine voice, and he wonders what has happened to the credit they were surely building up with Jesus each time they knelt before him in fierce and diligent prayer.

'*2. Keep them together. I don't want them splitting up. I don't want them adopting separately.*'

It seems as though their mother must have suspected, even as she wrote the letter, that their dadda would not return for them, and that Aunty Maureen would be reluctant to take her boys in alongside Eric. And she knew that, in the natural order of things, Liam would always lead and Patrick would always follow, and this is how it should remain, with the older, more worldly, boy protecting the younger one.

'3. *Princes of hope.*'

The man looks curiously at Aunty Maureen. Eric, his back now pressed against the wall, sniggers. Patrick knows the phrase. It was the one their mother had used each night when she put them to bed. Remembering it as he stands there in the waiting room brings back with a jolt the memory of her scent he had smelled each time she bent over him and whispered the phrase in that honey and sunshine voice of hers and stroked his forehead with her good hand.

'She always did have an imagination,' Aunty Maureen says in explanation.

Is it imagination? It is *something* that their mother had. Dreaming of angels before a birth; smelling violets in the night when someone she knew had died. Everyone on Patrick's street knew that.

The man goes on reading from the piece of paper. '*Two princes of hope – that's what I liked to call them. Remind them of this. Tell them that's what they were to me – my two princes of hope.*'

'It's just a fancy phrase,' Aunty Maureen counters. 'She was soft, our Jean. If she'd been firmer about not letting him saunter off to London, or not letting him into her bed in the first place, we wouldn't be in this mess.'

The man looks at his watch. 'Is there anything else, Mrs Mellor, before we conclude?'

Aunty Maureen takes in a breath through pinched nostrils and ponders the question, anxious, it seems, to convey at this late stage some kind of meaningful information.

'The older one's bright, but he's stubborn,' she says. 'The youngest, you can't get much out of. Can't do his letters yet, that's for sure. He doesn't sleep regular, either. I expect it's not been good for him, this, but I've done what I can. It's someone else's turn now.'

She stops there, satisfied that this is enough to confirm her credentials as their temporary carer.

'In that case,' the man says, looking around at the two brothers, 'I expect you'll be wanting to shake your aunt's hand to thank her for looking after you.' He seems to assume that they will and so, uneasily, they do, both of them shaking Aunty Maureen gravely by the hand, to her acute embarrassment, which generates another snigger from Eric.

And that is that. Aunty Maureen and Eric turn and walk towards the door, leaving the suitcase and the two duffle bags standing in the middle of the floor. Liam is already looking around, measuring his circumstances. Only Patrick is looking back at his aunt and at Eric. In the doorway, Eric pauses before descending the stone steps down to the street outside. He leans forward slightly and summons one final fart aimed in Patrick's general direction. And then they are gone, beyond the door, out into the street, to lives that will not involve Patrick or his brother again.

The welfare officer is still studying the piece of paper in his hand – their mother's letter – as if he is trying to decide what to do with it. He folds it in half.

'Can we have it?' Patrick hears his brother say.

The man looks at Liam. He seems taken by surprise by the request.

'Can you have what?'

'Our mam's letter?'

'That,' the man says, 'is now a legal document to be kept on file.'

'We should get to keep it,' Liam says. 'It was our mam's.'

'And it is now the property of the Corporation Welfare Office.' Then, as if to dismiss the query once and for all, the man slides the letter into his jacket pocket and begins to gather up the sheaf of documents he has put down on the table. As he does so, a betting slip falls out on to the floor from amongst the listing pile of papers. His face lights up.

It isn't until later that night, after they have been driven several miles out of the city and delivered to Providence House, that Liam finally produces the letter. He has somehow lifted it from the man's jacket pocket at some point during the day without Patrick or the man himself noticing. The two boys are sitting in the dormitory. There are four sets of bunk beds, one in each corner of the large room. Liam has unpacked their bags and organized their clothes into the drawers they have been allocated beside the vacant pair of beds. Patrick is sat on the bottom bunk watching him. He doesn't cry, but only because Liam does not. And it is then that Liam produces the letter and presses it into his brother's hand.

For a long time after that, whenever Patrick wakes up in the night and lays there fearing that the mysteries of their present lives might overwhelm him, he will feel for the piece of paper. It lies hidden from view, folded to a square and pressed between the mattress and the base of his bunk. He will lift it out and unfold it and look at the words he cannot yet decipher while his sparrow's chest pulls steadily for air. Above him in his high bunk, Liam's shadow will lay nestled among the ceiling's cornices like some protecting spirit. In those moments, with the letter safely in his hands, Patrick is sure that all will be well. He knows that eventually he will come to understand why all the things that matter happened in the way they have. He tries to imagine these things taking shape as if they are part of one of Liam's stories. He feels that everything, in due course, will fall into its rightful place.

Everyone in the room hesitated. Roland had made his allegation. Now he balanced his bulk on the front of his chair, staring at the carpet under his friar's fringe, challenging the world to respond. He made that habitual slow gesture of his, using the palm of his fleshy hand to rub his nose and then sliding it down over his big lips and the stubble on his chin.

Roland was a big man with a flop of unwashed hair. He had been a short-order cook until the day he held the manager hostage in the kitchen with a meat cleaver ('It was hardly sharp enough to cut ice cream'). They were in there for four hours before Roland finally surrendered himself to the police. When he let the manager go he told the police, impressed, that he'd never seen a man sweat so much.

'There was a full fucking SWAT team round the place,' he liked to tell people. 'There was probably raiding going on in every shop in Bury that day, 'cause everyone in a uniform for miles was surrounding the Happy fucking Eater.'

The other residents, folded into clumsy shapes in assorted armchairs around the edge of the lounge, kept their heads down, yielding to the authority that Roland's resentment gave him. It wasn't clear what might come next. Over the weekend the residents had learned about Edward's arrest. Many of them had come to know Edward in his year there as a resident, and his fate confirmed what many of them feared about the world. Over the weekend, as well, there had been another emergency admission, something which usually unsettled the residents. Now, Roland was falling apart again and it wasn't clear what might come next.

Patrick counted. One. Two. Three.

He felt the weight of the tension in the room like an object in his stomach, the size of an egg. He was using it, as Benedict had taught him, to measure the pace of his response.

Each of the residents took turns to organize the week's shared domestic chores at the Limes – gardening, vacuuming, cleaning the two bathrooms and the big kitchen. From Saturday it had been Roland's turn, but there had been problems. Now, in the Monday evening house meeting, they were trying to work out why.

'Him!' Roland had said, pointing across the room at Kenny, another of the residents. 'He wouldn't last two minutes in a restaurant. Two fucking minutes. That's why it didn't get finished.'

No one else spoke. Kenny's head was tilted sideways, away from Roland's glare. Kenny was tall, pale, thin, with a lifelong habit of easing himself away from the centre of things. For eight years, before he had come to the Limes, before the spell in the hospital, Kenny had worked nights as a baggage handler. Roland looked around the room.

'No one's saying anything,' he complained, aggrieved. 'No one's backing me up.'

The other residents in the room were tense with anticipation. Roland was looking at his hands. He seemed suspicious of them, as if they might do something unexpected.

'You sound angry about it,' Patrick said.

'Course I'm angry.'

'Do you think that might be making people nervous?'

'Why can't I be angry? Kenny just arses about, and that new guy's done piss-all – just wanders in and out all hours when he feels like it. No one's bothered except me.'

'Maybe it's not that people aren't bothered,' Patrick said. 'Maybe they're nervous of how angry you get about it?'

'I'm angry because we didn't get finished. And that new bloke Saul gives me the creeps. You bollock him for not doing a job and he just looks at you and smiles.'

'Did you ask Kenny what the problem was?'

'Course I did.'

'And what did he say?'

'Nothing.'

'Did you get angry with Kenny?'

'I asked him what was up and he wouldn't answer.'

'Why don't you ask him now?'

"Cause I'm sick of asking him.'

'Are you okay if I ask him?'

'Suit yourself.'

Patrick held a pause before he went on.

'Kenny?'

Kenny was sat bent into his customary corner seat. It was the best place to sit to block out the waves. They used masts to send the waves across the city. The government could broadcast that way directly into his head. The masts were anything up to forty feet high. Often they were designed to look like parts of buildings. The staff at the hospital, Patrick knew, had tried to persuade Kenny that the masts were erected by mobile phone companies to boost reception, and Kenny had humoured them because the authorities wanted ordinary people to think that. There was a heaviness in the air when the masts were transmitting. Kenny had explained the phenomenon to Patrick by likening it to the way the atmospheric pressure changed in the hours before a storm. At that stage, you couldn't always see a storm building, but there was a quality to the air that a barometer could read for you, or that you could feel if you were properly attuned. It was like that with the faint electrical charge in the air that indicated the masts had been switched on and were trying to locate him to tune into his thoughts or to broadcast the voices into him.

'There wasn't enough time,' Kenny said in answer to Patrick's question.

'In the kitchen?'

Kenny nodded.

Roland interrupted. 'We were short today,' he said. 'Muzzy went for his Depixol injection and Saul pissed off somewhere, and all Kenny can go on about is what's going on in his head.'

Patrick turned to Kenny. 'So what happened, Kenny?'

'Roland got angry.'

'What did he do?'

'He got a knife.'

'You got a knife out, Roland?' Patrick asked.

'He's still got it,' Kenny said.

Patrick glanced across at Roland. 'Have you still got it?'

'It was only one from the kitchen,' Roland said.

'Have you?'

'What if I have?'

'On you?'

'Maybe.'

'Where?'

There was a hesitation. Then, without looking, Roland slid his hand down between the cushion and the arm-rest of the chair and pulled the knife from where he had secreted it. It was an old steak knife – five inches long, wooden-handled, its serrated edge blunted by years of misuse as a general vegetable peeler.

'He wouldn't do anything except muck about,' Roland said.

'Remember, we talked about this,' Patrick said. 'No violence. Absolutely no violence or threats of violence in this place. Those were the terms of you staying here.'

'There wasn't no violence,' Roland said.

'So what was the knife for?'

'*Jesus*,' Roland said. 'I only *said* it. I didn't fucking *mean* it.'

'Okay,' Patrick said. 'So put the knife down, Roland.'

Roland was muttering to himself now. 'I've known chefs who'd fucking knife you for just over-boiling an egg.'

'Roland.'

'*And* stick you in the soup.'

'Roland.' Patrick was conscious of slowing his voice down. 'Put the knife down on the carpet.'

'What's the use of being in charge if no one does what you tell them?'

'Roland, just focus on the knife,' Patrick said. He was speaking quietly now so that Roland had to concentrate to hear him. 'Remember the knife. Put the knife down on the floor.'

Roland lifted the knife from his lap and inspected it. He ran his forefinger slowly down the edge of the blade. He smiled the *don't you fuck with me 'cause you can't ever know all of me* kind of smile he reserved for moments when he was under pressure. He waited. He looked at Patrick. He seemed to be debating which of the various options open to him here he might take. He leaned forward. Then with a sudden movement of his wrist he lobbed the knife out into the no-man's-land on the carpet in front of him. It rolled twice and then stopped.

Patrick let it settle. It lay there, seeming to contain in its inanimate shape the memory of Roland's rage. He let people get used to the knife lying out there in the open for a moment. Nothing wrong in waiting, Benedict used to say. Lot of good things happen after you've waited for them.

Patrick spoke. 'Can I come over and take it, Roland?'

'He hasn't fucking apologized,' Roland said. 'I just needed him to work a bit harder today 'cause we were short and he did piss-all.' He was looking hard at the knife on the floor in front of him.

'We'll sort that out later. I'm going to walk over there for the knife now. Is that okay?'

Roland's fists tightened around the arms of the chair. The rounds of his knuckles were raised and white. Patrick pulled himself up on to his feet and moved slowly across the lounge. He reached out for the knife on the floor. Roland had followed Patrick's movement across the room. He watched Patrick pick up the knife, then exhaled through his nose. He sat back in his chair, shaking his head in apparent disdain, perhaps for Patrick, or for Kenny, or for the whole fucking mess clouding his head.

Patrick walked slowly back to his chair. He slipped the knife behind him. He waited again for things to settle.

'How are you doing now, Roland?'

Roland shrugged. It was non-committal.

'You remember we said about the anger, when it came, Roland – we said we'd give it a name. We said we'd call it Joe when it came and you felt it inside you?'

Roland looked fixedly at the place on the carpet where the knife had been.

'You remember that, Roland?'

'Yeah,' Roland said reluctantly.

'Good. We said we'd talk about Joe. We said we'd think about why he comes on so strong sometimes, and how sometimes you regret afterwards that it happened. Do you know why Joe turned up today, Roland?'

Roland shrugged.

'What made him react like that today with the knife, Roland?'

'He was looking after me,' Roland said in a voice that seemed smaller.

'Why was he doing that?'

''Cause no one else does.'

'Because no one else does?'

''Cause he doesn't want me to get walked on.'

'Why does he think you'll get walked on?'

''Cause I'm not as strong as him. Not without him.'

'Not as strong as Joe?'

'Yeah. 'Cause he's the best bit of me.'

'That's what it feels like?'

''Cause the rest of me's shit sometimes.'

'So if you and I can persuade him that you're not getting walked on, then Joe might not go over the top?'

'Maybe.'

'Can we do that, Roland? Tomorrow morning, maybe? Can you and me talk about what you could do while you're supervising the work in the house that would help Joe. That would avoid him getting you to pull a knife?'

'I suppose.'

'Otherwise you can't stay here, Roland. You can't pull knives on people and stay here. You understand?'

'Yeah.'

'Okay. That's good, Roland. That's good.'

Patrick let the silence in the room run on for another

moment. He could hear the percussion of people's laboured breaths. 'So, then. How's the work going to be sorted tomorrow?'

No one wanted to say.

'Roland, why don't you let Kenny work in the garden tomorrow instead of the kitchen if he's unsettled at the moment? What about that for tomorrow?'

'I thought I was in charge this week?' Roland said sourly.

'You are in charge. So what about it, for tomorrow?'

Roland silently considered the option. Wedged now at the back of his threadbare chair, dislodged from the momentum that his wrath had given him, he pulled one knee up towards his chest with his cupped hands. Finally, he nodded in subdued agreement. The battle, it seemed, was no longer important to him after all, and the world could fuck off and leave him alone now for a while.

In the hallway, Sarah stood listening to the rise and fall of their voices. She had endured the strategy meeting to discuss Tusa and her daughter, and then driven across the city to the Limes, following the directions she had been given by a woman from the hospital social work team. She had walked up the drive and found the front door propped open in the evening sunshine under the dilapidated wooden roof of the porch.

She could hear the voices in the meeting behind the door of the lounge. If she put her eye close to the nick in the door where it was hinged to the wall she could see the legs and feet of one or two of the people sat in chairs around the edge of the room. The one person whose face she could see was Kenny, sat in the far corner of the room, pale and big-eyed, and she had watched him being subjected to the verbal assault from Roland, whom she could not see, while all the time Kenny glanced around the room, apparently looking for a way to escape.

In the hall where she stood there was dust spiralling across the lines of evening sunlight coming through the coloured panes of glass in the window. There was a fish tank, filled with tiny silver and grey fish, perched on an ancient cupboard. There was a handwritten sign on the door opposite the lounge that said 'Office'. The door was partly open. She tapped on it but there was no answer. There were two other doors but they were closed and she did not try them. She looked around at the high ceilings, the old-fashioned plasterwork. She smelled the age of the place. She felt the old ghosts and the silence in the big house. She watched the fish swimming around in the bowl for a while, and heard the drift of the voices from behind the door to the lounge. She listened again to see if she could hear Saul's voice in the meeting, but she could not.

The trust had sent someone down from Legal for the strategy meeting in Dr Vass's office. The meeting was chaired by the business manager, a woman called Claire with a stiff perm and a bright, shiny face whom Sarah only ever saw in committees when Vass feigned prior engagements and sent Sarah as a junior replacement. The man from Legal wanted to know why Dr Vass hadn't been able to persuade the patient to agree to an HIV test for the child. Why had they allowed the situation to run on like this for almost two months? Was the GUM department not clear that there was the potential for liability here under the Children Act? Vass himself, outnumbered and under pressure, had started sniping at Sarah.

'Did I not make my feelings perfectly clear to you, Sarah?'

Sarah looked across at him surprised.

'I said that the child needed testing, did I not?'

'You agreed that it's not that simple,' she said.

'Why isn't it that simple?'

'Because it's not.'

'You are paid a lot of money to give advice, Sarah,' Claire said, smiling reasonably. 'This was clearly your responsibility.'

'I'm not paid to bully people, or to harass them.'

'You think that's what this is?'

'You could not have explained to the woman that this is for her own good?'

'I tried to explain that. I did explain that.'

'How often have you been seeing her?' Claire asked.

'Once a week,' Sarah said.

'For two months?' the man from Legal queried.

'Yes.'

'And you still haven't got over the message that we need that child testing.'

'I think she understood that we thought it was a good idea.'

'You *think* she understood?' Claire said. The smile on her face remained static. It occurred to Sarah that the smile was a kind of reflex, adopted whenever Claire had to use up part of her working day in the hospital speaking to someone of lower rank or intelligence.

'I *know*.'

'Did you tell her we can get social services to take legal action? Did you tell her there's no *point* in refusing?'

'Why is she suddenly going to start trusting the authorities now?' Sarah said. 'She's lived her whole life in a place that doesn't even *talk* about HIV, never mind treat it.'

'Let's not get overdramatic,' Claire said. 'Let's assume for a minute that it's not a person we're talking about here. Let's just see it as a strategic decision we need to reach in order to take the heat out of the situation.'

'How do we assume she's not a person?' Sarah asked. Claire's smile stayed in place.

'I say we go to court now,' the man from Legal said. 'Get it over with.'

'Give me a week,' Sarah said. 'Let me have one more week before you go to court.'

'Another week? This has gone on long enough. This isn't playschool. Sometimes, you people don't seem to live in the real world.'

'That's not fair,' Sarah said.

'Do you know what the media would do,' the man from Legal said, 'if she has a baby that's positive before we've bothered to get around to testing the one she's got? Or something happens to the one she's got? We'd be sitting ducks. We've already got the minister going apeshit about the deficit of his local acute trust. We can do without another fucking own goal. When are you seeing the woman again?'

'Tomorrow,' Sarah said.

'Right, let's keep things simple, Dr Vass. If we've not heard anything from you by Wednesday, we start the application to go to court. Are we all clear? Have we got that minuted?'

Afterwards, Sarah could hear Vass huddled at his desk with the man from Legal. She could hear mumbles of conversation and then a sudden uproarious laugh. She had put on her coat and left the building.

Gary wasn't due home until nine. She had driven over to the hostel speculatively. She was curious. She had wanted to know how Saul was doing. She wanted to see that he had settled, that he was less likely to wander out again on to the nearest ledge, that he was at least still there and had not drifted out of her life and out of the city as casually as he had arrived. But it was the other man she had found herself listening to. She recognized Patrick Whatever's voice from the message he had left for her on the department's answerphone on the night he had been called out to the hospital. *Shepherd*. She remembered it. Patrick Shepherd. She hadn't met him. By the time she had returned from the hospital cafeteria he had already persuaded Saul to come in from the scaffolding and had left the hospital with him, and there was only the smirking security guard left to deal with.

Patrick Shepherd had rung the GUM department several hours later, leaving a message which confirmed that Saul had travelled back with him to the Limes and had agreed to stay there for the weekend. In the message, he had seemed hesitant. The ends of his sentences had dropped away. It made him sound as if he were not entirely comfortable in the world, even though he was clearly competent in what he did. Now, beyond the door to the lounge in the Limes, Sarah could hear that same voice prompting the residents, clarifying points, coaxing Roland from his rage. She was comforted by the quietness of his manner; by the way he understood the importance of the words he used to the residents; by how he used that knowledge not to speak more but to speak less. She had wanted to ask him about Saul. Usually, she was clear about the lines she needed to draw in dealing with her patients, but this time the situation was less clear for her. She knew that something was going on with Saul, and with her, but not what. Even when the policeman had been asking her questions about Saul on Friday night she had found it troublesome to work out how much of what was in her mind was him, and how much was her reaction to him.

'What did he talk about?' the policemen had asked her while Saul was out on the ledge and they were trying to work out what to do about it.

'This and that,' she had said. 'Nothing much about himself. He asked some things about the clinic, about the testing, but I don't think he was distressed about it.' She did not tell him about the secrets they had agreed to share – about the photograph of her daughter.

'Anything else?'

'He talked about the whale,' she said, grateful to find something else to bring up. 'We'd been looking at the picture up there.'

She had pointed to the picture on the wall. She had tried to remember things that Saul had said. She kept remembering how, while he was talking to her, he had picked up sugar lumps absent-mindedly from the bowl she kept on the coffee table in her office and made them disappear in his fluent fingers. All the while he talked, he seemed not to know that the sugar lumps were coming and going.

'Did you know,' she said to the policeman, suddenly anxious to keep talking lest he spot her confusion, 'that when whales are hunted by the whaling ships, the whalers attach a grenade charge to the harpoons?'

'He talked about hunting whales?'

'The harpoon is five feet long,' she said. 'The grenade is triggered to go off a second after its impact with the whale, so that it explodes into the whale's side. When the whale pulls away after it has been hit, the tension on the rope snaps open the steel barbs on the tip of the harpoon and they embed themselves into whichever internal organ the harpoon has struck.'

'That's what he talked to you about?'

'So the harpoon, with the rope attached to it, becomes anchored inside the flesh of the whale.'

She had gone to eat a sandwich and drink tea in the cafeteria, and when she came back thirty minutes later Saul and the man from the hostel had gone. And so, after the weekend, she had persuaded herself to drive across the city after work to find the hostel, to ask Patrick Shepherd if she was safe, if Saul was safe; whether she should exercise any particular caution around him when he came back for his appointment later in the week, in talking to him, in being alone with him. But each time she had rehearsed how she might ask such a thing as she had driven towards the Limes she had found herself smiling at its ridiculousness. Of course he was *safe*. He was Saul. Why wouldn't he be safe? Her compromise was that she had decided to ask Patrick Shepherd whether he had discovered anything more about Saul. Who he was. Where he had come from. Why he had turned up in the city. But the man was busy behind the door of the lounge with his roomful of residents, and the evening meeting ran on, and she did not hear Saul's voice and surmised that he was away from the house. She decided there was no point waiting. She decided that she would not come back again. She decided that Saul's life was none of her business. Whether he turned up for his follow-up appointment was up to him.

She went into the office to look for a piece of paper on which she could leave a message. The small room was crowded with furniture and files. Above the desk, a notice-board was crammed full of lists and forms, and postcards, perhaps sent from previous residents. At the top of the notice-board were two pictures which looked like they had been torn from magazine supplements, of two men high-wire walking. Next to the desk was a filing cabinet with a message pad lying on top of it. She picked up the pad and tried to work out what she should write. Above the filing cabinet a poster had been taped to the wall. It showed a medal ceremony in a night-time athletics stadium. She recognized the image from a documentary on the American Civil Rights movement she had watched alone one night while Gary had been out somewhere *getting it*. She stood holding the message pad, looking at the poster. It was a photograph of the Mexico City Olympic Games in 1968. Two of the men on the podium each had an arm raised in a black power salute. Martin Luther King had been murdered earlier that year. King had led the Civil Rights movement, he had won the Nobel Peace Prize, but by 1968, aged thirty-nine, he was gone. Perhaps, it had seemed, his non-violent approach had gone too. There had been riots in a hundred American cities following his death. And then two black athletes, at the crowning moment of their careers, had stood on the podium in the black Mexico night, and made their own silent protest to the whole world.

Sarah sat down at the desk, still struggling to work out what to write. In the end she wrote simply that she had called round, and to thank the man for coming out to the hospital on Friday, and for giving Saul somewhere to stay, and to describe a little of what Saul had been like that evening in the GUM department. She confirmed that Saul had made an appointment to come back to see her later in the week to hear the results of some of the tests. She said she liked the poster, and the pictures of the two high-wire walkers on the notice-board. She said the picture that kept *her* sane in her office was one of a blue whale in a big ocean. She left the finished note on the desk and silently she wished Mr Shepherd, whom she had never met, a good life.

4

THE NAMING OF PARTS

The light was gone from the sky now. From where Patrick lay on the grass, looking up at the heavens, he could see Venus. He supposed it was Venus. All that summer people were saying it was possible to see Venus clearly in the night sky. Whenever he went out after dark and stood on the narrow strip of worn and mossy lawn at the back of the Limes and looked up he kept seeing one substantial star that was vibrant, sharp as a pin, hanging low in the sky, and so he supposed that this must be Venus.

He had looked it up in the old encyclopedia on the communal bookshelves at the back of the lounge, in the volume that went from *Utilitarianism* to *Zwingli*. The book said that the closest Venus got to the Earth was twenty-six million miles. But it also said that the further away Venus was from the Earth, the easier it was to see. It was something to do with the reflection of the sun. Patrick supposed, in that case, that Venus must be as far away as it could be at the moment because it was so easy to see – because it was the brightest star in the sky.

By his side as he lay in the garden was the note left by the woman from the hospital when she had called at the Limes earlier in the evening. He had heard something out in the hallway during the house meeting, but by the time he had gone out to see what it was she had gone, and it was only later that he had found the note she had left addressed to him on the desk in the office.

He was lying on his back, breathing slowly. The autumn grass around him was shiny with its night-time lick of damp. He could feel the moisture starting to seep through his jacket and his shirt, numbing those parts of his back that were in contact with the ground. Soon, he told himself, he would lever himself gently to his feet and start to ease out the stiffness that had ebbed into his joints in the last half-hour during his bout of solitary stargazing. First thing in the morning and late at night were the times these days when he was suddenly aware of his age, when he was reminded of how surreptitiously he had crept through his forties, that his body was not an inexhaustible, unchanging thing, that he was in the second half of his life; that, although in his head he was within touching distance of the small boy he had emerged from, parts of him were gently wearing out. He looked at his watch. It was twelve fifteen.

'What do you want me to call you?' he had said.

'Call me Saul. Saul is good.'

'Not Liam?'

'I told you, Liam's dead. My name is Saul.'

His brother had been dead for years. Liam had died in New York. His friends had written to Patrick to tell him, and to dispatch the photograph and the jewellery box they thought Patrick might like to have. Patrick had spent the years since then periodically imagining what words he might have spoken at his brother's funeral. But his brother wasn't dead; he was here in Manchester; he had been coaxed in from the scaffolding cladding a hospital extension; he had been admitted to the Limes as a short-term emergency referral; he had spent the weekend wandering the streets of the city.

There was no doubt that this was Liam. It was of no relevance that Patrick had not seen his brother in the flesh since Liam was fifteen. The single photograph he possessed of Liam as an adult, sent by Liam's friends in America after his supposed death, demonstrated that this was clearly the same man. Patrick could *see* it was the same man. This *was* the brother with whom Patrick had shared a room on Walter Street for the first seven years of his life, shared a bath with every Sunday after tea. They had shared a bed for the six weeks they had spent in Aunty Maureen's box room after their mother died. Until their eventual separation, they had slept in twin bunks at Providence House where the last thing Patrick remembered before he fell asleep each night in the long room was the faint impression of his brother's shape, a familiar protective spirit curved into the mattress above him. A gap of more than thirty years didn't mean you couldn't recognize your own brother, no matter what he wanted to tell the rest of the world about being an angel called Saul, about having a dead man's unenunciated mission to carry out.

In the three days since Patrick had brought his brother back to the Limes from the hospital's GUM department, Liam had used the same phrase whenever Patrick had pressed him.

'*Liam's dead. My name is Saul.*'

He said it matter-of-factly. He said it looking straight at Patrick with the curious, blank gaze of a stranger. I don't know you, the gaze said. Truly, it implied, I wish I could be of more help.

Saul had been taken by Patrick earlier in the day to the office of the community health team. The duty psychiatrist had carried out the assessment.

'Depression?' the psychiatrist had asked briskly. 'On a scale from one to ten?'

'None.'

'Self-harm?'

'None.'

'Suicidal thoughts?'

'None.'

After Saul gave each answer, the psychiatrist ticked a box.

'Any thoughts of harming yourself?'

'No.'

'Hallucinations?'

'No.'

'Cognitive impairment?'

'No.'

'Sense of hopelessness? Helplessness? Lack of worth? Guilt?'

'That's a big shopping list.'

'Well?'

'No.'

'Problems sleeping?'

'It's not a problem for me.'

'Are you experiencing any form of disorientation at all?'

'No, but I'm hoping to save up for it.'

'I notice you are dressed in black.'

Saul considered the observation. 'You're good at this,' he said.

'I wondered *why* you dress like that. Is it, perhaps, a way of reflecting how you feel inside?'

Saul looked down at his clothes. 'They match my shoes,' he said.

The psychiatrist looked at the white plimsolls Saul was wearing. 'Is it your opinion that you are having fun with me?'

'I'm having a ball,' Saul said. 'Aren't you? Are you happy in your work, Doc?'

'I'm not here with you to have fun,' the psychiatrist said. 'I agreed to meet with you so that I could help you.' He wrote something down. 'Do you take drugs?'

'What sort of drugs?'

'Any sort of drugs.'

'I have a chemical imbalance,' Saul said. 'It happens a lot with angels.'

'You are a user?'

'I take things to help with my imbalance while I'm here.'

'What do you take?'

'I don't know. I can't remember.'

'Alcohol?'

'That helps.'

'I see,' the psychiatrist said. He made another note. 'You don't carry any ID, do you?'

'It seems not.'

'If you have no identification, and you can't give me a surname or any more information, it makes it difficult for me to substantiate anything about you. Don't you think?'

'I don't have a surname,' Saul said.

'Your brother tells me that your name is Liam Shepherd.'

'My brother?'

'The man who brought you here. He says you are his brother. Did you change your name? Did you used to be Patrick's brother? He says your name is Liam.'

'Liam is dead. I told you.'

'And you want to be called Saul?'

'That's my name.'

'As far as you know?'

'That's right. As far as I know.'

'And you're saying to me that, at this point, you are an angel?'

'Crazy, isn't it?' Saul said. 'If someone had said that to me, I'd have them locked up. Christ, I could be dangerous or something. Do you think I'm dangerous?'

'Are you dangerous?'

'I poisoned somebody once.'

The psychiatrist scribbled another note. 'Was it somebody you didn't like?'

'Well, she wasn't that keen on me afterwards.'

'What did you use to poison her?'

'Chicken.'

'Chicken?'

'She was sick for days. I left the giblets in the bag as well. Even they weren't cooked properly.'

The psychiatrist sighed audibly. He put his pen down. 'It is my belief that you might need some help.'

'You think I need some help?'

'Does that idea trouble you?'

'Do you know anyone who *doesn't* need help? Of course I need help. I mean, it's not much of an assessment, is it? It's like saying I need food. You think I need food as well? Not chicken, though. I went off chicken.'

'What kind of help do you need?'

'I don't know yet. I have this thing I have to do.'

'You have this task you have to perform?'

'I've got to save someone, Doc, but I'm not sure who it is. It'll come to me soon, I'm sure. But if it doesn't, I'll be sure to come calling to ask for your help.'

'Patrick – the man who runs the Limes – he says you go missing from the hostel for hours at a time. Where do you go?'

'I just like walking.'

'Patrick says you go walking the streets of the city. He says you seem to know where you're going. He says he knows because he has followed you.'

'I know he follows me.'

'You do?'

'Of course.'

'Why haven't you told him that?'

'Because it makes him happy.'

'Following you makes him happy?'

'It gives him a sense of purpose. He thinks that by following me he's finding things out about me. He feels that this way he can help me. It makes him feel better.'

'And you're happy to leave him following you?'

Saul shrugged. 'He's not doing any harm. It's not like he's dangerous or anything.'

The psychiatrist had spoken to Patrick on his own afterwards while Saul waited for him outside in the corridor.

'I'll complete a safety profile when I do the assessment. I imagine they'll pay for the bed for a few more days until then.'

Patrick nodded. 'Do you think he really doesn't remember me?'

'There are syndromes where there's a fixation on identity, but nothing that's much of a fit for this. I've read cases where the person thinks someone close has disguised themselves as someone else – Fregoli's. And Capgras, where the delusion is that someone has been replaced by a double. These things are fairly rare and very specific. This one is a delusion all of his own.'

'Caused by what?'

'Could be anything. Drink. Or drugs, if he's on them. Might be some kind of trauma. He seems very sure in his own mind that he only has a few days left to complete some task.'

'What about the angel stuff?'

'You said you and your brother were raised as Catholics?'

'Yes, until we went into the orphanage.'

'I suppose the angel fantasy might be a regression back to that, to the trauma of losing your mother and going into the home, brought on recently by a specific crisis, or maybe by drugs.'

Patrick shook his head. It was he who had wanted to be an altar boy, he who had yearned when he was older to be spirited away into the sacristy by his mother's priest, Father Jacobs, to be ordained in the mysteries of the mass. He had wanted to say the holy responses, to pour the wine and the water, to genuflect and kneel as he moved about his solemn business with God's priest at the altar. He had wanted to be dressed in the white surplice and black soutane, to ring the bell, to witness the hosts transformed in front of him by the conjuring priest into the body and blood of Christ.

'I don't think Liam believed in any of it,' he said.

'Well, he clearly wants to think of himself as Saul,' the psychiatrist said. 'Which suggests that, for whatever reason, he doesn't want to be Liam. The problem you have is that someone who thinks he has already died has nothing to lose. There's a chance he may go damaging himself, or get someone else hurt in the process.'

'So what do I do?'

'Well, the way he talks about it, the timetable in his head might be the trigger for psychosis. I'll prescribe him Clorazil for now. See if you can get him through the coming weekend in one piece.'

'Why, what happens at the weekend?'

The psychiatrist closed the file. 'That's how long he says he has to complete the task he's come to do.'

'And after that?'

'Apparently his human form will simply evaporate. He tells me that's what happens when their time is up. Assuming he doesn't go up in a puff of smoke, that's when his real problems are likely to start.'

As Patrick was lying on the grass, looking up at Venus, he realized he was being watched. He turned around. His brother was standing by the side of the garage that housed the ancient Lada, abandoned there since Benedict's day. He was smoking a cigarette. The nurse from the GUM department had described in the note she had left in the office for him how she hadn't been conscious of Saul entering the waiting room; she was just suddenly aware that he was there. Patrick watched the cigarette smoke rise slowly. It hung above Saul's head, forming a gauze around him. Patrick sat up. The two men, fifteen feet apart in the garden, observed each other in curious silence.

It was Patrick who spoke first.

'Do angels know the names of all the stars?' he asked.

Saul looked up at the sky and gave the question some thought. 'No,' he said. 'Do social workers?'

Patrick shook his head. 'I used to make them up,' he said, 'when I was a boy. It was a game I played with my brother. These days I lack the imagination.'

'That's a shame.'

Saul drew on the cigarette.

'Isn't there a rule,' Patrick said, 'that says angels aren't supposed to smoke?'

Saul looked down at the cigarette as though he were slightly surprised to find it there, pinched between the first two fingers and the thumb of his right hand.

'Maybe there is,' he said, after thinking about it. 'Maybe I'm not such a good angel.' He didn't seem troubled by this notion.

Patrick watched him as he spoke. He was examining the way his brother's face had changed, and the ways in a hundred minute shades and inflections that it had not. He was examining the middle-agedness of the face. He was scrutinizing the way in which Liam's face had altered from that of the young writer in the Brooklyn diner – the face Patrick had learned by heart from the photograph he had been sent in the aftermath of Liam's apparent death and which he had pinned on the notice-board in the office beneath the cuttings of the wire walkers he had preserved from magazines years before. One of the cuttings he had saved was of Karl Wallenda above the Tallulah Falls in Georgia, when thirty thousand people had watched Wallenda walk across the gorge seven hundred feet above the ground. The other photograph was of a young Frenchman who had strung up a wire between the two towers of the World Trade Center in 1974 and walked across while the New York traffic one hundred and ten floors below him had ground to a halt. The 25-year-old Frenchman Philippe Petit was everything that Patrick himself was not. Undaunted. Fearless. Free of constraints. Sure of who he was and what he could do. That was how Patrick saw Liam. It seemed natural, when his brother's photograph arrived, that Patrick should pin it up beside two other men who were similarly unbound.

The face looking back at him now in the garden of the Limes was the face of the same man who had gazed back from the photograph on the notice-board. Now, though, his brother's face was filled and lined and eddied by a life that Patrick himself had accrued so little knowledge of.

'You look tired. Not sleeping?'

Patrick gave a brief smile of acknowledgement. 'No.'

'Me neither.'

'So I heard.'

'The nurse at the hospital?'

Patrick nodded. 'It seems she called round here earlier tonight. She left me a note. She said in it that angels don't go to sleep. You want to read it?'

'No. What did she want?'

'I don't know. To be honest I think it was you she was looking for. I was in the weekly house meeting. You should have been there too. I get the feeling she wanted to check how you were doing. The last time she saw you, you were sitting on a scaffolding plank outside her office window with your feet over the edge.'

Patrick eased himself down on to the grass again and looked up at the sky. 'You know that Liam was my brother?'

Saul dropped his cigarette butt to the ground and stubbed it out with his borrowed plimsoll. 'I know that, yes.'

'He was smarter than me,' Patrick said.

'Yes?'

'He was my best friend.'

'He was?'

'After our mother died, he was the only person I could trust. That's the thing about an orphanage, you see. There are people who care for you, but nothing is ever unconditional. There are things that are unforgivable. That's what you have to get used to. That's why he was the only one.'

This time there was no answer.

'This thing you have to do, this errand. When you were given it, did you get any message from Liam to give to me?'

'I did get a message, yes.'

'What was it? Can you tell me?'

Saul thought about it for a while, apparently trying to remember what the message might have been.

'He said he was sorry,' Saul said finally.

Patrick didn't say anything. He lay on his back watching the ghosts of purple cloud edging across the night sky above him. Behind him, he could hear his brother lighting up another cigarette. It was some time before Patrick looked around again. When eventually he did, there was no one there.

He understood only that he had no answers to the events of the last few days. He wondered if it was some kind of test, although he didn't know what the test was, or why he was being tested. Before he went back inside the house, he looked again for Venus in the sky. He remembered how far away it was. He remembered how this was the reason he was able to see it so distinctly – how, the closer its orbit was to the Earth, the more it shifted out of focus and became harder to see clearly.

The water seems to hold its breath. The flat surface shimmers, bouncing light against the dark green tiles on the walls. The light from the high windows catches perpendicular lines of dust that sway this way and that until they seem to come to rest eventually on the surface of the swimming pool. The boys in their underpants are gathered at one end of the pool, fidgeting, jostling. The shoulders of their unfinished bodies are hunched, their arms crossed together in front of the flat of their white stomachs. Their voices, rising cleanly to the roof, are turned by the echo into the sound of guillemots squabbling. Even as the boys spar amongst themselves their eyes remain drawn to the water whose impossible stillness they dare not yet break, and so they wait for the signal.

To an outsider, the huddle of boys looks formless, but to Patrick's watchful eye there is order to it. He knows the weaker boys hold back. He knows the dominant ones line the edge of the pool, reserving the best vantage points for the dive that will mark the start of the warm-up when the register has been called. He knows they lay bets on who will be the first to hit the water. Although his view is obscured by twenty other bodies, Patrick knows which boys are already lined up at the front. He knows Kipper will be amongst them, will be at the centre of this carefully ordered world. He knows that Kipper is in charge. He can hear Kipper's voice now above the others, extolling with certitude the merits of resolute Henry Cooper over the disgraced Cassius Clay.

Patrick stands at the rear of the group. His back is pressed into the cold of the tiles on the wall behind him. He has made himself invisible. He is barely there at all. He is holding the most recent breath he took, as if to exhale now would break a spell that might momentarily be succeeding in holding back the passing of time and the inevitable treachery of the water. Liam looks around from his place in the pack and grins at him, as if to say it's all right, as if to confirm that soon it will be over with for another day.

There are other physical activities, but Patrick is excused those. Evening practice at Providence House means running or boxing twice a week before supper. Every boy is selected for one of the disciplines. Even Frankie Benn does evening practice. Frankie Benn wears elasticated slip-ons because he cannot tie his shoe laces, and he talks with an egg in his mouth (Kipper says), but in the gymnasium he boxes with a blank-eyed stubbornness that delights the physical education instructor, Jacko. Only Patrick is excused evening practice – he cannot run or box because of the asthma for which small white tablets of ephedrine are dispensed when he wakes up wheezing in the night, and so, instead of evening practice, Patrick is assigned to help Joe Swift, the handyman-gardener. But there is no escape from the swimming.

All the boys know the story of how the original charitable orphanage had been founded by the industrialist Dr Murdoch-Bannerman after his only son had drowned when his skiff capsized in the reservoir on the edge of the estate. They know that Murdoch-Bannerman had bequeathed his estate for the founding of an orphanage and that one of the conditions was that every orphan housed there must be taught to swim. They know that when the County Welfare Office took over the management of the orphanage in 1947 the trustees had insisted on this condition of their founder continuing to apply. And so, once a week, the boys attend the pool. But although it is Jacko who appoints the captains for the relay, although the whistle hangs on a piece of rope around his neck, although Jacko wears a tracksuit with 'Coach' sewn on the back, and was in the army before he came to work here, and hollers now and then at boys to point out defects in their technique as they swim, Patrick – with a young boy's perspicacity – knows that in truth it is Kipper who is in charge.

Kipper is the biggest of the boys in their block. He is not as natural a swimmer as Johnny Astle, who has swum breaststroke for Manchester Schools, but Kipper's exuberant and chaotic front crawl makes him effective enough in the pool, and anyway his boxing ensures his pre-eminence. Johnny Astle is just a pretty boy, a stylist. Kipper's grit is unappreciated by the Nancy-boys who coach the schools team. Kipper has swum in the Leeds–Liverpool Canal; he could swim to the Isle of Man if he needed, probably to France. He's confident of this. When he's older, Kipper will box at the Olympics, not at Mexico City next year but at the one after that – at Munich in 1972 – when he'll have grown to his full height and when he'll have a manager to drive him places and buy him food in restaurants with leather seats and waitresses serving milkshakes and hot-dogs.

After the warm-up of half a dozen laps (which, in Jacko's mind, is what constitutes their swimming lesson) comes the week's relay race. Each boy will swim two lengths for his team before handing over to the next leg swimmer by touching the side of the pool. Kipper and Johnny Astle are inevitably nominated as captains. Starting with the toss of a coin for first pick, the two of them will choose their teams one at a time. As each boy is selected, he will leave the line and join the group of boys forming behind their captain. Jacko makes the losing team stay behind afterwards to mop and clean the changing rooms. He tells them this is character-building. The stakes are therefore high, and selection is always an agonizing process, with the captains weighing up a myriad of competing factors including age and size and competence and form and allegiance. They must also contend with the urgings of those already picked and lined up behind them who hiss out their own suggestions over the captain's shoulder as to who should be picked next. The problem for both captains is that neither one of them wants to be left with Patrick on his team. Patrick and Frankie Benn are always the last two picks, but even Frankie Benn with his windmill arms and lack of fear of the water is preferable to Patrick.

Even now, as he presses his back harder against the tiles and tries not to break the moment's spell by breathing, Patrick understands that history is already written. He knows that shortly he will find himself once more the last man standing in the line, eyes down, trying to avoid the glare of other boys in this ritual confirmation of his place in the scheme of things. He knows that Frankie Benn will have been chosen. He knows that either Kipper or Johnny

Astle will, with a sigh, reluctantly signal for Patrick to join his team. He knows that, no matter how big a lead his team mates may gift him, they are condemned to watch him being overtaken on the last leg as his desperate doggy paddle disintegrates into mayhem, and that Jacko may have to get the bamboo pole out to drag him the final half-length. He knows that, like some latter-day Jonah, he brings a curse to those he stands beside.

Around the table in the kitchen, some of the residents were playing cards. It was almost one o'clock. This was their final game of the night. There were always a few poor sleepers who did not go to bed until the early hours, and the card game was the customary way for them to wind down after the inevitable trials and confrontations of the house meeting. In the quiet of the house they could hear the tapping of the keyboard in the office next door where Patrick was still working, and it comforted them. Kenny felt safe enough not to have to sit in the corner seat. It felt like there were no voices being transmitted in the air tonight, just the sound of Patrick's keys being steadily tapped next door, and the routine of the Monday card game.

Saul lit a cigarette. He had drifted back into the house an hour ago. The conversation as they played their cards was punctuated by Muzzy tapping the table lightly with a pen to some unheard rhythm inside his head whenever it was someone else's turn to play a card. He was always like that after his Depo injection. Saul took a long drag on the cigarette. His fingers trembled slightly as he held it.

'Well, I don't want to leave here,' Brenda said, going back to the previous conversation. 'I'd rather stop here for ever.'

'You have to go,' Kenny said.

'Look what's happened to Edward,' Brenda said.

Muzzy was tapping with the nib of his pen. In front of him on the table was a notepad. Muzzy made notes of all the thoughts he had. Back in his room, the others knew, he tried to organize them by laying them out and colour-coding them through the night.

'Sometimes,' Brenda said, 'I just wish I was someone else. I don't want to be me for ever.'

'Who d'you want to be?' Kenny asked.

'Someone who wasn't afraid of things.'

'What sort of things?'

Brenda laughed briefly. 'Doctors,' she said. 'Dogs. Wasps. Dentists. People. Supermarket checkouts. Anniversaries.'

'Anniversaries?'

'Once,' Brenda said, 'I cried in a store because I was in the wrong queue.' She smiled.

'I wouldn't get on a plane one time,' Kenny said. 'They got mad at me, but I wouldn't get on.'

'Olivia Newton-John,' Brenda said.

'Who?'

'That's who I'd like to be.'

'Why do you want to be her?' Kenny asked her.

'She's pretty,' Brenda said. 'I expect she didn't want to be anyone else.'

'What about you?' Kenny said, looking over at Saul.

'What about me?' he said.

'Who'd you want to be? If you could choose?'

'I'd be a cat,' he said eventually.

'What'd you want to be a cat for?' Roland asked him.

Saul smiled – a brief smile that came and went in an instant, and then he recited something from memory.

> *The dog is a baffled lion,*
> *The engineer wants to be a poet,*
> *The fly studies to become a swallow,*
> *The poet tries to imitate the fly,*
> *But the cat*
> *Wants only to be a cat.*

Muzzy had picked up the pen again and was knocking it absently against the side of the table while he waited for his turn to play. He scribbled something down in his notepad, then resumed his tapping.

'What is it?' Kenny asked.

'It's part of a poem.'

'It doesn't rhyme.'

'No, it doesn't,' Saul said. 'I'll be sure to tell him when I see him.'

'So what *were* you?' Kenny asked.

'What was I?'

'Before you ended up here. What were you? What did you do?'

'You want to know what I was?' Saul said.

'Yeah.'

'I was alive,' Saul said, 'and now I'm not.' He took another drag on his cigarette. Then he raised the smoked-out stub and held it pinched between the tip of his thumb and the first two fingers of his right hand. He moved it slowly over to his bare left forearm and pressed the smouldering tip against the veined white flesh below the crook of his arm. The hot ash slowly blistered his skin. His face registered nothing. Muzzy's pen had stopped tapping. Saul held it there until each person's breath around the kitchen table, without them being conscious of it, was held, hanging on the cusp of an exhalation.

When Saul finally pulled the stub away, the mark was scalded purple on to the underside of his forearm. The action released them all silently back into their breathing rhythms. They could smell the faint trace of burning.

'Sometimes,' Saul said, 'you have to see things yourself before you can understand them.'

'Someone said you reckon you're an angel,' Brenda said.

Saul took a drag on the cigarette, watching her. He smiled.

'Does that mean you can do things?'

'Course he can't,' Kenny said.

'What sort of things?' Saul asked.

'I don't know. Things.'

Saul was looking out of the window. 'I know the next card is a three,' he said vaguely.

'What?'

'The next card in the pack,' Saul said, 'is a three.'

'You think you know what the next card up is?' Kenny said.

Saul shrugged. 'Try it. Turn it over. You never know.' He didn't seem to care whether they did or didn't.

Kenny reached over to the pack in the centre of the table. He picked up the top card. He drew it close to his face and examined it.

'This thing you have to do?' Kenny said. 'What is it?'

They sat waiting for Saul's reply. Muzzy had picked up the salt cellar and was rocking it almost noiselessly in his hands. The rest of the house was quiet. They were the evening's last few survivors. Roland had pulled a knife today, and somewhere across the city Edward was under arrest, and the only sound they could hear above their breathing was the ticking of the kitchen clock on the wall, and all of them were hoping that it would be a three.

Kenny flicked the card out across the table towards Saul. It landed face up for everyone to see. It was the seven of diamonds.

'I thought you said it was a three?' Kenny said.

Saul shrugged. He looked out of the window again where it appeared the answer might lie.

'I must have got it wrong,' Saul said. He seemed unconcerned. Then something occurred to him. 'It was on the top of the pack,' he said. 'Maybe it wandered off on its own somewhere. Maybe it's hiding. Have you looked in your shirt pocket?'

Kenny watched him for a moment, incredulous, then wary. He felt at his shirt. There was a playing card in his breast pocket. He pulled it out, looked at it, dropped it onto the table in front of him as if he didn't want to hold it any longer than he had to. It fell spot side up. It was a three.

The game had broken up and the residents had gone to bed. Only Patrick, not yet ready to drive home across the city and with no sleep in him, was still downstairs. He was sat in his office, jabbing at the keys with his two deliberate forefingers. There was only a wall between the kitchen and Patrick's office and he had sat there listening to their conversations about Edward's arrest, about Saul and his lunatic notions. He enjoyed being there when the last of the residents had gone to bed. He liked the stillness in the old house, the sense of another day passing and the residents safe. The hush reminded him of the nights at Providence House. As a boy, he would lie in his bunk in the dormitory room and drink in the noiselessness, savouring the spaces this opened up inside him. The people charged with running Providence House had meant well in their own way; their intentions had mostly been honourable. But it was a compromised life – in the way they lived and breathed as a single group, in the limited attention each child received from those in charge, in the regulation needed to bring order to seventy children's lives. There were rules, and broken rules led to punishments, and each punishment was graded on a scale as fixed and immutable as the laws of physics or the verses of the catechism, and what passed for love or came close to it was contingent on following the rules, and it was so far away from the unconditional white light in which their mother had bathed them.

The mug of tea beside Patrick had been Roland's peace offering before he had gone to bed. Roland couldn't ever bring himself to say sorry, but whenever there was a confrontation Patrick knew that he would appear at the door of the office some time later with a brew with the same three sugars in that Roland himself took.

'I just thought you could use this,' he'd say, and put it down on Patrick's desk and leave. And Patrick would thank him as he left, never finding a way of telling Roland that he didn't take sugar in his tea.

He was writing up his notes on Edward's arrest. In the eyes of the Hobart Trust, Edward had progressed and that was an end to it. Payment had been made and he was off the books. There was no need to keep any records of further contact. There should be no further contact. But Patrick had continued to keep in touch with Edward as he did with a number of other ex-residents across the city, and to keep notes of his support.

He had tried a number of times in the last few days to speak on the phone to Lillian. He needed to explain to her that the police had been granted a warrant to search the flat. He needed to tell her that he had been called to the police station a second time while the police questioned Edward again, this time with the duty solicitor in the room as well. But however often he rang through to Bolton, Lillian's sister would not pick up the phone.

Patrick had observed the romance unfolding between Edward and Lillian with curiosity. It occurred to him that he had never been so close to love. Not since his mother had died. Not, at least, since his brother had left Providence House. When Patrick was very young, he had assumed that love grew easily and everywhere, like dandelion or meadowsweet. Only when it was gone did he come to understand its elusiveness, its miraculous improbability. By then, by the time he was on his own at Providence House, he could imagine it but he did not expect it to happen, in the same way that he could imagine the sky raining frogs.

With Edward and Lillian, he had felt a kind of alchemist's power, and an alchemist's ignorance, in the way his limited interventions with two people had set off a much larger, more powerful reaction between them. He sought to name the parts of their love, but could not. He understood that they had crossed to a place beyond his reach. Although Patrick had needed to explain the mechanics of sexual intercourse to a baffled Edward, Patrick understood that with love itself it was he who was the novice.

As Edward had fallen in love with Lillian he had started to walk better. It was as if the pieces of his body had begun to fit together more pleasingly. His hearing was sharper. He could remember things that had previously eluded him. Although he still did not smile, there was a new sense about him that he could if he chose to. In those last weeks in the Limes, and then perhaps fleetingly in their life together in Gallowfield, Edward's hesitancy seemed less like the prison it had once been than a kind of anticipation of some small good thing lying ahead.

At the police station, they had started by going through the same questions again to establish the basics, to set a rhythm to the interrogation. Edward's name and address. That he lived with Lillian. That Lillian had gone. The details of Edward's previous offence. The terms of his licence as a schedule one offender. How long the licence had been lapsed. The young girl who had gone missing on the Gallowfield estate. Whether Edward had ever spoken to her, seen her. Whether he knew what had happened to Lucy. Whether he knew where Lucy was.

The questions about the girl's coat. The circumstances of his arrest on the estate. What he was doing with the coat in the middle of the night. Did he understand he wasn't doing himself any favours by not giving answers to these questions? And from the rhythm of the questions came the rhythm of Edward's rocking in his chair, back and forth.

Finally, the new information. Edward's flat had been searched. What did Edward think they might have found? Did Edward want to help them out here? Starting to talk would help him and them. What did he think they might have found at the flat? Look at us, Edward, while we're talking to you. Look at us! What do you think? Anything? Anything belonging to Lucy? What about a bobble hat? Do you think we might have found that in your flat? Lucy's hat? How did it get there, Edward? Did you put it there? Did you take it from Lucy? Was Lucy in your flat, Edward? What about the Spiderman figure? That's Lucy's as well, isn't it? We know it is. We checked with her parents. Lucy's step-dad says it's been missing from her room. We found the Spiderman in your flat as well, Edward, didn't we?

Edward, did something happen with Lucy? Tell us, Edward. Tell us what you did, before it's too late.

Edward had not spoken since the policeman had asked him to confirm his name and where he lived, and he had nodded. He had found a spot slightly to the left of the door in the interrogation room and had fixed his gaze on it. He maintained it even now as he rocked, two inches back, two inches forward. His left fist was clenched white and bloodless beneath the table. Patrick could see it from where he sat. It seemed to Patrick, watching him, that at any moment Edward might forget to breathe and fall dead there and then of fear and asphyxiation.

Only when the questions at the end switched to Lillian did Edward break from his self-imposed trance. The policeman wanted to know whether there had been an argument. Could the argument have been about Lucy? Perhaps Lillian had not liked what Edward had been saying about the girl? Or what he was doing with her? To her? What was it that had persuaded Lillian to pack a bag and leave? Was it something to do with Little Lucy? On the table between the detective and Edward, the machine recording the evidence of his non-co-operation ran on in a conspiratorial hum.

Only at that point had Edward finally addressed Patrick, but without turning around or shifting his gaze from the spot on the wall to the left of the door, or pausing in the steady motion of his rocking, as if he knew already that Patrick would fail him.

'Help me, please,' he had said.

But even before he had formed the words, his voice was breaking into pieces.

5

THE RULES OF FLIGHT

The little girl kept looking at Saul. She had startlingly big eyes. She was facing backwards on the chair in front of him in the waiting area, kneeling with her legs tucked beneath her. Her mouth was resting on the top lip of the chair's moulded plastic backrest. She gave no indication of wanting to speak.

The girl's mother was a hesitant African woman whose communication with her daughter seemed to be entirely in the form of small whispers. The girl had been sitting in the corner of the waiting area which was given over to a collection of children's toys. She had been looking at the multi-coloured building blocks and apparently making a series of calculations about them in her head. When the woman's appointment with the health advisor had been called, there was a murmured conference, the result of which was that she had gone into the room alone and the little girl had stayed outside in the waiting area. After a few minutes, the girl had started to drift around the room. She seemed curious about people's faces, gazing hard at them as she wandered past. One or two people said hello, but she didn't respond. Mostly, people had avoided her gaze or taken refuge behind magazines. Eventually she had come to rest in front of Saul.

Above their heads, the clinic's wall-mounted television pumped cartoon noises out across the waiting room. The girl seemed oblivious to them. She kept her eyes focused on Saul. He looked back at her, mirroring her solemn gaze. It seemed possible that the two of them might stay staring at each other in that way for the rest of the day.

'Is this where the 42 bus stops?' Saul asked eventually.

The girl didn't reply.

'Someone said the 42 came past here,' Saul lamented. 'I've been here for ages and there hasn't been one yet.'

'This isn't the bus stop,' the girl said seriously. Her accent had the elliptical vowel sounds of southern Africa.

'No?' Saul queried.

She shook her head.

'That would explain it,' he said. He shifted his weight in the chair and crossed his legs by placing one white plimsoll over the other.

'How long have you been waiting?' the girl asked him.

'Since Christmas Day,' he said. He seemed only vaguely aggrieved.

'You have not.'

'No?' He seemed ready to be corrected.

She shook her head again in confirmation.

'I must have miscounted,' he said.

She didn't answer him.

'So if there are no buses,' he asked her, 'what's everyone queuing for?'

She rested her forearms on the top of the chair. 'It's a hospital.'

He nodded that he understood. 'What do they do here, then?'

'They treat you for germs.'

'Is that so?'

'Have you got germs?' she asked him.

'Yes, I have,' he admitted.

'What sort do you have?'

'Blue ones,' he said. 'I've got blue germs.'

'You've got *blue* germs?'

'That's right. Most people have pink ones, but these are harder to deal with than the pink ones. That's why I came here. They said this hospital was the right place for blue germs. Is that why you're here?'

She shook her head. 'It's my mother.'

'Does she have blue germs?'

The girl shrugged. 'She gets sick sometimes. But she's going to have a baby, so she'll be better then.'

'Did you know I had blue germs?' he asked.

'No.'

'I wondered if it showed,' he said. 'You look like someone who would know that kind of stuff.'

'Where are they?' she asked.

He paused, as if weighing up whether to confide the information to her. 'They're in my coat pocket,' he said finally, as if the information had been coaxed reluctantly out of him.

'Can I see?'

'Only if you're training to be a doctor.'

'I do spellings,' she said.

He nodded. 'That's close enough.' He peered into the pocket of his long black coat, then looked back at her, obviously puzzled.

'Funny,' he said. 'They were there the last time I looked.' He pushed his hand inside and felt around. The girl waited for him to report his findings. Then he stopped searching. 'I remember now,' he said. 'They're in my other coat.'

The girl's mother emerged from the health advisor's office. It was clear that she was heavily pregnant. She looked around the room for her daughter and beckoned for her to come. The girl saw her mother but did not seem ready yet to acknowledge her.

'Can you die from blue germs?' she asked Saul. She was still looking steadily at him.

'*Grace*. Leave the man alone, please.' Her mother's voice had the same African inflection.

Grace glanced around. Her mother was moving slowly towards the door, hoping to draw her daughter into following her. Grace slid her knees off the chair and drew herself reluctantly to her feet. She was still looking at Saul, though. She was still waiting for an answer.

'Only if you lose them,' Saul said to her. 'And I'm sure I put mine in my other coat.'

Sarah was crossing the waiting area after her appointment with Tusa had finished when she heard Tusa's daughter talking to Saul. She hadn't heard the little girl speak before. She knew that, in theory, the girl spoke English, but in Tusa's visits to the clinic Sarah had been unable to coax any words out of her.

From the start of her visits to the GUM department, Tusa had talked about her own situation to Sarah almost matter-of-factly – as if she were describing the story of another person she barely knew. She had been raped, she said, by soldiers.

'Did you see the authorities to press charges?' Sarah had asked her.

'They *were* the authorities,' Tusa had said. She was not angry or outraged. She was simply explaining a fact about her life in Angola.

'Why you?' Sarah had asked.

'My husband,' Tusa had told her. 'The MPLA soldiers said he was working for the rebels and they did not like that. They made his life very difficult. He lost his job. We were both teachers. When they arrested him, they said it would be for one or two days for questions. We did not see him again after that. I went to stay with my parents in Malanje province. The soldiers came there too. That was when they did the thing.'

'Were your parents there too?'

'Only my brother.'

'What about Grace?'

'They took her to another room.'

'Did she hear what was happening?'

Tusa had shrugged. 'I suppose so.'

'Was she hurt?'

'One of the soldiers hit her, I think, when she was crying for me. Afterwards, we were taken by friends to be treated. The doctor looked after us both. I was sick for three days – I don't remember much about those days.'

'You couldn't take the matter up with anyone? I mean, if they broke the law?'

'They are the law. It is the law which does these things. At a time like that, you must accept that you are not a real person, a full person. Not one of the big people. You are a small person and you must resign yourself to what is offered.'

The situation, she said, had been difficult enough before the soldiers came back, but after that she made the decision to flee from Angola. She had travelled with Grace in the back of a lorry to get to Namibia, then crossed into South Africa when she feared the Namibian authorities would send her back. In South Africa, she was advised not to claim asylum because she would be sent back to Angola. She paid a Nigerian called Innocent four hundred rand for a South African passport.

She was six months pregnant when she arrived in England on the passport she had bought. The Home Office said it was false and confiscated it. At her screening interview at the airport, she was given a registration card. It had the name from the passport on it. Tusa told them it was not her name, but they wouldn't change the name on the card.

Within a month of arriving in England, Tusa had been diagnosed as HIV positive. She was attending Sarah's GUM clinic so that the medication regime she had been put on as a pregnant HIV positive mother could be monitored. Sarah used the sessions in part to try to get Tusa to talk, but they had been difficult. Tusa did not know how to trust her. She had lost faith in the possibility of trusting anyone. Her most frequent form of communication was a shrug of compliance. Almost unconsciously, as an attempt to bridge the gulf between them, Sarah had begun to knit a baby quilt at home with the intention, when it was done, of giving it to Tusa for the baby. After a month of working on it at home, she brought it to the office and knitted during the sessions while they talked.

'What is that thing for?' Tusa had asked her finally.

'It's for your baby,' Sarah had said. 'Do you like it?'

'It is not necessary,' was all Tusa would say.

'Do you have anyone you can talk to about things?' Sarah said. 'About the baby?'

'There was someone,' Tusa said.

'Who?'

'There was a man called Findlay. He was another man claiming asylum. He was someone to talk to. Sometimes we laughed.'

'How did you meet him?'

'At the welfare rights office.'

'What happened to him?'

'He went away. When I went to the place where he worked driving the taxis, they said only that he had gone away.'

'Do you know where he went?'

'Perhaps he meant for me not to know.'

'And he didn't leave a message or anything?'

There was that shrug again, an acceptance that a man like Findlay would not choose to stay around, that he would inevitably drift away. There was a hesitation in Tusa's voice in recounting the story in which, momentarily, she seemed to be recalling the memory of laughter.

It was some time after this that she had told Sarah about the rape, and how her brother had died that day at the hands of the soldiers. She would not, however, consent to

Grace being tested. Tusa already knew it was possible that the baby she was expecting would be HIV positive. She didn't know for certain, though. Even when the baby was born, she wouldn't know for sure because Tusa's antibodies would still be in the baby's system. The hospital would pump the baby with AZT as a prophylactic as soon as it was born, but the early tests would be inconclusive. In her heart, Sarah felt that Tusa knew the baby had the virus, but it would be up to a year after the birth before the authorities would know for sure whether the baby was positive.

Sarah had tried on several occasions in the sessions to talk to Tusa about having Grace tested for HIV. She knew that she had the authority to seek legal sanction if it was absolutely necessary, but so far she had resisted telling Tusa this. It seemed better to carry on trying to persuade Tusa rather than marching her off to court. But while Grace stayed apparently healthy, it would not be easy. To have Grace tested, Sarah knew, was for Tusa to admit the possibility that her daughter had been raped in the other room. To learn she was positive was to be sure of what the soldiers had done. To delay the test on Grace was to keep alive the chance that her daughter had not been harmed, and that – with the baby awaiting its sentence at twelve months – some small element of innocence still prevailed in their lives.

This was the knife-edge on which the life shared by Tusa and Grace was balanced. This was the secret that the little girl carried inside her, that only she knew and that her mother dare not ask about. Grace was an intelligent little girl, but she would not talk to Sarah or to the department's nursing staff, even about the dress she wore or the toys she would not play with. She would not let down her guard. She shared her thoughts only with her mother. Yet Sarah had watched the girl talking to Saul in the waiting room.

She was still reflecting on this when she caught sight of Saul outside the hospital. She was making her way across the car park. She was carrying a copy of the *Evening News*, which she had spent her lunch break studying. As was her custom, she had read through the property section and concluded by ringing the ones she liked and then scoring them to review her favourite for the day. She would take the newspaper home and confirm her choice at the kitchen table before she threw the paper in the bin so that Gary wouldn't see it, and then start the preparations for supper.

Saul was sitting on a wall with his back to her, a few yards away from the bus shelter. At his appointment earlier in the afternoon she had told him that his test for HIV had come back negative. The remaining tests for chlamydia were not in yet and she had asked him to wait in the clinic afterwards while she tried to establish whether the tests had been carried out and, if so, where they were in the system. It was while Sarah was checking this that he had come across Tusa and her daughter. That was when Sarah had seen Grace talking to him. Now he was sat out in the car park staring up at the new hospital wing being constructed.

'Something interesting up there?' she said.

Saul turned around. He smiled. There was a thin stubble spread across his face. 'Lot of building going on,' he said, pointing towards the box lines of grey girders forming a backdrop to the car park.

'It's the new extension. They're closing St George's and amalgamating both hospitals up here. It's all borrowed money. As long as we don't hire another nurse for the next forty years we'll just be able to afford the rent.'

'Good news for the builders, then.'

Sarah shrugged. 'It's progress, I suppose. Do you need a lift anywhere?'

Saul shook his head. 'I'll be fine. Thanks.'

'No, really. I can drop you off somewhere. It's no trouble.'

He thought about it, then shrugged to confirm a reluctant acceptance. He stood up. The two of them walked through the car park together.

'I saw you talking to Grace,' Sarah said.

'Grace?'

'The little girl in the clinic.'

'Ah!'

'How did you do that?'

'How did I do what?'

'Talk to her.'

'I don't know. We just talked.'

'I've never managed to get a word out of the child,' Sarah said. 'What did you talk to her about?'

'I complained about the service.'

'That's different.'

'The girl's mother . . .' Saul said. 'Is she sick?'

'I'm not really supposed to talk about patients' medical issues,' Sarah said.

'What about the girl? Is she sick?'

'I don't know. I hope not.'

'I don't think she's sick.'

'Is that your medical opinion?'

He shrugged. 'I don't know. I just have a feeling. I think the mother is sick. I think the child isn't. Haven't you ever known something without knowing why?'

'No. Yes. I don't know. No, not really.'

'I'm sure you do. You just don't trust yourself with it. You've taught yourself not to trust yourself.'

'How do you know?'

'I'm right, aren't I?'

'Tusa said something to me once,' Sarah said. 'She told me that there are moments when you can look at something and see things as they really are.'

'She's right.'

Sarah reached for her keys and pressed the remote locking fob. She opened the driver's side door and lobbed her shoulder bag and the newspaper on to the back seat.

'Where do you want dropping?' she asked.

'I'm going back to the hostel.'

Sarah nodded. 'I know where it is,' she said.

'Patrick said you called in there the other night.'

'What's he like?' Sarah asked.

Saul settled himself in the passenger's seat and fastened his belt. 'He's a good man,' Saul said, 'who's lost his compass.'

'I never got to see him,' Sarah said. 'He was in a meeting with the other residents in the big lounge. I don't think you were there. I couldn't hear you.'

'I know. I got a reprimand for missing it.'

'Where were you?'

'I was out. I had some stuff to do.'

'Is this the errand you have to carry out?'

Saul smiled, but he didn't say anything.

While Sarah was manoeuvring out of the car park, Saul reached for her copy of the evening paper on the back seat and began to flick through it.

'How long before the baby's due?' he asked Sarah as they drove.

'I'm sorry?'

'The girl's mother. In the clinic.'

'Not long.'

'She's HIV?'

Sarah glanced across at him but didn't answer.

'What'll happen to them then?'

'She was turned down for asylum. She's trying to appeal but they're stuck in some bureaucratic black hole. She can't get any benefits, and the council seem to have washed their hands of her, mostly because no one seems to understand the rules because they keep changing, so they're living hand to mouth at the moment.'

'And you still don't know if the daughter is sick as well?'

'No.' Sarah looked across at him. Saul was engrossed in the property section. He had reached the page where, as was her weekly custom, she had ringed several of the houses. Her scores ran down the paper's margin.

'Was your daughter sick?' he asked. 'Before she died, was she sick?'

Sarah changed down gears as she approached a junction. She brought the car to a halt and looked right for a gap in the traffic.

'She was out playing,' she said. 'She was knocked down by a car.'

The traffic cleared. Sarah pulled away and accelerated into second and then third gear. Saul appeared to be considering her answer. He let her work out what to say next. They were a mile further along the road before Sarah spoke again.

'It took a long time before Tusa trusted me enough to confide in me. Then after a while she started telling me things. She told me one day that she had come to the conclusion that the world is made for important people. *Big people*, she called them. Where she came from she meant the ones who own the cars, the food supplies, the government – but it's the same everywhere. She said the immigration people in London were big people. She said the little people didn't count, except to each other. She said that all the little people like her just got in the way of the big people. She said little people just had to find their own way in the dark.'

'Are you one of the little people?' Saul asked.

She smiled at the thought. 'What makes you say that?'

'I just wondered.'

'That's what life makes you feel sometimes,' she said. 'Not in the way Tusa meant. Not in dramatic ways like that. It's just . . . You marry a shit, you drown in your job, you lose your daughter. Things like that make you feel smaller. Like you're just finding your own way in the dark.'

'Turn left up here,' Saul said.

Sarah looked up, glanced instinctively in her mirror, signalled and hurriedly turned off the main road.

'Can we get to the hostel this way?'

'Just carry on driving up here for a minute or two,' he said. 'There's something I want to show you.'

They drove on. The neighbourhood became leafier.

'Stop over there,' he said.

She pulled over and stopped the car. She put the handbrake on, keeping the engine running.

'Why have we stopped?' she said.

Saul passed the open newspaper to her.

'See,' he said. He pointed to one of the properties for sale in the paper. Sarah had drawn a black circle around it at lunchtime with a marker pen. She looked at the photograph and description, and then looked across the road. It was the same house – a stone-fronted cottage with black-leaded glass, one of four in a row. There was a 'For Sale' sign planted in the postage-stamp front garden. This was one of the properties she had chosen a few hours earlier as one she might live in if this had been the direction of her life. If she had the choice. If such things lay open to her.

She sat looking across the road at the cottage. She kept remembering how she had circled it with a pen as she ate a sandwich in her office at lunchtime. Is this what angels do? she thought. Do they offer you a glimpse of the future in return for four hundred milligrams of Cefixime? Not my future, obviously, she thought. My future is with Gary. But someone's future. Someone could be happy here, in this house that I ringed casually a few hours ago. Is he showing me that somewhere happiness is possible? That *someone* could make a new life here? *Someone* could start again?

'Are you going to be late getting home?' he asked.

'No,' she said. 'Gary's out on business tonight.'

'Do you ever think of leaving him?'

Somehow, the question did not feel improper or out of place. So she answered it.

'He'd kill me,' she said.

And she laughed.

When Lillian first arrived at the Limes, her world had shrunk to the size of a pomegranate. It was the circumference of her two palms, pressed together, into which she habitually gazed, and her actions said she had lost faith with whatever lay beyond that space.

The night her mother died, her father had taken Lillian into his bed for comfort. After a week, he moved her clothes into the double wardrobe he had shared with his wife and they turned her old room into a spare bedroom so that Margaret would have a place to sleep when she came to her senses and returned home, which she never did. They shopped together. Lillian's father liked to hold her hand. He needed her so much. He was a man who needed a lot of love. Margaret wrote to Lillian sometimes. Lillian saw the envelopes on the mat and recognized the writing, but she was never sure what was in them because her father only ever gave her a précis of their contents and kept the letters for himself. When Margaret starting ringing, wanting Lillian to come and live with her, he unplugged the phone.

Lillian began to see herself as an astronaut, looking at the outside world from an unimaginable distance, relying on a smaller and smaller number of routines to keep her safe, dependent for survival on maintaining a sterile environment, being unable to make the sounds of words carry beyond her own small space, losing any sense of gravity. She narrowed the orbit of her life in order to fight off infections. She scrubbed herself with greater vigour in the bath. She couldn't get clean enough.

She began to cut herself out of curiosity. She wanted to know if the badness could be bled from her. It didn't hurt. She was too busy finding things out. The first time she did it, her father was out of the house. After she had made the incision, she called the ambulance. In the hospital, her father explained to her how sick she was, how much looking after she needed. Lillian told the doctor everything was fine. Her father, standing next to her, nodded. Whenever she cut herself after that, she waited for her father to find her and patch her up. Each time, he rescued her.

It seemed to Patrick that Lillian had too many teeth in her long, Saxon face. Her brittle hair was drawn into a bun that pulled her face back into a kind of mask of stoicism. She was the first person Patrick had seen Edward look at directly. Usually, Edward's gaze slid to the side of people, into safe nooks and crannies, but when Lillian wasn't looking he would cast glances towards her surreptitiously.

A week after Lillian's arrival at the Limes, Edward bought himself a new suit. He brought it back to the Limes in a carrier bag from the Oxfam shop where Patrick had arranged for him to do some voluntary work one day a week, sorting and steam-cleaning the donated clothes. It was an expensively cut pale linen suit with a discreet cigarette burn by the left cuff. It was designed to fit a man thicker set and two inches taller than Edward, but it was the best suit in the shop. He had to work a little at wearing it, sliding his hands in the trouser pockets as he walked from one room to another so he could lift the waistband back on to his hips. When he turned corners he swivelled slightly faster than the shoulders of his jacket. He didn't mind. The suit allowed him to be someone else, someone better than the person who had stuffed pillows and baby mattresses in the factory because he wasn't fast enough to be a packer or a checker – as if the suit itself carried the memory of a previous, more accomplished owner. His mouth had a tendency sometimes to hang slightly open as if the world were still surprising him, but the suit made him appear, finally, to be the proprietor of his own body. It hid the tension holding all his bones together. It gave him courage, and he courted Lillian in it.

When Edward had been admitted to the hospital, he had by then taken refuge in some out-of-reach place. Even when he had finally arrived at the Limes, he talked only sparingly, as if he had lost some sense of who he was and how he was meant to be connected to the everyday world around him. After a month, Patrick had persuaded Edward to start attending the local college once a week. The tutor gave him a spiral-bound notebook to use as a journal. The idea was to practise using words by keeping a diary or writing down things that were important to him and then bringing the book into class the following week. Edward wrote nothing in the first week, not because he couldn't be bothered, but because he could not work out what to write. He didn't know what he thought of anything. When he looked for himself, he wasn't there. He had become invisible. Patrick sat with him and wrote 'Edward's Book' on the front cover. Beneath it he drew two circles next to each other.

'What are they for?' Edward asked him.

Patrick pointed to each of them in turn. 'What we are,' he said to Edward, 'and what we think we are.'

Edward asked him what the difference was.

'Sometimes,' Patrick said, 'other people see qualities in you that you can't see yourself.'

Edward looked at the two circles often after that. Then, suddenly, he began to write – one problematic, ill-fitting word at a time. Now and then he showed Patrick what he had written. On the front page of the notebook, where Patrick had drawn the two circles, Edward had added a thin line, as if at some point he had grasped the way in which those two things were held tentatively together – who we are in the eyes of others, and who we sometimes think we are to ourselves – and how there was always the danger of them drifting apart.

With Lillian, all the therapy had been Edward's, not Patrick's. After she arrived, Edward had started shaving every day. He brought back items he had been given from the Oxfam shop – they were a kind of wage for his labours – and offered them to the residents. More and more he chose things with Lillian in mind. He couldn't offer them to her face to face, and so he left things on the landing outside her bedroom door. If she ignored them and they lay there untouched for a day or more he took them away. If she claimed the item, his heart rejoiced and he wrote down the details in his journal.

One day Edward heard Lillian talking to Patrick in the kitchen about things she liked: the colour of the single dress she owned but had never worn (she always wore trousers), the notion of dancing with a man (she had never danced), the flowering of spring bulbs (she had never had a garden). Edward persuaded Patrick that the garden needed spring bulbs and he planted two hundred and twelve purple irises in the narrow soggy border alongside the lawn at the back of the Limes, waiting after that for the garden to turn the colour of her single dress as proof of love. Only when the bulbs came up and Lillian understood what he had done did they exchange their first words.

They took to playing Scrabble to help Edward with his words. Lillian corrected his spellings. They learned between them how to sit in close proximity to each other without alarm sirens sounding in their heads. When Edward played the word 'please' on a double-word score, Lillian walked out into the garden and cried. She was only used to her father. She was used to people taking what they wanted. The word made her into something she had not been until that point. When she had plunged the kitchen knife into her father's stomach, it was the first time she had done something for herself since her mother had died when she was thirteen years old.

When Patrick put the phone back down in its cradle, he sat in silence for a long time. He didn't know what to do. Lillian's sister had finally rung him back. Margaret had told him that Lillian was not going to return to the flat. She had told Patrick to leave her sister alone. Patrick tried to tell her about Edward's arrest. She said she knew – that the police had been round about Edward. Patrick tried to reassure her by saying he was certain it was a mistake, even though he didn't believe this himself. It was the only way he could think of persuading Margaret to let him talk to Lillian. He told her that Edward really needed Lillian at the moment, but Margaret had put the phone down on him.

In front of him on the desk was a newspaper cutting. It was a book review. He didn't know which newspaper it had come from. Patrick had kept it with the other cards and notes his brother had posted to him over the years from London and Spain and America. The review of Liam's book said that the author was an Englishman now living in the United States. It said *The King of Providence* was a quietly magnificent debut that celebrated the resilience of the human spirit. Patrick picked up the cutting and read it again, though after twenty-five years he knew it now by heart. He glanced up at the notice-board on the wall above the desk, at the photograph of the young man in the creased linen suit in the diner in Brooklyn, holding a copy of his newly published novel beneath the two photographs of high-wire walkers. In the photograph Liam was twenty-four.

The computer screen was still showing the American website Patrick had been examining when Margaret had rung him. The website was maintained by a group of independent booksellers centred on the San Francisco Bay area. It was a mixture of stock lists and articles and customer reviews, with links to other websites and an online checkout facility for ordering books. It seemed to be the independents' way of competing with the nationwide chain stores who undercut them on the bestsellers and sold books the way supermarkets sold meat. It was a way of making the buying and selling of books a personal thing. Patrick had stumbled across the site by accident. He had been moved to search for information about his brother following the events of the last few days. It was when he looked up the name of an American journalist Liam had quoted in one of his letters that Patrick had been led to this website. And there in front of him on the screen, after an hour of digging and several red herrings, was the same review of Liam's book that he had sent Patrick.

Instead of a creased and yellowing T-shaped cutting, the review was laid out on the screen in an unfamiliar block of clean text, but it was the same review. *The King of Providence* by L.S. Shepherd. Liam's book. At the bottom of the page there were links to a couple of other websites. Patrick clicked on one of them. It took him a while to work his way around the site. Eventually he found the page he wanted. He typed in 'Shepherd'. There was some background information on *The King of Providence* and on another, second book the author had written. The biographical details that followed said that L.S. Shepherd was married and lived in Berkeley, California. There was an option to click for a photograph. Patrick clicked. At first, the image was a blur. It shifted into focus in stages as the information downloaded. It took about twenty seconds until it came fully into focus. Patrick sat looking at it.

The bedsit for emergency admissions on the top floor had for years been the staff flat until the Hobart Trust finally abandoned the practice of staff sleeping in to provide night-time cover. When Patrick knocked on the door there was no answer. He pushed the door open and stepped inside. It was dark and stiflingly hot. The windows in the galley kitchen and the bedsitting room were closed. The central heating radiator was on. He checked the thermostat. It was turned up as high as it would go. Patrick pulled up the blind and opened the window. He turned the radiator thermostat down a few degrees. As he did so his foot toppled a saucer left on the floor. There was a skim of curdled milk hardening at the edge. He picked up the saucer and put it on the work surface. He mopped up the spilt milk and walked through to the bedsitting area.

In the former lounge there was a single bed positioned in the corner of the room where once Benedict had propped the portable TV on which he and Patrick had watched interminable snooker matches into the early hours and discussed the imperceptible progress of the current group of residents. The set of drawers was still there, now serving as a bedside cabinet. There was a second saucer perched on top of the drawers. It was filled with cigarette stubs and flakes of ash. An empty cigarette packet had been scrunched into a ball and thrown under the bed.

'You know you can't smoke in here,' Patrick had said when he had checked on him on the first evening and found him smoking as he lay in bed scrutinizing the ceiling. His brother had examined the cigarette dreamily, then taken another drag and finally leaned over from the bed and stubbed it out in the saucer. But whenever Patrick returned to the room after that, the saucer would be filled again with ash and Patrick would make a mental note to seek out his brother once more to confront him about it.

Back in the galley kitchen Patrick scraped the sour milk away with a spoon. Saul, like the other emergency admission before him, was allocated four pounds a day to buy food. On each of the days he had been there so far he had signed for the money each morning in the office. When Patrick looked in the fridge to check whether the rest of the milk had gone off he found nothing inside. He looked in the bin. There was no sign of food having been bought or eaten there since Saul had arrived. There was nothing in the drawers by the bed except for the tablets he had been prescribed by the GUM department. Patrick cleaned the saucer under the hot tap and stacked it in the drainer. He went back downstairs to his office. The computer screen on his desk still had the American website up when he cleared the screensaver. It was still showing the photograph of the writer L.S. Shepherd. The man's face was cast partly in shadow by the portrait photographer for artful effect. The face looking back at Patrick was patient, tired, lined. It was not his brother's face. *The King of Providence* was not his brother's book.

*

'It's a test,' Kipper says. He is definite.

Kipper is twelve. His youthful bulk makes it seem as if he is made up of a series of random adult pieces jammed together. Lloyd is the same age, but he is skinnier, and he has a hare-lip. Kipper says that when the superintendent is off site, he and Lloyd are in charge. Patrick has reported Kipper's claim back to his sceptical brother.

Kipper is clearly mulling over a decision. 'Don't know that I should tell you,' Kipper says. 'I don't think you'll be ready for it yet.'

Patrick has been at Providence House with his brother for eleven days.

'What test?'

Kipper confers quietly with Lloyd.

'It's the test,' he says again, nodding. 'It's what parents do – if they want to see if their children love them enough.'

'What do they do?'

'They put them in here and say they've gone away, or they can't live at home any more, or one of them's died or something. Did you see your mam after they said she was dead?'

Patrick shakes his head.

'See! That's classic,' Kipper says. 'It's perfect. It's the perfect test. It's like when Jesus got tested by the Devil in the desert. You'll learn all that in Sunday school. They're testing you to see whether you'll go back home – or whether you don't want to any more. I mean, it's obvious that Jesus wouldn't leave you without parents. He wouldn't be doing his proper job if he did that, would he?'

'So how come you're here?' Patrick says. It feels like a risky question to ask. So far they have got through this whole conversation without either of them calling him Toad. Kipper had christened him by the second day on account of Patrick's ungainly mouth and his overlarge eyes that forget to blink when he gets anxious, and he doesn't want to prompt either of them into remembering.

'I'm different,' Kipper says. 'I didn't get sent here as an orphan. I *know* my mam and dad are at home. The court sent me here instead of remand home 'cause I was nicking stuff, and if I nick anything else I have to go to remand home, or else Borstal if I do something really bad. You've to be really bad to go to Borstal. I mean, like, kill people and stuff. But Lloyd, here, and most of the others who are meant to be orphans – they're still here 'cause they didn't work out it was a test, or they didn't dare try to get back home, or else they couldn't find the way. That's what happened to Lloyd. He tried to walk it all the way when he worked it out. He didn't have the money for the bus. They told him his mam had died, but it was the same test they've given you. It's classic.'

'How d'you know she wasn't dead?' Patrick says.

'My uncle said. My uncle knows her. My uncle and my dad come to visit me sometimes.'

'His uncle told me,' Lloyd confirms.

'But when he tried to get home,' Kipper says, 'he got lost. Isn't that right, Lloyd?'

Lloyd nods.

'Up there, past the reservoir on the moors, wasn't it?'

Lloyd nods again. Kipper points in the general direction of the boundary fence. Patrick knows about the reservoir. He knows about Dr Murdoch-Bannerman's drowned son. The reservoir lies just beyond the grounds of Providence House and is out of bounds to the boys. To go up there is a caning offence.

'Lloyd lived in Oldham, see,' Kipper says, 'and you have to go over that way to get to Oldham, but there weren't any proper signposts and he couldn't find his way. They found him starving on the moors after six days and brought him back. He was like a skeleton when he got back here. He had to eat grass and stuff on the moors like a wild man just to survive.'

Kipper shakes his head sadly at the missed opportunity that left Lloyd stranded on the moors and which has condemned him to a childhood at Providence House.

'Why didn't your mam just come for you after that?' Patrick asks.

'I heard they waited for me for three weeks,' Lloyd says. 'That's what Kipper's uncle said, wasn't it, Kipper?'

Kipper nods in confirmation. 'But when he didn't come back,' Kipper says, 'they must have thought he didn't love them enough so they went and moved to somewhere in Liverpool 'cause their hearts were broken.'

'Why doesn't the superintendent tell the boys it's a test?' Patrick asks.

'Because that's *part* of the test,' Kipper says, 'like Jesus in the desert.' The weary tone in his voice says it's obvious. 'To see if people have enough *faith*. That's what the people working for the welfare have to do. That's their job.'

Patrick is sure in his heart that Kipper must be right. The world is not so random as to have Jesus leave people without parents. It must be a test – to make sure he loves them enough, to see if he dares to undertake the journey back to them. Liam would do it easily, but they have chosen to test Patrick.

He keeps thinking about the stunning possibility that their mother is waiting at the house for his return. Maybe his father is waiting for him too. Maybe his father's absence for all those years was part of the test. He keeps thinking about Lloyd's family moving to Liverpool because their hearts were broken, because they thought he didn't love them enough to make his way back. He thinks about telling Liam. He knows he should, but something stops him. He knows his brother doesn't like Kipper, doesn't trust him, and Patrick doesn't want Liam's pride to get in the way of this. He doesn't want to do anything that might spoil their chances of being reunited as a family.

The thought bubbles up inside him like the gas bubbles from fizzy pop. He keeps marvelling at how simple it all seems, at how obvious it is. Patrick already knows all about running away from watching his brother. His mother had observed that Liam had been running away since he was three. Usually, Liam would announce it before he set off, and he had set off most weeks. In the coal merchant's depot, which faced their line of back yards on Walter Street, he was always asking van drivers to give him a lift to his imagined destinations. Once, the assistant from the grocer's shop two streets away found him sitting on the bridge over the Manchester to Leeds railway line. He had apparently run away to spend the afternoon dropping pebbles on to the metal rails, and when their mother went out to collect him and asked him why, he had said, 'So I can hear the ones that go *ping*.'

Liam's running away had never seemed to worry their mother unduly. Usually some neighbour or other brought him back from his wanderings, or it would turn out that he had only travelled as far as the privy, or the back alley behind Walter Street, and she would find him an hour later unmoving and engrossed by a line of ants or a slopstone sink someone had thrown out. When he did venture further and she thought it was time to coax him back home she would set out after him, pushing Patrick in the pram. More often than not, they would find him in the cab of one of the coal merchant's lorries in the depot talking to one of the drivers, or at the allotments where Rossiter's cat lived and where Rossiter, who lived two streets away, kept his two donkeys, and Liam would be sat watching the animals in rapt concentration.

The day after his sixth birthday they found Liam in the park. He had run away for longer than usual that day. It was almost tea time when Patrick and his mother got there. The boat hire kiosk by the side of the boating lake was still open, but all the hired boats had been returned and most families were already heading home. The man had shut the wooden boards on the refreshment hut and was patiently heaving his vacated boats out of the water one at a time and turning over their wooden hulls on the little jetty. Liam was standing on the edge of the small three-tree island in the middle of the boating lake, a good twenty yards from shore. He saw them coming but didn't wave. He didn't seem wet and yet there was no sign of a row boat for him to have made the crossing and so, in the way it was possible to do as a small child, Patrick simply imagined that his brother must have flown across the water to get there.

His mother cupped her hand around her mouth to help her voice carry across the water.

'Are you the man in charge of this island?'

She seemed in no great hurry to resolve the situation. There was still warmth left in the day and there was an hour's light left in the sky.

'It's a country,' Liam shouted back.

'Yes,' she said, 'I can see that.'

'You can't live here too,' Liam shouted. He said it as though it were a simple statement of fact.

'I imagine not,' his mother said. 'It looks like an ideal country for one single boy.'

Liam looked around at the island he had seemingly commandeered.

'I'm going to live here,' he said.

Their mother nodded and weighed up the possibilities. She walked across to the man who was stacking the boats for the night. They spoke for a few moments before coming back together for Patrick. The man helped them both into one of the remaining boats tethered in the water, then climbed in himself. He rowed them across to the island in hardly more than half a dozen sweet strokes of the oars, with Patrick sat in the middle seat facing his mother, her quiet arm resting in her good arm's embrace. When the boat came to rest against the grassy bank of the island, Patrick's mother climbed out. The man heaved Patrick out and deposited him next to her.

'You want me to wait?' he asked her.

She shook her head. 'Knowing him,' she said, 'it might take us a little while. I'll give you a wave when we're ready.'

The man slipped back in the boat and rowed back to the shore. Patrick's mother turned towards Liam who was standing defiantly ten feet away.

'You can't come any further,' Liam said.

'I was hoping,' their mother said, making no attempt to move closer, 'that someone in charge of this island might grant us permission to come ashore.'

'I'm making up laws,' Liam said solemnly.

'Always a good idea for a new country.'

'No one else can come here until I've done it.'

'Apart from a lord mayor, surely?' their mother queried.

Liam eyed her. He was suspicious of his self-imposed solitude being undermined, but she had said it with such matter-of-factness that the proposition seemed too reasonable to object to.

'I suppose so,' he said cautiously, 'apart from the mayor.'

'You know, of course,' their mother said lightly, almost in passing, 'that as a former alderman of the city I was invested as lord mayor in 1957?'

Liam shook his head. 'You weren't the mayor.'

'Oh really, Liam Shepherd! You were there, were you?'

'I would have known about it. You would have told us before now.'

She shook her head. 'It was before you were born,' she said. 'And besides, I had to take the traditional vow of silence when my work at the town hall was done. That's why I keep my ceremonial chain in a wooden box in the pantry under the shoe-polish things.'

'You said it was Dadda's jazz records you kept in there, for when he comes back.'

'*Underneath* the records,' she said patiently. 'That's where I keep it. Purely for ceremonial occasions, when we ex-mayors get together to remember the old days and raise money for retired donkeys.'

She waited for Liam's next move.

'I want to live where there's a law that dead things can come back to life,' he said.

'That would be a useful law,' their mother said.

'There's no law for that at home,' Liam said, 'so I'm starting a new country where they can.'

Their mother, the former mayor, took a couple of tentative steps forward.

'I've got something that needs a new country,' Liam said.

'Why don't you show us?' she said. 'Mayors always need to be shown things. We're very literal creatures as a rule.'

Liam walked to the raised centre of the tiny island where the three trees were huddled together. He returned holding a dirty cotton sheet with an object wrapped inside. He held it out. It was Rossiter's cat.

'Eric killed it,' he explained.

Aunty Maureen and Eric had visited the house the previous day.

'Rossiter said you can't have things back to life in this country. It's the law.'

'Did Rossiter say what to do with the cat?' their mother asked.

Liam shook his head. 'He just said it was dead. I saw him cry.'

Their mother looked around the island. 'It was a fine idea to bring him here,' she said. 'But I think you'd need more jurisdiction to pass that sort of law.'

'What's that?'

'Jurisdiction? Well, it's funny you should ask me that, Liam Shepherd. You see, as a former mayor of the city, I have just enough jurisdiction under the corporation's charter to permit the naming of islands in the borough, and to allow an official burial of Rossiter's cat before sunset.'

And so they buried the animal under a pile of stones, and christened the place Rossiter's Cat Island under powers granted to their mother by Manchester's charter of incorporation, and after that they signalled for the rowboat man to come for them to row them back to shore and then they headed for home, until the next time Liam ran away.

But since they have moved to Providence House, Patrick's brother hasn't run away once. Patrick doesn't understand why. He wonders if it is because Liam has never succeeded, and that finally – at exactly the wrong moment, at the very time they are both being tested to see how much they love their mam – his brother has lost heart, and so it is up to Patrick alone to rescue them.

Their old address is in the top corner of the letter their mother had written for the welfare officer. With the letter in his pocket, Patrick slips out one morning after breakfast with the shilling Kipper and Lloyd have saved up for him to help him get home on the bus. The Austin is parked up outside the coach house. Patrick creeps on to the coach and crawls under the big sheet at the back that Jacko uses to cover the spare tyre and the toolbox. Then he waits, lying as still as he can. Eventually, he hears Jacko climb into the driver's seat to make the weekly journey to buy provisions in the small town two miles away. Patrick feels the coach jerking into life. Jacko revs the engine for a few minutes to warm it up. Patrick hears Jacko expel a gob of spit and light up a cigarette. Then he feels the pull of the coach moving slowly out of the yard. Patrick lies unmoving at the back of the coach under the sheet. Eventually, he feels the coach come to a halt. He can hear people walking past, and the sound of stallholders and shoppers. He hears Jacko get out and slam the driver's door. When he is sure it is safe, Patrick pulls the sheet away and climbs out of the coach. The high street is busy with women threading their way between the lines of stalls and along the row of shops. Patrick asks a woman who is pushing a pram which bus he needs to get. He shows her the address on the letter. She seems suspicious.

'I'm with my aunty,' he tells her. 'She's waiting at the bus stop for me.'

The woman nods and points to where the bus goes from. When he gets on the bus, the conductor asks him where he is going. Patrick shows the man the address on the letter and gives him the shilling. He says his mam has been sick but now she is better. When the bus arrives in Manchester, the man puts him on a local service and arranges for the conductor not to charge the boy.

All the way back to Walter Street on the second bus, as the streets become gradually more familiar, Patrick keeps thinking about how Lloyd had missed his chance, and how Liam has lost faith in the business of running away, and how it is Patrick who is going to make it home. He keeps thinking about how his mam will be there, and his dad, and that they'll go back to Providence House to collect Liam and that the superintendent will be pleased that Patrick has shown faith in Jesus. He looks out of the window and sees the coal merchant's yard. His heart is quickening in his chest. When the conductor tells him they have reached his stop, he leaps from the bus with his head full of reunion kisses.

The back door is on the latch. He pushes the door and goes inside. There is no one in the kitchen, but the wireless is playing. The cupboards are the same, but there is a different table with a red and white tablecloth laid over it.

'Sometimes,' Kipper has said, 'they decorate it new for you. Like for a party, because you believed that they loved you and you knew they would never leave you, and you managed to get all the way back. Lloyd never saw it set out new, but my uncle said that's what they did for him.'

Patrick walks through the downstairs rooms. There is a different settee, and a sideboard with a lamp on it that hadn't been there before, but the dining chairs that Aunty Maureen donated to them when she bought new ones are still there. Patrick can see the stain near the hearth where he caught the carpet with black shoe polish when he was practising cleaning his shoes and which his mam hadn't been able to scrub out completely. He wonders if she is out getting the shopping for the party they will have. He sits down on the settee and waits.

The man who wakes him is holding his arm. There is a woman standing over him as well. A second man is checking the sideboard cupboard to see if the housekeeping money is still there. The man who has hold of Patrick is asking him what he is doing. Patrick doesn't answer. The man grows angry and says it's his house and wants to know what is going on. Someone says the police have been called. Patrick starts to shake. He keeps looking at the polish on the carpet, and Aunty Maureen's stand-chairs. Another woman comes in. She recognizes Patrick – she lives across the road. She says something. The man who is holding Patrick's arm lets go. He sits down on one of the stand-chairs and rubs his head with the flat of his hand as if defeated by the logic of the situation. After a while, Mr Briffet arrives from the welfare office. He tells Patrick that his aunt has overseen the sale of the house. He says it isn't theirs any more. He says Patrick's mother is dead. Patrick hears Mr Briffet say it was the upset. He hears him tell them it won't happen again. He asks Patrick what he thinks he is playing at. He says Patrick is a stupid boy. Patrick opens his mouth to speak, but no words come out.

6

THE FAITH OF ANGELS

Sarah was driving to work. As she passed under the bridge with the graffiti on it – *Pass here, you princes of hope* – she wound down the window and let the few strands of hair she was clutching fly from her fingers and be picked up by the wind, and then she sped on.

Each day, while the child from the Gallowfield estate was still missing, Sarah cut off a small lock of her hair and released it from her car window as she drove through a different part of the city. It was a token, but for whom or what she did not know. It was a duty because there was nothing else she could give. She knew it would continue until the girl was found, or until her hair was all used up. She was like a peasant from some ancient tribe making offerings to the sky in the hope of saving the season's crops.

After Katy died, Sarah had cut off all of her hair. She came home from the hospital and took the scissors from the kitchen drawer and sat down at her dressing table and cut it off in chunks until all that was left were tufts sprouting from her clean scalp. She watched herself in the mirror as she did it. She was not distraught or enraged. The act of cutting off her hair felt like a balm. It was a reasonable measure. They had turned the machine off and Katy had died, and so she was cutting off her hair.

Afterwards, she had no desire to hide it. She consciously slowed to catch sight of her reflection whenever she passed a mirror or the plate-glass window of a shop front. It allowed her to appear on the outside the way she felt on the inside, and she took comfort from this.

Only once did she put on a hat. In the days leading up to the funeral, Gary pestered her to wear a hat in the church to cover up what she had done.

'It's a mess,' he said.

'It was meant to be.'

'You'll feel better with a hat,' he said.

She considered his request. 'Fuck off,' she said.

'What are people going to think?' he countered later on.

'They're going to think my daughter died,' she said.

'I didn't mean that.'

'I know you didn't.'

'I mean we have to be strong,' Gary said. 'I mean we have to get through this.'

We are two ships passing in the night, she thought. We flash messages to each other with lanterns about the storm that is sinking us, but we are powerless to save each other.

She tried to explain why it was important that she didn't cover up her hair in the church.

'It's a way of speaking to the world about myself while my voice cannot,' she said.

'They're all gonna think you can't cope,' he told her.

'I *can't* cope,' she said.

'Just wear a hat for me,' he said. 'Wear one for Katy. What would Katy think if she saw you going out looking like that?'

'Katy's dead.'

'I'm not letting you go out looking like that,' he said. 'I'm not having it.'

On the morning of the funeral, Gary retrieved her favourite black beret from the wardrobe as she was showering and left it out on the bed. She caught sight of it while she was dressing. She could hear him on the phone downstairs. His voice was lowered so as not to alert her. She went to the top of the stairs. The conversation was about overtime payments. She went back to the bedroom and looked at her strangely shaped, comforting scalp and cried for the first time.

'This is who I am,' she said out loud as her fingers touched the remnants of her hair. She realized that she was talking to Katy. She looked at the hat lying on the bed.

When she finally came downstairs she was wearing a hat. It wasn't the beret but a squashed felt cap she'd had for years. Gary's face lit up in relief. He squeezed her arm. For the rest of her life she would recall how, as she bent down to get into the big black car waiting for her on the road in front of the house, she was thinking, If I was somebody else, I would leave you.

She wondered if it was true, as she had read somewhere, that you could only fall in love with someone more intelligent than yourself. As far as Sarah could tell, Gary was a smart operator. He had confidence in his own right to succeed. He held authority over some other men. But he was not more intelligent than her. He was a fixer. A controller. He reduced things to their lowest common denominator. He had no sense of apprehension about life's significance; no notion that there might be vast things of which he had no knowledge.

The next day – a cold, bone-dry winter's morning – she burned both hats in a fire she set in the metal dustbin in the garden. She talked comfortingly to Katy while she did it, allowing the edges of the smoke to cloud her face and make her eyes water. She savoured the feeling of growing cold, the cinnamon sting of the wood smoke. She watched the hats reducing to ash. It was a reward she had granted herself for not embarrassing Gary in the church; for keeping her hacked-off hair covered up from the rest of the congregation; for pretending she could cope.

The phone rang for a long time before someone answered at the other end. The speaker was suspicious of Patrick's questions. He kept wanting to know if Patrick was from 'the Benefits'. It was only when Patrick finally managed to convince him that the man he was enquiring about really was his brother that the landlord began to offer small pieces of information.

Patrick had spent the morning ringing round places in the city. The landlord admitted that he had a tenant who matched the description Patrick gave. The man had been living there for a couple of months. He'd gone missing a week ago. He owed rent.

'Was there anything about him that gave you cause for concern?' Patrick asked him.

'What d'you think this is, the fucking health spa?' The man's accent was Mediterranean – maybe Greek or Turkish. 'Everyone who's here,' the man said, 'I have cause for concern. You know what I'm saying? They're all not here if they could choose. They're here since they can't afford to be somewhere else, or since nowhere else takes them.'

'I'm asking if he was all right. He's my brother.'

'He doesn't trash the place, if you're asking for this. He doesn't commit crimes. Not any that make people notice him, anyway, unless you counting him walking round with no shoes like he's on the beach or something.'

'You think he was doing something? What? Drugs?'

'A man in my position, I have to be careful. I have a living to make, you know? You don't notice things, before you know it, things are out of control.'

'You think he was dealing, using, what?'

'I'm not saying.'

'Did you see him using anything?'

'No, I told you, I'm not saying. I'm saying he had that look about him sometimes, that's all I'm saying. You know, that sick look they get, that white face, like a ghost. Like they're a ghost. I seen it many times. You do what I do, you see it. And he disappears at nights. Then I don't see him for days. This is normal? Nah, I seen that look before.'

'What about before he moved in?' Patrick asked. 'Do you know anything about that, about where he came from?'

'Don't know where he came from. Just arrives here one day. Most of them do. He arrives here blown on the wind. Like I say, they all do. It's that sort of place.'

'Did he talk to anyone else much while he was there?'

'Not much.'

'What did he do during the day?'

'What am I, his minder? Jesus, I just run the place, mister.'

'What did he do?' Patrick persisted.

'He keeps himself to himself, that's what.'

'What about at night?'

'I'm telling you – he comes and goes a lot. Don't sleep much that I can see.'

'Can I come over and see the place? I want to show you a photograph to make sure it's him.'

'You think I've nothing else to do, mister? I've got plenty things to do. Anyway, your brother owes me rent when he goes. Two weeks. I don't owe him no favours.'

'If I bring you the money will you wait for me to drive over? I can be there in half an hour.'

'You want to bring me the money, it's no skin off my nose. You want to pay me what I'm owed, I reckon I can wait around.'

'I'll be there.'

Patrick ended the call. Then he rang the police to report that the house car, which had been parked up in the garage at the Limes, untaxed, undriven for the last four years, had been stolen. He had discovered it that morning when he arrived at the Limes and found the garage lock broken, the doors prised open and the ancient Lada gone.

The light entering her office turned the wall into the colour of the favourite Alice band Katy had liked to wear. Sarah was watching it, and when she looked around he was there again, standing in the doorway. He smiled.

'I thought you might have called me,' he said.

She shook her head.

'I can go back outside and wait. There's a *Scooby Doo* episode on.'

'No, it's fine. I was about to call you.'

'Are you sure?'

'It's fine. Honestly.'

He nodded, but still waited at the door.

'Come in,' she said. 'Please.'

He came in and sat down. She noticed that he was still wearing Dr Vass's white plimsolls, and the same black coat and shirt and trousers. She asked him how he was feeling. He said he was fine. She opened the notes that were ready on her desk. She went through the remaining results of the previous week's screening with him. She said he had tested positive for gonorrhoea. She said it wasn't as bad as it sounded. She said it was more common than people thought. She said she would get Dr Vass to sign the prescription for the antibiotics for Saul to take away with him.

'Will the ones I've got not do?' he asked.

Sarah shook her head. 'The tablets you have for the urethritis are just a general antibiotic. You need something more specialized for this. It's nothing to worry about. It's not a problem. It's completely curable. Unless there's anything else you want to tell me.'

She knew that the tests had picked up an abnormality. She had asked for a haemoglobin check on his blood sample as a precaution. She knew that the test had shown up anaemia.

'You mean the blood thing?'

'You know about it?'

'We have that problem,' he said.

'We?'

'Our immune system doesn't work properly. We start to get weaker as we get closer to the end of the time we've been allocated.'

'For the task that you have to complete?'

'That's right.'

'And how are you doing with your task?'

He made a gesture that seemed to indicate there was still some way to go.

'Have you worked out what it is you're meant to be doing?'

Saul smiled. He put his hand in his coat pocket and scooped out a fistful of the business cards with people's names on them. He piled them up on the coffee table. He fished for the remainder in his other pocket.

'I've been trying to contact them,' he said.

'Who?'

'The people whose names are on these cards. I figure if I talk to each of them, I might be able to work it out from there. Maybe one of them will know what I'm supposed to do. Maybe it's one of them I'm supposed to save.'

'How many have you contacted so far?'

'Seven.'

'Is that all?'

'And I've got the addresses for another four. It's not easy, you know, tracking these people down. I'm busting a gut here.'

'I just mean seven isn't a lot. Not if you're planning to get round to seeing all of them.'

'The problem is, they're not all in the phone book.'

'Isn't there any other way of looking for them?'

'Like what?'

'I don't know,' Sarah said. 'Registrar's office?'

'They wouldn't release the details.'

'You could advertise in the paper. Ask people to contact you.'

'Takes too long. I need to find somewhere that has a list of all the addresses for these people but I don't know where else to look.'

But Sarah already knew where to look. 'I do,' she said.

'Sorry?'

'I do. I know where to look. I've just realized.'

'Where?'

'*Single assessment*.' She pushed at the cards on the table. 'All these names,' she said. 'They're all people who might need saving, right? They're probably all people who need some sort of help.'

'So?'

'So, maybe they're on our computer. Maybe they've been sick. Maybe they are hospital patients, or they've been assessed by social services. There's a single assessment now for everyone who needs anything to do with health or social care. You know how many people that is in the city? Thousands. You want a place to look for people who need saving? Look on there.'

'I can't look on there. How would I do that? I'd need someone to hack into the system for me. There'll be passwords and all kinds of things.'

'I can look for you,' Sarah said.

'Won't you get into trouble?'

'Only if you intend to shoot them, or steal their savings. You don't, do you?'

'There'll be rules against you doing this. I don't want you getting into trouble. All this stuff is crazy enough as it is.'

Sarah shook her head. 'I spend half my life looking up addresses on the computer. What's another few? If anyone found it on the hard drive I can just say I was tracking some more transmission routes from names given to me by anonymous patients. I send letters out every day to addresses

I've had to research. If you leave the cards with me, I can do a search for them all on the database.'

Saul looked at the pile of cards in front of him on the table.

'What do you have to lose?' she said.

'I'm still not sure.'

'How long have you got before you need to have talked to all these people?' Sarah asked him.

Saul flicked at a couple of the cards. 'Three days,' he said.

The Somerset Hotel was in an alley backing on to the railway sidings close to the line coming out of Salford Crescent. There was no parking and Patrick drove around for a while looking for a side street where he could leave his car. He could see the confident glass and steel skyline of the new Beetham Tower and the Salford Quays development in the distance, but this, a mile away, was another country.

The front door to the Somerset was shuttered. There was an intercom fixed to the brickwork next to the door, but it had been broken off. He banged on the door with the palm of his hand.

The man who finally answered looked about the same age as Patrick. He was wearing a decent suit with a collarless shirt underneath and hair shaved down to the bristle.

'You the man?' he said.

Patrick nodded.

'I'm Savos,' the man said.

Patrick followed him into the hallway.

'What line of business you in?' Savos asked.

Patrick thought for a moment. 'Repairs,' he said.

The man nodded. 'There's money in that.'

Patrick showed him the photograph of his brother, taken in the Brooklyn diner when Liam had been twenty-four. The man peered at it.

'He was younger then,' Patrick explained.

'Jesus fuck,' Savos said, 'you're not kidding.' He handed the photograph back. 'It's him, I think. About a hundred years younger. About three lives ago. You know what I'm saying?'

'Can I see his room?' Patrick asked.

'There's still rent outstanding.'

'How much?'

'One sixty.'

'Did you report it to the police?'

'What do you think?'

Patrick counted out the money in twenty pound notes from the cash he had withdrawn from the ATM machine on the way over. The man watched him reeling them off.

'There were breakages, too.'

'How much?'

'Another forty, give or take.'

Patrick counted out another forty. 'I want a receipt,' he said, 'showing he's all paid up.'

Savos shrugged. 'Sure,' he said. 'Clear the air. Me and you, we're both businessmen.'

In a small windowless office leading off the hallway Savos took a blank piece of paper and wrote out a receipt for the money. Then he led Patrick upstairs.

'There's no one move in this one since your brother clears off,' Savos said as they climbed the first line of stairs. 'Truth is, there's no time to get the cleaner to sort it out yet. I guess he's not coming back?'

'No,' Patrick said, 'he's not coming back.'

They carried on climbing.

'He wants the top floor,' the man said. 'I have others. I tell him there's always a smell up there, but he wants this one. I can see him sometimes. He has the window pushed right up so he sits on the window sill looking out. He says he likes being up here. He says he doesn't like to feel cramped up anywhere.'

At the top of the final flight of stairs Savos produced a set of keys and unlocked the single door off the landing.

'It's the plumbing,' Savos said, looking at Patrick's face. He shrugged. 'I tell him about it when he turns up here. Smells of piss, yes? It's the plumbing. He says he doesn't care about the smell.'

Savos opened the door. Patrick walked in. With his arms outstretched he could have touched both walls simultaneously. There was a bed, a free-standing fifties wardrobe thick with varnish and a sink with a mirror fixed above it. A single crack ran two thirds the way down the mirror in a meandering diagonal. Patrick sat down on the edge of the bed and looked around. He could see linoleum where the carpet didn't reach the skirting boards. The walls were papered with stick-of-rock stripes. There was nothing on the walls – no pictures, no photographs, no decoration. There was a single brown curtain hung on one side of the window.

Liam was going to be a writer. He was going to live in a skyscraper in London or New York, and watch the lives of people unfolding below, and tell stories about them, and become the remarkable person he was destined to be. He was from the angels, their mother had said. But somehow, as Patrick now understood it, his brother had endured some terrible fall from grace. He had invented his own death, or else his madness was so enduring that he truly believed it. And he had ended up here. Patrick opened the wardrobe. A metal coat hanger on the empty rail was dislodged and fell to the floor. There was a saucer in the bottom of the wardrobe with a ring of scum where the milk had evaporated over several days. There were three shelves fitted inside the wardrobe. Two of them were empty. On the third was a page ripped from a newspaper. Patrick lifted it out.

'Your brother, I think he leaves it in there,' Savos said from the doorway. He was twirling the keys around the index finger of his hand, signalling that he had his money and that there were other things that needed his attention.

Patrick looked at the newspaper page. It had been torn from the *Manchester Evening News*. There were two stories on the page. One was the controversy about the private finance initiative being used by the local health trust to pay for the extension to a local hospital, and its amalgamation with a second hospital. There was a photograph of the new wing being constructed. The other article reported the disappearance of a little girl the previous day from the Gallowfield area of the city. It mentioned the theories the police were working on about the presumed abduction.

In the grounds of Providence House, Liam is sat with his back against the side of the laundry building. Beside him on the ground is a brown paper parcel. It was previously held together with a loop of white string and tied with a rough knot, but now the string has been pulled to one side and the parcel has been opened at one end and then roughly folded over again.

'I think Aunty Maureen sent them,' Liam says. 'I had a look but they're for you, really.'

Patrick sits down beside him. He has not spoken since he was returned to Providence House by Mr Briffet following his flight back home to Walter Street. Liam passes the parcel over to him and he rests it on his knee.

'It hasn't got stamps on,' Liam says. 'She must have got Uncle Frank to fetch it in the car.'

Patrick can see Lloyd swinging on the rubber tyre tied to the branch of a tree near by. Kipper is using the snapped-off branch of a tree to hit the outer rim of the tyre in a desultory rhythm. Other boys are mooching around in the sunshine in twos and threes, or flopped on the grass, talking, laughing. The noise of an impromptu game of football drifts over from the field behind the laundry. And in this steady rise and fall of speech across the grounds, Patrick is an outsider. He doesn't think of himself as living in a silent world. The world is as full of noise as ever, and he hears everything, but something inside of him has slipped away, something more than his words. When they tested him, when the welfare officer brought him back to Providence House and they realized that he was not speaking, they could find nothing physically wrong with him. The superintendent told him so, that the tests they had carried out in the infirmary had shown nothing, but Patrick knows that something has slipped out of reach, that his wordlessness is merely a symptom of this, and that somehow he is drifting alone.

Patrick feels the smooth exterior of the shiny brown paper on the parcel Liam has passed to him. Cautiously, he unravels the parcel. Inside is a small wooden box and two separate objects wrapped in newspaper. The box, made of rosewood, is the one that was used by their mother to keep her trinkets of jewellery in. Patrick opens it. It is empty. He puts it down and concentrates on the other two packages, starting with the smaller, heavier one. When he has unwrapped it, he holds it up. It is a book.

'It's a bible,' Liam says. 'It's got Mam's name in the front.'

It is the one she had kept in her bedroom and taken to mass each Sunday. It seems that Aunty Maureen didn't want to keep it herself after all, but perhaps a bible is a troublesome object to throw away. She could have sold it, or given it away, but then it has their mother's name and address imprinted in black ink on the inside cover and Aunty Maureen may have worried about the possibility of someone known to the family coming across it, or about the morality of ripping out the offending page. Maybe she has heard about Patrick turning up at their old house. Maybe Mr Briffet has told her. For whatever reasons, she has arranged for the delivery of the package including the bible to them.

Patrick picks it up and begins flicking through the pages. He hands it to Liam open at the page where he has stopped. Liam looks at the page and reads a sentence from it.

They said to Moses: we went into the land to which you sent us and it does flow with milk and honey.

Patrick likes the stories Liam tells him from the Bible. They make him feel safe. He likes Noah and the Ark. He likes David overcoming the giant Goliath. He unties the second bigger, flatter parcel. It is a long-playing record. There is a picture of a man on the record sleeve. Patrick doesn't know who the man is. Liam says the record belonged to their dadda. Patrick wonders if the photograph on the sleeve might be his dadda, but he doesn't say this out loud. It seems likely that the record has been uncovered in the pantry when the house was being cleared. Perhaps the idea has been to leave the brothers with several mementos of their parents to share. Or perhaps the idea of sending them the bible on its own seemed too severe and reproachful, and so the dispatch of the record and the jewellery box offer a kind of balance, in Aunty Maureen's eyes, to this final act of hers in their lives.

Kipper is still swishing his stick against the tyre.

'What you got there, Toad?' he shouts.

'His name's Patrick,' Liam says.

'So what's he got?'

'It's none of your business,' Liam says.

Kipper ignores him. He wanders over in Patrick's direction. Lloyd follows on his heels. 'What you got?' he says to Patrick.

Patrick holds up the bible.

'Not that – the record. Give us a look at the record.'

Patrick picks up the record from where it lies on the ground.

'Who is it?' Kipper asks.

Patrick turns to Liam for help.

'Charlie Parker,' Liam says.

'Never heard of him. Can I have a look?'

'No,' Liam says.

'I only want a look,' Kipper protests. He lifts the record from Patrick's grasp. He slips the vinyl disc from its sleeve, passing the sleeve back to Patrick, and holds the disc expertly up to the light in both hands.

'It's got a scratch,' Kipper announces. 'About an inch in. It'll probably jump, will that, on the needle.' He continues to inspect the record. 'Don't know, though. It might not. It's hard to tell with a scratch like that. What's it sound like?'

Patrick shrugs.

'Think we should have a go and see what it sounds like?'

Kipper finishes examining it, then brings it down from eye level and takes a grip of it in his right hand. He lets the record rest between his fingers for a moment, then draws his arm back slowly across his chest and fires it. It sails out across the grass, making the faintest of swooshes as it travels.

'*That's* what it sounds like,' Kipper shouts jubilantly.

The disc rises sharply, then levels out again. It sails over the flat roof of the laundry and out of sight. There is a noise like a twig snapping as Patrick hears it smack against the bitumen roof. He feels a sudden sickness rising in him.

'You know what, Toad?' Kipper says. 'It sounds like it's busted to me.'

Patrick is still focused on the laundry roof, on the end of the disc's flight. He is vaguely aware that Liam has stood up.

'Toad's brother's gonna smack you,' Lloyd says.

'I was just testing it,' Kipper says innocently. 'I told him it would jump on the needle.' He is untroubled by Liam rising to his feet. He has an advantage of more than two years on Liam.

'He's gonna fight you!' Lloyd says again. 'Ha ha!'

Liam stands watching Kipper carefully. Kipper grins. Liam waits until Kipper's grin is hard to hold any more.

'You have to hit me,' Liam says.

'What?'

'You can have three hits.'

'Kipper's in the boxing team,' Lloyd protests. 'They nearly sent him to Borstal before he came here. He'll kill you.'

The word goes round the grounds in a moment. Boys gather round. There is a hubbub of voices, and then they all go quiet.

'You want me to hit you?' Kipper says. 'Are you daft?'

'You get three hits,' Liam says again. 'You can wear your boxing gloves. If you knock me down, it's quits.'

'What d'you mean, quits?'

'About the record getting broken.'

'And if he doesn't knock you down?' Lloyd asks gleefully.

'Like I'm not gonna knock him down,' Kipper says. 'He should stick to running.'

'If you don't knock me down, you and me both have to jump in the reservoir to show we're not scared.'

'We're not allowed at the reservoir,' Kipper says. 'The super'll kill us.'

'Bet's off then.' Liam shrugs.

There is a murmur from the ring of boys.

'Go on, Kipper – not frightened of a swim, are you?'

'Three hits?' Kipper queries again. 'And you don't get to cover up or dodge out of the way?'

Liam nods his agreement.

'And if he knocks you over, it's quits?' Lloyd says.

'Yes.'

'All right,' Kipper says. 'You're on. And if you duck out of the way, I get the bible as well.'

'What d'you want the bible for?' Lloyd asks him.

'To see if it flies as good as the record did.'

There is laughter. Someone is dispatched to fetch gloves for Kipper. More boys arrive on the scene to watch. Someone is posted to keep a look out for staff.

'Stand there,' Kipper says, as his gloves are being fastened at the wrist.

Liam takes up his position.

'First hit!' Lloyd announces. 'You and you!' He points out two of the boys in the enclosing circle. 'You check with me that he doesn't move while Kipper's swinging.'

Kipper flexes his arm, then plants his feet. Standing face to face with Liam it is plain that he is several inches bigger than his adversary. He grins, and swings. Liam stands his ground as the blow comes. It whips into the side of his face. The punch jolts him on impact. He flinches, his eyes closed. His back foot jolts back to enable him to stay upright.

'Wuu-one,' Lloyd announces loudly. There is a cheer, partly for Kipper, partly for the fact that Liam has at least survived the first blow and is still somehow on his feet.

'That was just my sighter,' Kipper says. 'He's too small for me to hit him properly first time.' He flexes his arm again. 'I'm warmed up now.'

He jockeys for position this time as if looking for an opening, moving his weight from side to side with his hands up in a sparring position.

The second punch when it comes is perfect. It strikes Liam flush in the face. There is a gasp from the watching circle. The force of the blow jams Liam's head backwards. The initial spurt of blood from his nose shoots across his cheek and down across his mouth. Patrick waits for his brother to drop to the ground from the weight of the blow, or dizziness, or from the pain. If from none of those things, Patrick hopes that Liam will fall in order to avoid the third and final hammer blow that will surely kill him. Kipper examines the blood on his glove. Liam doesn't move. He doesn't even wipe the blood from his face. He is just staring at Kipper.

There is no cheering this time from the circle – just the anxious hum of murmurs as they wait to see what will happen next. Kipper stands there, waiting for Liam to drop. Liam does nothing and says nothing. He just stands there looking at Kipper, the blood dripping from his nose.

'Ah-two!' Lloyd announces.

'Shut up, Lloyd,' Kipper says.

Lloyd shuts up.

'I hope you can swim, Kipper,' someone says.

'I said *shut up*,' Kipper snaps.

Silence falls abruptly.

'Make sure he doesn't move,' Kipper demands. He steadies himself again, takes a breath, concentrates, and winds up into his final swing.

The last punch, although it catches Liam on the mouth, is not as clean a hit as the one before. It hardly seems to matter. It will occur to Patrick, looking back on the incident years later, that his brother would never have fallen that day. It is as if Liam has simply decided not to fall. By then – by the third punch – perhaps Kipper knows this too. In its lack of timing, his final blow carries a sense of desperation. Of the three punches, the last one is the one that is thrown more in hope than expectation.

It was after dark when Patrick took the call telling him they had recovered the house car from the Limes. The woman told him to go to the police station. She said his brother was there.

'My brother?'

'Liam Shepherd. We're holding him.'

Patrick had grown used to people calling his brother Saul over the last few days. The use of Liam's real name dislodged something inside him.

'I'll be ten minutes,' he said.

'He's not going anywhere,' the caller told him. 'He's in the cells under caution.'

Patrick drove fast to the station.

The custody officer slid open the viewing panel to the cell. Patrick peered inside. His brother lay on his back on the narrow mattress. His brother who had not written the novel he had claimed. His brother who was not the *King of Providence*. The custody officer nodded for Patrick to go inside, then closed the cell door behind him.

Patrick stood by the door, looking at him, not speaking. His brother's eyes were closed. His head was still. His hands hung loosely by his sides. His feet were together. Patrick noticed that the laces had been taken from his plimsolls by the custody team. He seemed to have been lying in that position for a long time. Patrick understood that his brother knew who was in the cell with him. When they were boys on Walter Street the two of them had played a guessing game in the tin bath they shared in front of the fireplace each Sunday evening. Their mother, ironing in the background, would look on as the game unfolded. One boy, sitting behind the other, would slowly bring his finger to within half an inch of the other boy and, without looking around, each had to guess in turn where the touch was coming – shoulder, arm, back, neck, head, ear. Invariably, Liam would guess correctly.

Standing at the edge of the police cell, Patrick waited for his brother to speak.

Saul, his eyes still closed, raised a hand and scratched briefly at his ear.

'Do you know if they've found the cat yet?' he said.

'What cat?'

'He must have wandered off. I asked them to look for him.'

Patrick ignored him. 'Someone could have died,' he said.

'No one died.'

'Someone *could* have. Someone could have died.'

'I scraped a wall, that was all. The police car came from nowhere.'

'What were you doing?'

Saul opened his eyes. He was staring straight ahead at the ceiling. 'I was minding my own business, driving along.'

'You were driving a car with no brake lights – one that I'd just reported as stolen.'

'I was driving your car. The Lada.'

'And that makes it all right does it?'

'I shouldn't have taken it without asking.'

'You shouldn't have taken it at all.'

'It's just a few paintwork scratches,' Saul protested. 'I'll pay for it.'

'I don't care about the car. It's not worth anything. I'm amazed the damned thing still works.'

'It wouldn't have done without some of your residents. Kenny and Muzzy got it going for me. They're smart lads.'

'You don't think that's a bit irresponsible?'

'I thought it was a miracle, to be honest. The electrics were completely shot. But like I said, I'm sorry about the scratches.'

'I told you, I don't care about the car. I do care about you involving the other residents in whatever stunt it is you're trying to pull.'

'They didn't mean any harm. Don't get mad at them.'

'I'm not mad at them, I'm mad at you for involving them.'

'They just wanted to help. They're just a bit lost and lonely. It gave them something to do for a couple of nights while we fixed it up.'

'Well, it was good of you to give them a bit of therapeutic activity. Look – get yourself killed by all means, but if you kill someone while you're out joyriding in that death-trap, you're implicating them.'

'No one died,' Saul said.

'That car's not been driven for years. It's not been serviced, the brakes were knackered years ago . . . Christ! It's a lethal weapon.'

'It's a *Lada*, Patrick. Get a grip.'

'It's illegal!'

'I told you already – no one died. No one was ever going to die tonight. I just had some people I needed to see.'

'And you knew that, did you? You knew it wasn't a death-trap? That the brakes weren't going to give out at sixty?'

'I wasn't doing sixty. Not till the police appeared anyway.'

'You knew the car was safe? You had . . . what? . . . divine intuition that no one would get hurt? What are you telling me, that it wasn't *time* for anyone to die tonight?'

'That's right, it wasn't time tonight.'

'Liam would have said that was bollocks.'

'I mean, I wasn't going to let it happen.'

'The police said you tried to ram them to get away. They said you didn't stop when they sirened you.'

'I did in the end.'

'After you'd collided with their panda car.'

'I told you – it's a scratch. They came round that corner at a hell of a lick, you know. I was lucky they didn't hit me head on.'

'What was it that was so urgent that you had to drive round Manchester like Stirling bloody Moss at ten o'clock at night?'

He saw that his brother was smiling at him. 'What's so funny?'

'They told me you didn't swear.'

'Who did?'

'The residents at the Limes. They said you never swore.'

'I've taken it up recently.'

Saul shrugged. 'Everyone needs a hobby.'

Patrick rubbed his forehead with the palm of his hand in a gesture that was equal parts anger and impotence.

'I told them at the desk,' he said. 'I don't want to press charges about the car. But there's nothing I can do about driving without a licence, or insurance, and the MOT stuff. They said you haven't . . . they said *Liam* hasn't got a licence. You knew that, didn't you? That's why you didn't slow down.'

Patrick looked around the cell. He squatted down cautiously on the floor with his back against the door. 'You know, I can't help you if you won't let me.'

'You don't need to help me.'

'You look like death.'

'It's fine. It's a blood thing. It's just an imbalance.'

'You need help.'

'I don't need help. I just need to get out of here. There are things to be done.'

'Things to be done?'

'That's right.'

'That's why you took the car? To do these things?'

'I only have a few days left.'

'I went to the Somerset Hotel today.'

Saul, still laid flat on the mattress, didn't react.

'I showed the landlord your picture. I know you were staying there. I know you owed him rent when you turned up here. I paid him off.'

Saul levered himself up on to his elbows. He looked across at Patrick, examining him.

'Your face is full of discoveries,' he said.

'Is that right?'

'So what other things do you think you know?'

'I went on the internet,' Patrick said. 'I found a website with a picture of L.S. Shepherd. I know it's not you. I know it wasn't your book. *The King of Providence*. You didn't write it. You weren't the author. Liam wasn't the author.'

'Is that it?'

'No, that's not it. I know the police in Manchester have this thing, this technology. Livescan. He called it Livescan. He said when they arrest someone they use it to check the person's fingerprints to see if there's a match with any of those they've got a record of on the computer. When they took yours, after they arrested you because they thought you'd stolen the car, there was a match.'

'Really?' Saul sounded amused at the notion.

'He said the computer found your prints on the database. It means you . . . it means Liam has a criminal record.'

'Had,' Saul corrected him.

'Had?'

'Liam's dead.'

'Saul, has Liam been to prison?'

'Why are you asking me? Won't the police tell you that?'

'They say they're not allowed to tell me how many convictions, or what for.'

'You told them this thing about you being my brother?' The idea sounded faintly preposterous as Saul said it.

'Yes.'

'And they still wouldn't tell you?'

'No. The custody officer said he'd be breaking data protection if he did.'

Saul weighed up the information. 'While he was telling you this, did he say when I could get out? I need to find the cat.'

'Will you stop talking about the cat?'

'He'll be getting hungry.'

'There *is* no cat. There is *no* cat. They said they'll give you bail if I vouch for who you are and you agree to reside at the Limes until the hearing. The custody officer's doing the paperwork now. You're down for the magistrates' court on Monday morning.'

'Do they know I won't be here on Monday?'

'You need to be there. Why not?'

'Because I'll be finished by then.'

Patrick rested his head on his clasped knuckles. He breathed out steadily.

'You steal a car. You drive it round the city even though it's falling to pieces and hasn't been MOT'd in years. You refuse to stop for the police and finish up ramming them. You won't give them a full name. You get locked up in a cell. You've got a criminal record come to light. And you still want me to believe that you're not my brother? That angels are real? That the world is awash with them? That they're all busy intervening on heaven's behalf, fighting against the forces of darkness? You know what? Let me tell you something about what I do. Let me tell you something about the life I lead. Kenny still thinks on his bad days that the thoughts in his head are transmitted from mobile phone masts. Muzzy won't eat anything unless he's microwaved it for sixty seconds because he's worried the microbes will eat him from the inside if he doesn't. I've got Brenda sat in front of the television exchanging secret signals with Johnny Depp while she plans her elopement with him. You think somebody's angel story is so different from that? It's not so different.

'Your name is Liam Shepherd. You are my brother, who I haven't seen since you were fifteen years old. You have probably been to prison. You lived in a dosshouse in Salford. You have alcohol in your bloodstream that registered over the legal limit. You've turned up here, for reasons none of us can fathom, and you are sick. Something happened to you, that's all. You're not the first, and you won't be the last. And while you're busy playing dodgems on the A56 and getting yourself arrested, I'm trying to piece some of these people back together. And I'm trying to get the police to allow me to see Edward. And I'm trying to coax Lillian back to give him some kind of lifeline – so they and I and the others can go back to falling apart quietly again without anyone else noticing. And you know what, Liam? You know what? You're right. We're all frightened and alone. We're all drowning out here – all of us. My life's slowly falling apart around here along with everyone else's, but at least some of us are trying to swim to the fucking shore.'

Neither of them spoke for a while.

'Anyway,' Saul said finally. 'You got screwed. I didn't owe Savos any money. He was just pissed off at me after I cleaned him out playing cards with him and some of his mates.'

There was a knock on the cell door. It meant the paperwork was sorted. It meant the custody officer was ready for them now.

When they look down from the top of the rise, the black water of the reservoir seems to stretch away from them like an ocean. It slaps and swells below them, its percussion serving as a backdrop to the shriek of an occasional gull in from the coast and the whine of a car that none of them can see passing now and then in the evening gloom on the Oldham road.

Seven or eight boys have followed the main protagonists through the fence that marks the boundary between the grounds of Providence House and the rise that leads to the reservoir. They edge down the grassed embankment, feet shuffling sideways against the incline to balance themselves, until eventually they all make it down and stand in a huddle by the edge of the water.

The basin of the reservoir itself is constructed of rows of cobblestones cemented together. There are six or seven rows of cobbles running down to the lip of the water, sloping away from the boys in a steep gradient. Below the waterline they can only see a single row before the cobbles become invisible beneath the black swell. For all they know, the depth immediately beyond that drops to infinity.

A metal pipe, running from the purification plant, juts out from the bank above the level of the water until it meets a jetty half a dozen strides away. Liam walks over to the pipe. His face is flushed and meaty from the punishment it has taken from Kipper's three strikes, and there is swelling beneath one eye. He takes off his boots and his shorts and pulls off his shirt. He pulls himself up on to the pipe and stands there in his underpants. He looks back to see where Kipper is.

'You're allowed to push yourself in from there if you want,' Liam says. 'I'm going to jump from the end of here.'

Kipper is looking at the water.

'Are you gonna jump in from up there like him, Kipper?' Lloyd asks.

Kipper scowls. He walks across to the pipe. He hauls himself up and balances upright. He holds his arms outstretched to avoid falling off the pipe that suddenly seems narrower under his feet than it did under Liam's.

'We can walk out and jump together,' Liam says nonchalantly. He takes several steps forward and then looks back. Kipper hasn't moved. Kipper still has his arms stretched out wide to keep his balance, but he seems unable to shuffle forward any further.

'What's the matter?' Lloyd shouts over to him.

'It's these stupid boots,' Kipper says. 'They're too slippy on the pipe.'

'So take them off.'

Kipper twists around and jumps back down to the ground. 'It's stupid trying to get in from up there. I'm gonna dive in from the side.'

Liam seems unperturbed. He takes half a dozen more steps along the pipe until he is above the deeper water. He waits for Kipper, still fully clothed, to take up his own position on the cobbles.

'Shout,' Liam says, 'and we'll jump in at the same time.'

Kipper watches the movement of the water.

'He's ready, Kipper. Just go – he won't dare jump in from up there. He'll drown.'

Kipper bends over the lapping water. Three or four times, Patrick watches Kipper's centre of gravity start to tip forward as if he has made up his mind to plunge headfirst, only for him to pull back at the last second. After that, he crouches low with one foot behind the other, as if he is waiting for a marksman to fire a gun. His face, Patrick can see, is screwed into a mask of concentration, or of fear.

'One. Two. Three,' Kipper yells out. He takes a breath. 'Jump!' he screams, as if in imitation of the starting pistol he has been waiting to hear in his head.

Patrick's eyes flash across to the jetty pipe. At the snap of Kipper's shout, Liam leaps. He seems to hang in the air for an age, both arms raised above his head so that the tips of his fingers touch. Then he crashes into the water. Patrick looks back. Kipper is still standing in his crouched position, one foot still behind the other, still seemingly waiting, in his head, for the gun to go off. He stays there for a moment longer, then turns. His face is pale. His eyes are staring. He doesn't see Patrick. He doesn't seem to see any of the other boys. He starts to run back up the slope in the direction of Providence House. Twice, he slips and falls and struggles urgently to get back to his feet again as if something is chasing him and he is in danger. No one says anything. They watch him flee in silence.

When Kipper has vanished from sight, the attention of the small group of boys reverts to the water. Liam has swum the short distance towards where they stand. He is treading water in front of them.

'What's it like?' Lloyd yells out at him.

'It's cold,' Liam gasps, but he is laughing. 'Are you coming in?'

Lloyd shakes his head.

'Come on, Lloyd.'

'I can't,' Lloyd says with a tone of infinite regret in his voice.

'Why not?'

'I just can't.'

'I'll show you.'

Lloyd shakes his head again.

'Someone else come in with me,' Liam says.

One by one, the boys shake their heads. No one comes forward. They know that the black water is cold. They know it is a hundred feet deep at least. They know that Murdoch-Bannerman's son drowned in its depths. And they know that all of this has broken Kipper.

'Patrick,' his brother hears him say gently after that, 'I'll show you. Let me show you how to float.'

Patrick does not understand if it is courage, or fear, or faith. Perhaps at another time he would have stayed where he was. But somehow he knows at that particular moment that it will be all right. He takes off his boots and his jersey. The other boys watch him. He stands on the edge of the reservoir in his shorts. He looks into Liam's face. He falls forward into his brother's embrace in the water.

When Kipper finally reappears on the crest of the hill he is running. His eyes are red as if he has been crying. He is accompanied by the superintendent and by Jacko. They are both running. They must both think that the bodies they can see in the water are the torsos of drowned orphans. They must wonder whether there are others sunk beneath the surface. They must see the group of breathless boys huddled on the lip of the reservoir and assume that they are children mute with horror at the tragedy unfolding before them. They must be convinced that the water has claimed new victims. They do not know the truth as they shout down the hill in desperation. They have not yet guessed that the two brothers lying still in the water, their limbs outstretched in the blackness, are resting on the surface in suspended star shapes, heads stilled and raised to heaven, knowing with the faith of angels that they will not sink, that they are safe, that – held in the singular moment as they float – they are triumphant, perfect, blessed.

From up at this height, Sarah could see the whole illuminated city before her, spreading back to the darker silhouettes of the Pennines ten miles away. Saul was right; up here there was room to think. Beneath her was the hum and pitch of night-time: distant sirens, single shouts, the smoke of city streets, rain falling softly from a black sky through arcs of yellow light. Sarah knew that at this hour, in this place, the world was more primitive and fragile than it sometimes appeared in the rawness of daylight, and that remarkable things might still sometimes be possible.

Several yards away, Sarah knew, her office window was propped open. On her desk was the information she had spent the evening retrieving from the hospital's database – the list of addresses in the city of the people whose names appeared on the business cards Saul had discovered in his coat pockets, each of them with the design of Leonardo's *Vitruvian Man* on the front. Sarah had been right. Every one of the names had been on the computer system that the hospital shared with social services. And when she had finally finished transcribing the list for Saul, she had levered up the window and climbed out on to the scaffolding.

It was possible, she had discovered, to walk a full circumference of the new hospital wing by starting outside her office window and traversing the scaffolding. It was astonishing; revelatory – to be able to walk about at that height with the sweep of night-time sky above her and the theatre of lights all around. It had made her seem, at one and the same time, enormously significant and infinitesimally small in this elegant scheme of things all about her. And now she was looking out at the city's lights from the very spot where Saul had positioned himself on the scaffolding on the day he had turned up at the GUM for the first time, her own feet swinging casually over edge of the ninety-foot drop, and she realized that she, too, was not frightened of the fall.

She wondered what would happen to Saul after the weekend. She thought about his blood tests. He had dismissed the anaemia. He had wanted her to believe that his metabolism was different to hers. She could choose to believe that if she wanted. She could also, if she wished, elect to see it as a symptom of internal bleeding, or one of several developing cancers, or any number of things, and she wondered if any one of those might start to explain the pallor of his skin and the sense that he had that he was running out of time.

'What would *you* do,' Saul had asked her this morning, 'if you had one day left?'

'What would I do?'

'How would you spend your final day. If you knew for sure it was your last one.'

Sarah had pondered the question for a long time before answering. 'I would go somewhere to see whales,' she had said. 'And I would have a picnic.'

She realized, even as she recalled these things now from her vantage point on the hospital scaffolding high above the city she had lived in all her life, that not for a moment had she considered spending any part of her final day with Gary.

'I think there's an investigation going on,' Gary had told her at the weekend. It seemed amusing to Sarah. Irrelevant. She herself was wrestling with the dilemma of whether to allow herself to believe that an angel had turned up in the city.

'The VAT, the inland revenue,' Gary had said. 'One of them. Someone's put them on to me. I think I'm being investigated.'

'Have you got things to hide?' she asked him.

'It's not that simple,' he said.

'Why's it not that simple?'

She could sense him shifting onto the back foot. Soon he would start to get riled, but not enough for his temper to blow. Sarah could usually control these conversations. Only a couple of times had she misjudged them, or grown too angry herself and missed the signal to pull back, and then he had hit her. On both occasions she had been more angry at herself than at Gary. He couldn't control it, but she could and she had missed the signal.

'Because it's business,' he said.

'Have you done anything wrong?'

'I told you, it's not that simple. It's business. You need to be careful if anyone turns up here or rings out of the blue asking questions – the VAT or anything.'

'What do I need to be careful about?'

'It's not a game, is any of this.' His voice had that *talking to a child* irritability that she knew well. He knew she wasn't taking his predicament seriously.

'Okay. So what do I need to be careful about?'

'I mean, if they ring up. If they turn up.'

'If who turns up?'

'Any of them. You know what they're like.'

'Do I?'

'Don't be telling them about who's rung up, who I'm dealing with.'

'You think I *know* who you're dealing with?'

'I mean, someone might ask you. Say you don't know. Say you can't remember.'

'I'll try to get my lines right,' she said.

He missed the sarcasm. He was looking at her strangely. 'Have you done something to your hair?'

'How do you know there's an investigation?' she said.

'There's something up,' he said non-committally. 'There's somebody been asking questions. That's how these things start. Some little shit will have rung them with a titbit to get even for something. They're gutless, these people. They don't come out of the shadows until they think they've got something on you. Someone I know got broken into, but nothing got taken.'

'That might not have anything to do with you.'

'No,' he said, 'it might not.' But she knew he didn't believe this. She knew he thought he might be in trouble. And she realized that she didn't care, and that she was happy to let events take their course.

Sarah divided up her life into pieces. There was no single thread. There was no narrative any more. There were duties and rewards. The duties were the things she did for other people. She went to work; she paid the mortgage; she deflected Dr Vass's crude overtures for sex; she compensated for Vass's inability to address the rampaging transmission routes for chlamydia and a dozen other STIs across the city. She put up with Gary's nonsense. She held back from goading him. She resisted running a knife across the metallic paintwork of his convertible in the way she had once done with his treasured black Audi. She didn't grind laxative into meals she left standing on the hob for him to reheat noisily at two in the morning when he finally returned home.

In return for carrying out these duties, she allowed herself rewards. She gave herself permission sometimes to read a book instead of doing the housework; to buy the local paper each week and give marks to the houses for sale; to cook good things for herself on evenings when she knew Gary was out; to talk to the kindred spirit she had created for herself when she finally took the decision to stop conversing with Katy; to let her daughter lie.

Now there was another reward. To keep alive in her mind the notion that Saul was someone different. That he was special. That he was here for a purpose. That his arrival augured something, though exactly what it was she did not know.

7

THE WEIGHT OF DREAMS

As Sarah drove she could feel herself becoming someone else. She had been driving for fifteen minutes, but she was unsure where she was and unclear how she had got there. She was simply following the directions Saul was giving her. She struggled to read maps. She had no physical sense of the geography of the city. She could not arrange its districts in sequence in her head. She could not calculate that if she drove from A to B she would then be closer to C than to A. The advent of sat nav had been a revelation to her. Sometimes she would get lost even when, only a moment before, she had been driving on familiar roads on a well-rehearsed route, and whenever it happened she could not explain why. The intuition that served her in dealing with people's feelings and fears failed her completely when it came to the mechanical process of mapping the physical world.

Letting Saul take responsibility for navigating as she drove allowed her to surrender the anxiety that usually accompanied travel. It was comforting that someone else was making the decisions. It was like being a little girl again when she travelled on two buses to get to the grammar school. Although she rode the same routes every day, she could not describe the journey. She knew that home existed in one location and school in another, but not the relationship between the two places. In her mind the two were akin to separate pages in the books she read. Different places lay like layers, one on top of the other. She read so much as a child that real places and imaginary ones felt like pages being turned in the same book. The forests and kingdoms of the stories she devoured nestled side by side with streets and shops and Trafford buses. And so she turned left or right at the request of her passenger and she fell upon new scenes and neighbourhoods like the pages of a storybook, turned one at a time for her, and she waited for the story to unfold.

The previous day Tusa had rung her to say she had decided to allow her daughter to be tested for HIV. Tusa had indicated that she was finally reconciled to the testing. As chance would have it she was scheduled to visit the hospital the following day to discuss the impending birth of her second child with the maternity staff, and so, after the phone call, Sarah had arranged with Paediatrics to fast-track the test and book Grace in for the same day. It was the culmination of all those weeks of work to persuade Tusa that it was the right thing to do. It had justified Sarah's patient approach. It felt like a victory, like a small good thing had happened in Sarah's own life. Like a reward had been earned. And the reward she had given herself, because there was no clinic scheduled, was to ring work on an impulse to book a day's leave and to use the day to take up the offer Saul had made.

She didn't know where they were going, or why. She didn't ask. That was part of the game. The game was playing hookey for the day. It was a reward, because Tusa had finally consented to the test for Grace.

'What are you thinking about?' Saul said.

He had been watching her with that same intensity he had shown when he had first turned up at the GUM department a week ago. It occurred to Sarah fleetingly that she was trusting herself to a patient, a virtual stranger who might choose to do her harm. But it didn't feel dangerous. It felt comforting. Perhaps it was the comfort of madness. Who was she to judge any more? It felt like it might do if an angel really had turned up to guide her gently towards the possibility of a different kind of life.

'I was thinking about *The Wind in the Willows*,' she said. 'You know, when Mole says, "Hang spring cleaning."'

'And they go boating on the river?'

'Yes. Is that what we're doing? Boating on the river?'

'Sure,' he said, 'we're boating on the river. There's just a bit more traffic than there used to be.'

'How much further to the first stop?' she asked, but the truth was that she did not really need to know, that she was content to drive like this across the pages of the landscape all day.

At the back of the church Patrick stood watching Margaret for a long time before he said anything. She was wiping and polishing the pews. There was no one else in the building. Margaret was narrow-shouldered, small-breasted, small-faced, thin-lipped, thin-wristed, economical, adept. With each pew her technique, honed over any number of selfless years, was to shuffle along, straddling the knee rest bit by bit with a damp cloth and then come back the other way with a dry one. The preparatory work done, she then shifted to her knees to apply the polish with a dozen vigorous circular motions using a yellow duster to rub the polish smoothly into the age-stained, black-brown sheen of the bench, the back panel and the prayer rail. As she worked she kept her head bowed in concentration. Every now and then she rose, unhurried, like a sea mammal coming up to breathe, glancing each time at the altar, at the crucifix with the dying Christ suspended from the high vaulted ceiling, as if there might be something unexpected or remarkable there to see. Then, satisfied there was nothing, she returned to her crouched position, comforted by the physical nature of the work and the amount of it that lay ahead.

When, finally, she sensed his presence, she turned around and looked. She didn't speak. Her silence said she was not wary of him. It occurred to Patrick that perhaps she was not wary of anything any more. He sat down in the back pew.

'The church is closed,' she said when it was clear that he was not leaving.

Patrick looked around. 'I didn't know that churches closed.'

'Where've you been for the last twenty years?'

'Not in churches.'

'The place gets locked up between services except on Sundays,' she said. 'It's too handy otherwise.'

'For what?'

'Drugs, kids, you name it. The door's only open now because I'm in here cleaning and it doesn't feel right bolting the door when I'm inside.'

'What do people do round here if they have the urge to pray?'

'They go to bingo instead.'

'Do you think they pray at bingo?'

'Perhaps they pray to win.'

'Do you play bingo?'

She shook her head.

'Do you pray?'

She held up the bunch of keys linked to her waistband. 'I'm all right,' she said. 'I get to come in and pray any time I want.'

'What do you pray for?' Patrick asked.

'I pray for my son, not that it's any of your business.'

'No, it's not.'

'I pray that he won't mix with bad people any more. I might as well pray for the sky to turn yellow.'

'You don't pray for your sister?'

'My sister?'

'Lillian?'

'No, I don't pray for Lillian. I don't need to. I can see to Lillian myself.'

'I'm Patrick Shepherd.'

'I know who you are.'

'Can I call you Margaret?'

'No,' she said, 'you can't.'

'What should I call you, then?'

'Don't call me anything. How did you know to come here?'

'I went to the house, but there was no answer. Your neighbour told me you were on the church cleaning rota. It wasn't her fault. I told her it was an emergency – a family thing.'

'So what's the emergency?'

'The police came to search Edward and Lillian's flat. I wanted to tell you – to tell Lillian. I want her to come back and see Edward. I want him to tell the police what he knows. About the girl. I want him to say where he found the girl's coat – Little Lucy. Why he was carrying it. The things they found in his flat. Edward must have found them somewhere. When he couldn't sleep, when he was wandering round the city at night – he must have found them. I want Lillian to get him to talk to the police. To sort it all out.'

'Don't want much, do you?'

'Will you ask her to come back with me, Margaret?'

'She's not going back. She doesn't live there any more. She lives here.'

'I don't know what's happened between them but it can't be more important than what's happening now. They have Edward locked up and he needs to see her. I need her to see him. He has to know that she's not abandoned him.'

'The door's over there, Mr Shepherd.'

'You have to let me see her. I know she's staying with you. Let me talk to her. I'll make sure everything's all right.'

'You're going to make everything all right, are you?'

'Yes,' he said.

Margaret stood up, unfolding herself from her penitent's position. 'Do you know what it is to have no power, Mr Shepherd? Do you know what it is not to be able to mend what is broken?'

It was not a question to be answered and so he stayed silent.

'They didn't do anything,' she said. 'I told them all along and they didn't do anything.'

'Do you mean your father?'

'Of course I mean him. They were all like you. They were plausible. Well-meaning. Full of clever words. I kept telling them what was happening and sometimes they sent someone round and sometimes they did assessments and wrote reports, but they did nothing. They didn't even take Lillian away. Just because she said everything was fine. In front of him. He was standing in the kitchen and she said everything was fine, and so they did nothing, and now it's happening again. You're all the same. You all do nothing. You achieve nothing. So now it's my turn. Now I'm going to look after her.

'Do you know what I dream about sometimes, Mr Shepherd? Sometimes I dream about one of you people getting knocked down by a bus and you're shouting for help. And do you know what happens, Mr Shepherd, in my dream? It's the same thing. It's always the same thing. I cross over and I walk right on by on the other side.'

She wouldn't let Patrick speak to Lillian. She wouldn't tell him what had happened, or try to persuade Lillian to come back and visit Edward. She wouldn't step aside. *She* was Lillian's protector now, and everyone else could go to hell.

There are nine choirs of angels. They rehearse them in their Sunday school lesson each week, the other boys reciting them out loud and Patrick forming the shape of the words in his speechless mouth. He practises the sequence in his head after school as he walks down to the barn to help Joe with the cows, lining up the ranks of angels in his head so that he will recognize them when he is confronted by them in his future life.

The Seraphim are the highest. They attend God's throne. Seraphim have six wings – two covering their faces, two covering their feet and two for flying. Cherubim are guardians of God's glory. Thrones are the gatekeepers to God for the other angels. Dominions pass on God's commands; they organize the duties of the other angels. Virtues control the seasons, the stars, the moon and the sun. They are in charge of miracles. They give out courage and grace to men.

Courage and grace to men.

It is sometimes hard to remember what comes next, and now he has been distracted by something glinting in the undergrowth. He looks around to make sure no one is watching, then stoops, gathers it in his fist, moves on.

Liam can rhyme the whole sequence of angels off without thinking, but then Liam says it's all tosh. He does it only because he has to. Why does an angel need wings to cover its feet, Liam wants to know. Why does God need all these beings flitting about doing stuff for him? Can't he do these things for himself? Patrick listens to him but doesn't respond. The idea of the angels is wonderful to him. His mother, Patrick understands, knew it all to be true. So does the superintendent with his saint's face and his baggy suit and his smell of cigars. Before him, so did all those men who spent their lives populating their paintings with angels filling their medieval skies.

Patrick passes the superintendent's office and doffs his cap in case the superintendent or the secretary is watching. He grips the coin tighter in his fist. Through an open window of the Big House near by he can hear boys being directed in choir practice. Below stairs in the Big House, he knows, is the cool, brick-lined basement where boys will be pounding ancient leather punch-bags, and swinging heavy Indian clubs, and grappling awkwardly in the ring under Jacko's dissatisfied eye, and where Kipper and Lloyd host their illicit card games with real money being bet, and drink beer from bottles because Kipper has somehow procured a key to the small door at the bottom of the cellar steps. And in the distance, in golden autumn light, Patrick can see the remainder of Providence House's boys padding steadily around the wooded grounds in white vests and shorts.

For a month now, evening practice has been increased to twice a week in the run-up to the match against Jubilee House, the Welfare Department's sister orphanage on the other side of Manchester. Jubilee House is bigger, Kipper says, and the boys there are harder, meaner, sent there from a tougher part of Manchester where there isn't always enough food and people steal from each other like rats. The match is held every two years, and Jubilee House usually wins, Kipper says. But this year, for the first time, Providence House has a real boxing coach, Jacko, and a real possibility of winning. Jacko himself has said that a number of boys are showing promise.

'He means me,' Kipper has explained.

'Since when?'

'Since I won against that lad from the YMCA when Jacko took us sparring there.'

'He was a titch.'

'He can't have been that much of a titch if that trainer asked if he could sign me.'

'He wasn't any trainer.'

'He frigging was. He showed me his card.'

'I bet he wanted to show you something else.'

'Get lost. I'm an exciting prospect. He told me.'

Virtues give out courage and grace to men.

Through the pattern of trees across the grounds, Patrick can see Liam in the distance at the head of a long line of runners. The others ranged behind him, some of them older and taller than him, labour in his wake, grim-faced, over-striding. Liam's stride, in contrast, is short and sweet. From this distance, Patrick's brother, in his noiseless pumps and simple, steady cadence can seem to glide over the ground like one of the visiting angels.

Patrick opens his fist and examines the coin he has found in the shrubbery. It is a threepenny-bit, chunky and satisfyingly shaped by its series of edges. Threepence is what Rossiter used to give Liam for helping with his donkeys. Patrick knows that God is not clumsy or inattentive. He understands that everything happens for a reason. Nothing is by chance. Nothing happens that is not desired by God, that is not observed and catalogued by His angels, or how else would each boy be accurately reckoned and held to account? This is why Patrick collects these tokens when they are offered to him. They are part of the revealed ordering of the world. They are evidence of God's unfolding narrative, after which everything will become clear. Heaven is order, Patrick understands, and chaos is hell.

Courage and grace to men. Patrick's mind slips back to the choirs of angels. He strains to remember the rest of the sequence. Virtues give out courage and grace to men. Principalities are next. Principalities are the angels who have turned against God. Powers are the warrior angels, defending men against evil. Archangels are God's messengers to men at important times – like in the Bible. Angels pass down God's messages to men. They are the closest of the nine choirs to men. They sleep at night in the eaves of Joe Swift's barn, nestled like indistinct and ghostly birds. Dominions gather in the trees, chattering like starlings, their flight causing the trees to rustle. The Powers live in the woods that fringe the grounds; they wear green like Robin Hood and raise the alarm for the superintendent if danger is approaching. The Cherubim on earth take human form, working for the good of men. It seems a possibility to Patrick that his mother was one of these and this is why she was called back early to heaven. At night before they go to bed the Cherubim hang up on doorframes the wings which have been folded into their belted coats and smocks during the day so they can sleep more easily.

By the time Patrick arrives, Joe has already coaxed the cows into the barn. Patrick remains nervous of the animals, of their bulk, of their passivity which he doesn't trust. Close up, they always seem to him as big as countries. He loves Joe for not being afraid of them. The nine cows stand close together, heaving, steaming, shitting, shuffling, patient as the day is long, comfortable around Joe, indifferent, save for an occasional vague flick of the tail, to the late summer flies which have followed them in from the bottom field, unconcerned about Patrick, who retrieves his bucket from its usual place on the long nail and goes to the feed box. He fills the bucket up to the line Joe has shown him using the metal scoop. Joe is ushering the first cow across the barn into the milking stall. He knows each of the cows by name. He uses the name to cajole each animal along to where he wants it to go.

'Come on, Dorothy, keep going y'awd bugger. Go on, girl.'

Patrick pours the bucket of grain into the trough at the head of the milking stall. Joe manoeuvres the cow in. She shifts her bulk, blinking at the flies, then notices the feed and bends to it, satisfied. Joe and Patrick glance at each other, acknowledging each other's presence in the exchange, before Joe bends to attend to the cow.

Joe is unperturbed by Patrick's wordlessness, happy most of the time to match it except for occasional instructions or commendations. He makes a few short pulls on the teats of the udder to start the milk coming, then attaches a suction cup to each of the teats. Patrick watches as the always astonishing first spurt of milk is suddenly drawn through the tubes and into the container. The cow munches, oblivious to the industry beneath her. When the flow of milk from the cow is done, Joe disconnects the cups. He checks with his hands to make sure the udder is properly drained. When he is sure the cow is finished he backs the emptied beast out of the stall, holding its collar, and leads it back to the others before selecting the next animal to coax forward and so begin the unhurried, unthinking process once more.

It is a mystery to Patrick how one man can have as much knowledge as Joe possesses. He can grow cabbages and lines of potatoes and runner beans on the allotment. He knows how to nip out carrot fly. He can drive tractors and plant shrubs and mend tables and rewire fuses and milk cows. He has honoured God by mastering all these disciplines, and Patrick supposes this is why God has chosen to place him here, amongst orphans and angels, in the work of leading the boys towards heaven. In contrast, the only things Patrick knows are the nine choirs of angels, and how to measure out the grain rations for the cows, and how to position Joe when he has one of his fits in the barn so that Joe can breathe properly in the half an hour it takes for him to come round, and not to panic, and not to tell the superintendent, and to know that keeping this secret is a sin but that he will continue to do it anyway.

Joe leads the nine cows back outside, across the yard whose sides are formed by the barn and by the long L-shaped red-brick coach house. The coach house is where Jacko keeps the coach parked up at nights. It is where the tractor and the mowing attachments are housed. It is where Joe keeps the shotgun he uses on the foxes that menace the chicken coop and the rabbits that dart across the allotment at dusk, and the US army pistol he found in the grounds. The coach house is also where Joe keeps his collection of engine parts from the Jeep the Americans abandoned there in the war. Joe remembers the Yanks. He was an orphan at Providence House himself when they were stationed in part of the grounds in the lead-up to D-day. The engine parts from the Jeep are scattered across two long work benches.

They absorb Joe on his weekends off. One day he will get the old Jeep working properly, he says. One day her engine will start and then . . . and then, he tells Patrick, like the Yanks he will ride away into the sunset.

Patrick stands at one side of the yard watching the cows, lighter now, emptied of their milk, lugubrious and satisfied, still mammoth to the boy, encouraged back into the field by Joe. Patrick knows they are all God's creatures. He supposes, since they, like him, live in an orphanage, they too must be orphans, and the thought comforts him. When the superintendent talks about heaven in his weekly Sunday school talk, Patrick pictures it to be full of cows being moved slowly to and from milking by taciturn people like Joe, unafflicted by hurry and made content by the sameness of the days and the regularity of the tasks.

The two of them dismantle and disinfect the milking equipment. After that they load the milk container on to the tractor ready to be transported up to the Big House so the milk can sit on the marble block in the pantry to keep it cool overnight. With the milk aboard, Joe sets off on the tractor. Patrick makes his way behind the cows' barn and past the chicken run to his own shed. It is the smaller of the two wooden structures running alongside the allotment (the other is where the chickens are rounded up to sleep at night in an effort to keep them safe from the foxes), and Joe has bequeathed this second shed to him. On the day Joe officially made it Patrick's shed, he had produced a Huntley & Palmers biscuit box. Inside was a selection of padlocks. Patrick had pointed to the biggest one, with a brass key longer than the boy's index finger.

Beyond the allotment is a patch of scrubland, good for nothing and backing on to the woods. Joe says that a grenade exploded there in the war when Yanks were billeted on the estate. In the middle of the clearing is the Jeep, covered with a tarpaulin sheet. Joe has it jacked up on bricks while he works endlessly on it. Patrick pulls back the edge of the tarpaulin to reveal a key. He takes it over to his shed and unfastens the door.

Inside the shed an ancient spade and fork are hung on two galvanized nails Joe has punched into the wooden panelling. Joe has made the tools half-sized for the boy by cutting them down and re-splicing the handles so that Patrick can work alongside him on the allotment. On the floor of the shed, two upturned tea chests have been pushed together. A tablecloth, buttery with age, is draped over them. Standing at one end of the cloth-covered chests is a small chalk statue of the Virgin Mary. At the other end, propped between two half-bricks that function as bookends, is the cover of the Charlie Parker record sleeve. In the centre is their mother's bible. It is folded shut. The cover has a cross engraved into the wine-coloured leather. It is flanked by two candles that are wedged into the necks of pale ale bottles retrieved from the bin outside Jacko's lodgings. In front of these is an assortment of objects: the wing mirror of a car, an empty Robertson's marmalade jar, a plain metal ring, a posy of April bluebells, now grey and dry, a wooden jewellery box. His mother's. He lifts the lid and places the threepenny-bit inside, then closes the lid again.

He steps back and examines the array of objects, checking as always that everything is as he left it last time. He picks up the metal ring and turns it in his fingers so that it catches the light from the open door. Then, as he has seen the priest do each week at mass with Liam and his mother, he kneels. He makes the sign of the cross, and then brings his two palms flat together in front of him to pray.

To what – for what – he isn't certain. For Liam's wellbeing, of course, and for Joe's. For Liam to win the cross-country in the match against Jubilee House. For Joe to shoot straight at the rabbits that threaten the autumn crop of vegetables on the allotment. But for something else as well. For something like a dream that weighs on him. For something that pulls invisibly at his heart, like a tide on a moonless night in waters for which he has no charts. There was a time when he prayed for his mother, but now he is no longer sure what she looks like, how she sounded, who she might have been. She is more feeling than thought in his head. She is a name. Whenever he tries now to imagine what she looked like, her face in his mind is vague and irretrievably merged with the face of the statue of the Mother Mary in the chapel – apple pallid, blank, cheeks clumsily rouged.

Mary, Mother of God, Mother of Patrick and Liam, pray for us sinners now and at the hour of our death. Amen.

Outside, he hears the sound of Joe's tractor returning from delivering the evening milk. He stands up, ready to join Joe for half an hour tending to the allotment before he makes his customary way back up the hill in time for the supper bell. He stands there, examining curiously the patterns from the rough wooden floor impressed on to his knees. There were saints, he knows, whose devotion to God was such that the marks of the crucifixion would appear on their flesh while they were sleeping. Sometimes, when Patrick wakes up in the dormitory during the night wheezing, he will examine his palms and his feet to see whether any slowly emerging goodness in him is causing the stigmata to emerge, but whenever he looks his hands are always flawless; the slopes of his feet are milky white and crossed only with faint blue veins.

Of the forty-seven names on the business cards, Saul had tracked down seven people by criss-crossing the city on foot in the days since his arrival. He had managed to contact several others on the day he had borrowed the old Lada from the Limes before crashing it and getting arrested. There was a further group who, it appeared, had moved on from their addresses and for whom there were no contact details. There were, by his calculation, nineteen people left to find.

Sarah was content to play chauffeur. Saul navigated. On his knee was the printout from the hospital database she had given him. It contained the addresses of everyone whose name he said he had found on the back of the white business cards embossed with the name 'Saul' and the symbol of the *Vitruvian Man*.

Saul directed her first to an address on the Gallowfield estate. As they drove down the road running through the centre of the estate, Sarah recognized it as the backdrop for numerous television reports she had seen covering the disappearance of the missing girl, Little Lucy. Saul asked her to turn left into a small cul-de-sac and pull over. Saul walked over to one of the houses and knocked on the door. A woman appeared. Sarah could not tell what Saul said. From where she sat in the car she could only watch Saul's face, and the face of the woman he was speaking to. She could see Saul's concentrated gaze, his stillness as the woman talked to him. After a few moments, she watched Saul produce a white calling card and Sarah knew that it would be the one with the woman's name on it. The woman did not shut the door on Saul in response to his possibly lunatic ramblings, to the story he was telling, his need to work out what he was meant to do in the short time he believed he had left. As she watched, she was reminded of Tusa's child – of Grace – who would not speak to anyone, but who had felt comfortable enough to talk to Saul at the clinic as if there were already a bond between them, as if Saul had always been her friend.

When he got back in the car, he asked Sarah to drive to the end of the road and turn left at the junction heading towards Cheetham Hill. After that, he told her to stay on the road until the lights. The sky promised rain. Saul directed her to make a couple of right turns before he asked her to pull over again. He got out and knocked on the door to a flat over a chemist's shop. It was a while before anyone answered the door. Sarah turned the radio on. Radio 3 was playing something severe by a Scandinavian with a difficult surname. She flicked stations to Classic FM. She watched people walking by while Samuel Barber's *Adagio for Strings* played in the car and Saul talked to the man who had appeared in the doorway.

It was strange to use up a morning in this way, but not unpleasant – to let the hours idly run through her fingers like sand as they drove around the city and music played on the radio. Sarah traditionally used up any spare leave days or lieu time to catch up on the housework, or to get the supermarket shopping out of the way. Somehow the same rules didn't apply to Gary when he had unallocated time, yet it had come to be an understanding between them. But today she was taking a day off for herself. She was playing hookey. The only thing of substance she needed to do was to be back at the hospital for four thirty to meet up with Tusa and Grace after Tusa's prenatal check and take them through to Paediatrics for Grace's test.

Each time someone opened the door to Saul, Sarah searched for some kind of sign, some clue in their unremarkable faces. She knew that all their names had appeared on the hospital database. She knew that in some way they had all been through bad times. Some of them, perhaps all of them, needed something to reassemble the damaged pieces of their lives. She wondered how Saul would calculate which one of them needed it the most, and what he might say to the others – to the ones he was not here to save and who would be left to struggle on alone. Each time Saul returned to the car, Sarah refrained from asking him what he had said, or what each of the people in turn had said to him. She didn't want to ask. She didn't think it was right. It wasn't why she was here. It wasn't something she could demand of him. Each time he slid back into the passenger seat of the car she waited for Saul to give her the next set of directions and she let him tell her what he wanted to about the person he had just met – as little or as much as that might be.

He said, 'Brian has two boys from his first marriage and a little girl from another relationship. He doesn't see the two boys because their mum got remarried and lives in Leeds. He sees his daughter, but it's a supervised contact set up by the court. He goes to a community centre once a week and there are always two workers in the room with him while he's with his daughter. That's because his ex-partner says he hit her. He says his favourite thing there is the doll's house. He says he and his daughter play with the dolls the whole time and before you know it the hour's up and he leaves the building though the side entrance before the girl's mother arrives to collect her.'

He said, 'Seth works in a garage. He has a condition called Raynaud's. The blood supply isn't reaching his fingers and his toes. He's had two fingers off so far, and he'll lose another three before the end of next year. He says his hands and feet are always cold. His boss has rigged up a heater in the workshop but it doesn't do much good in the winter. He says he used to love fishing but he can't use the rod now. He says he goes fishing with his sister's boy and shows him what to do. He says his sister is grateful. He says he wishes his own daughter was still in touch with him, but that's water under the bridge. He says sitting on the canal while Ben fishes is worth everything.'

He said, 'Janine worked in a supermarket. She was a supervisor. She used to alternate between home & leisure and poultry, but the management kept wanting more. She said they were bits of kids in suits, not understanding how things worked and telling you to do stuff that was impossible. But you couldn't argue with them, and anyway you always knew they'd be transferred to another store after four or five months. There was one man particularly – Lance. He was the worst. She said she still gets panic attacks, but they're not as bad as they were. She said it's hard to describe them. She said it's like the world speeds up inside your chest to a thousand miles an hour with your heart beating, but in your head it's going really slow like you're under water and something's coming after you but you can't get away from it. She said her mum was wonderful. She said her mum died of cancer when she was seventeen and things were never the same after that. She said the best time at the supermarket was when Lance got fired for defrauding the books.'

Saul's route took them in a wide sweep of the city, through Miles Platting and Hulme and Urmston, to raw and unregenerated neighbourhoods she did not know existed and to which she knew she would not return.

He said, 'Lisa's boy is struggling a lot at school and she is worried about him because he doesn't talk to her about it. He sits there quietly after school and he says everything's fine, but she can see it gnawing at him inside. He's had a lot to put up with, she says. There was a time he had to look after her when she was ill and he did it, not complaining. Now, she says, I see him coming home like this from big school and I could rip somebody's heart out for it. Lisa says she and Luke have a Chinese takeaway together every Friday evening at the end of another week and she says it's like a blessing. It's like the blessing of the bread and wine in church because the weekends are just holy because it's just her and Luke.'

He said, 'Jesse is making a pie. She is going to spend the evening playing cards with her sister who has MS and she will take the pie with her for them to eat. She says she knows the person she will marry is out there somewhere, it's just that she hasn't met him yet. She's fifty-two but she knows he's there, the person she was meant to be with. Late on, she says, they'll do the tarot cards. Her sister makes money from it. Her sister does the cards for her. Even when she was in the hospital and then recovering, her sister came to do the cards for her. The cards always say the same thing, that the person she's going to be with is out there and it won't be too long.'

He said, 'Ronnie drives haulage in forty-tonners. He likes the way everything in the truck gets packed in neatly. He likes things organized. He needs things that way, even at home – in the kitchen, the cupboards. Sometimes he'll get up in the night and feel the need to check that the coat hangers in the wardrobe are all evenly spaced and everything's hanging in the right sequence. Ronnie's dad lives in a nursing home. He's eighty and sometimes he forgets who he is, who Ronnie is, but when Ronnie sings to him he remembers things.'

Saul guided them out of the city towards Wigan, ten miles away. They stopped there twice, then drove further north to a house in Leyland, and finally to a housing association complex on the edge of Preston where Saul disappeared inside one of the flats for twenty minutes with the woman who answered the door. When he finally emerged he was clutching a carrier bag.

'Supplies,' he said, holding up the bag as he approached the car.

'Supplies for what?'

'For the picnic.'

'What picnic?'

'Well, we have to eat.'

'It's going to rain,' Sarah said, smiling, and she drove on.

They headed west out of Preston on the Kirkham road. They drove through villages and along roads with fields on either side. The sun appeared briefly and then slid away behind clouds.

'I can see Blackpool Tower,' Sarah said.

'Where?'

She pointed to her right across a field high with corn waiting to be harvested. 'There, on the horizon.'

'Good. Just keep heading in that direction.'

'We're going to Blackpool?'

'The only place to have a real picnic,' he told her, 'is when you can hear the sound of the sea.'

'Who told you that?'

'It's a rule,' he said. 'I read it somewhere.'

'I used to come to Blackpool with my mum and dad,' Sarah said. 'My dad had an old Morris Minor. I think we used to come this way. I think I remember parts of this route. We used to have a competition to see who could see the tower first. The winner got candyfloss on the prom.'

'Who used to win?' Saul asked.

'Funny, that,' she said. 'It always used to be me. I used to take it really seriously. I was convinced my dad was trying to beat me. Of course I didn't realize until years later that it was always going to be me who won. What was really happening was one thing for them and another thing for me.'

They skirted the edge of Blackpool and picked up signs for the North Shore.

'You need petrol?' Saul asked.

Sarah looked at the dial. 'I'll need some before we head back.'

'There's a place about half a mile further along here on the left.'

As Saul promised, the petrol station came into view a few minutes later. Sarah drove on to the forecourt. There was a mini-supermarket attached to it and a car wash round the side.

'Need anything?' Sarah asked.

'I'm going to stretch my legs and take a pee. See if they do take-out coffees with lids on. We'll take them with us and have them on the pier with the picnic.'

'You take sugar?'

'Three.'

'How many?'

'I'm cutting down.'

She winced.

'It's for the energy,' he said. 'It's a metabolism thing.'

'You'll rot your teeth.'

'You ever see an angel with bad teeth?'

'No,' she said. 'Fair point.'

Sarah filled the tank and then joined the queue inside the

mini-market for the cashier. When she came back out after paying, the car was empty. She looked around. She saw Saul over by the car wash. He was talking to a man in overalls. She walked over. Saul saw her coming and smiled.

'Sarah, this is Findlay.'

'How are you, Findlay?'

She marvelled again at Saul's ability to strike up conversations with anybody.

'Good, thank you, ma'am.'

He was a black African. He had a cautious smile. His gaze dropped away from hers. He held out his arm stiffly for her but it wasn't enough to disguise a small tremor. When she took his hand it was large and warm. His left arm, she noticed, stayed down by his side. The fingers of his left hand were turned into an odd shape, as if Parkinson's or MS had deformed them.

'You work here, Findlay?'

'Yes, ma'am.'

'Sarah,' she said, smiling.

Findlay nodded seriously. 'Sarah.'

'Have you worked here long?' she asked.

Findlay glanced across at Saul. He seemed to take comfort from Saul's expression. 'For one year,' he answered, 'maybe a little less.'

'Where were you before?'

There was another glance at Saul before he answered.

'Manchester.'

'You like it here more than Manchester?'

Findlay nodded. 'Good a place as any to start again.'

A car horn sounded behind them at the entrance to the car wash. They all looked around.

'I have to go,' Findlay said. He turned to Saul. 'Thank you.'

Saul shrugged and nodded in a single movement. Findlay stepped back, raising his good arm in acknowledgement as he did so.

'Nice to have met you,' Sarah said.

'Yes indeed, ma'am,' Findlay said, and Sarah saw as he moved away that in his big warm left hand with the bent fingers by his side he was holding one of Saul's calling cards.

'Tusa knew a man called Findlay,' Sarah said as they pulled away from the forecourt back on to the road. 'He disappeared.'

'Is that so?'

'What can you tell me about him?'

'He used to work as a driver in Manchester. The firm employed a lot of foreign drivers, mainly doing the night-time shifts – airport runs, that kind of thing. The foreign drivers cost less. They worked longer shifts. They didn't do undeclared runs and keep the money for themselves. Findlay had been the first. He was legal, from Zimbabwe, but some of the others were working illegally while they waited for their asylum applications or their appeals. Findlay used to teach them the routes. He kept them in line. He said he used to love working nights. He said it was like freedom, driving alone in the city in the middle of the night under the stars.'

'But he doesn't do that any more?'

Saul shook his head. 'There were some problems. It didn't work out.'

They drove on into the centre of the town and found a place to park.

The North Pier stretched out on its stilts into the sea. They paid their fifty pence at the entrance kiosk and elected to forsake the small train that rode out to the end of the pier in favour of walking the quarter-mile. Sarah carried the two cups of coffee with the lids still fixed on. Saul carried the bag with the food the woman had given him in Preston. By the time they were halfway along the pier, beyond the shops and the arcade, there were very few other people around. There was drizzle drifting in on the breeze. The sky was the colour of pewter. In the glass-roofed sun lounge at the end of the pier half a dozen people sat in chairs facing down the line of the shore. They all seemed to be asleep.

'Inside or out?' Saul asked.

'Outside, definitely.'

Sarah ignored the wrought-iron benches running around the edge of the pier and sat down on the floor with her legs dangling through the slats of the guard rail. We're playing hookey, she thought to herself. Hang spring cleaning. She smiled. Saul joined her down on the boards.

'Did you know,' he said, prising the lid off his coffee and taking a slurp, 'that once a year they have a whale-watching week along the Fylde coast?'

'Whales?' she said. 'Here?'

Saul shrugged. 'I think it's a bit hopeful. A bit of a marketing ploy by the council. It's not impossible, but it'd be pretty rare. I think they get a few dolphin sightings these days, and seals – stuff like that.'

They drank coffee and ate lemon drizzle cake and apples and looked out at the sea. Sarah had taken her shoes off and placed them next to her on the boardwalk. She could feel the breeze at the very edge of the pier whispering past her feet. She watched the small breakers flick the surface of the sea a hundred yards offshore and froth white. If she pressed her face to the gap in the rail she could almost be out at sea, disconnected from the multitude of things that bound her to the life she had. She wriggled her toes. She breathed the salt-laced air and ate more lemon drizzle cake.

'I used to think there must have been signs that I'd missed,' she said.

'Signs?'

'That something was going to happen. That something so bad couldn't have happened without there being indications that it was coming. For months afterwards I used to go through things in my head. I was convinced I must have missed things. I used to search for them, events that would have been premonitions that I was going to lose Katy.

'But that's the thing in the end. The thing is that before it, everything is so ordinary. There aren't any premonitions. There isn't any way to have seen it coming. There are just ordinary things. Her netball shirt needed washing. Her room was going to be redecorated. We were going to go over and see her gran, but she persuaded me to let Emma come over after school and play so we put her gran off. You go through the story a thousand times trying to find premonitions and all you find is stuff that's ordinary. So then you go through it and think about all the ways it could have been different. A hundred little ways it could have been different on the day, a hundred possibilities, none of which were fixed and locked into place until the moment it happened. I'm sorry, this is all stupid.'

'It's not stupid,' he said.

'But you think you can undo it. Unfix that one possibility and replace it with one of the others where she doesn't die. We're only talking inches. We're talking seconds. There's another universe where the measurements were slightly out and a different reality could have occurred, and maybe *that* one could be jammed back into play here, and in that way, if I go over it enough, I could still take her and Emma to see Gary's mum, and if that involves having to like the woman half an inch more I'll take it. I'll take it. I'll take it. Half an inch. A second or two. I'll take it.

'If they'd been round the back. If I'd called them in for a drink instead of deciding to load the washer first. If I'd made her go to her gran's. If I'd taken Emma with us. If I'd liked Gary's mother enough to want to go instead of agreeing to put it off. Any one of them and it would have been different. And if you go through it a thousand times maybe eventually it will be different. And though it never is, it never stops you.

'I was shouting at them not to move her. All I could think was that if I got her back in the house, if I gave her a glass of milk and got her laid down on the sofa she'd be okay. In the end I think they had to hold me back while they got her into the ambulance. I just wanted to get her back inside the house. It would have been all right, then. Things would have gone back to being ordinary. It's just this small thing you want. It's so ridiculously small. Just for it to go back to being ordinary.'

'But the ordinary never came back?'

'No,' she said. 'I understand what Findlay meant. About starting again. About going to a place where nobody knows you after something bad has happened. Bereavement's meant to make you invisible. That's what they say, but it doesn't. It means everybody knows you, everybody knows your story. *That's* what your story is and you can't hide from it. Your story's not ordinary any more. You're the woman who lost her child. And all I wanted to be was the woman putting the washing in the machine. The woman getting the milk for her and Emma. The woman finding excuses for not taking Katy round to see Gary's mum. The woman who is just bringing her daughter up. But you can't be that any more. That's gone.

'A part of you is supposed to die when it happens. But the thing is, it didn't. It didn't die. It kept on living. Living and feeling and hurting. So you build a wall round it. You build a shell, not because something's died but because something's still alive.'

'That's what you did?'

'Yes.'

'To survive?'

'Yes.'

'To get to the last day?'

'Yes.'

'And then, on the last day, you have a picnic and you see whales?'

She half laughed. There was a catch in her voice. 'Yes,' she said.

'So what happens after the last day? What happens after the picnic and the whales?'

She shook her head. 'I don't know.'

'What would happen after that if there was the chance of a different story?'

'I'd let it go by. Because it's not for me. It's not for me. It's not my story any more.'

There were tears falling quietly down her face. She hoped he couldn't see them. She hoped he would mistake them for the rain that was falling on the two of them. She looked steadfastly out at the sea. She concentrated on the waves. And then she saw it in the white cut of the breakers. It dived and rose again, and again she saw the fin slide through the surface into view. She put her hand to her mouth.

'Look,' she said.

'I can see,' Saul said. 'You think it's a miracle, don't you?'

She didn't answer him. She was watching the fin slipping gracefully through the water. She didn't want to let it go. She didn't want to lose the moment.

'You think it's a premonition,' Saul said. 'You think it might be *something*. You think . . . you don't know what to think. You know what you *should* be thinking?'

'Is it a whale?' she asked.

'You see the short head? You see the fin in the middle of its back? It's a harbour porpoise.'

'How big is it?'

'Four feet, maybe five. It's hard to get a sense of perspective against the water.'

'Why's it here?'

'You mean, why's it here for you?'

She looked around at him for a split second and then turned back to the porpoise. It was rising and falling through the troubled surface of the water in front of her, sleek and sure and pale-flanked.

'It's here because it's meant to be here,' he said. 'A harbour porpoise – thirty, forty sightings a year off Blackpool. You drive half an hour from here into North Wales, you see dolphins in the sea if you know where to look. You go up to Morecambe – to Silverdale – now and then you see a long-finned whale. You go to Cornwall, you see humpbacks every summer and fin whales in the winter. Second largest whales in the world, fin whales, and you can stand on a bit of England in December and watch them swim past. Did you know that?'

She shook her head. She was still crying and she didn't care now. 'No,' she said, 'I didn't.'

'That's the thing,' he said. 'You have to know what you're looking for. Dolphins, whales – you have to be looking for them before you'll find them. I think mostly you have to be looking for stuff before you have a chance of seeing it.'

Something occurred to her. She turned to ask him. Before she could phrase the thought she glanced back out to sea again, and the porpoise had gone. The sea was just breakers and swell again, and drizzle falling noiselessly into it from the sky. Her thought had evaporated. She let it float away. She watched the sea for a long time without saying anything. She pressed her face to the gap in the rail.

Eventually she stopped crying.

She said, 'If we stayed here long enough, would we see a whale?'

'Probably,' he said, 'but my bum would get too wet. Let's go home.'

Patrick knocked twice on the door of the flat. He waited, then knocked again a third time before he opened the door with the spare key Edward had entrusted to him. He had come, he told himself, to make sure the flat was secure. He had knocked in case Lillian was inside, because he had hoped to find her here, but he knew it was a forlorn hope. He knew that Lillian was still with Margaret. He knew he wouldn't be able to tell her about Edward's arrest. He knew she wasn't coming back.

The police had left things strewn about after their search of the flat. Patrick checked the windows in the bedroom. He straightened the curtains. He picked up the shirt lying at his feet. He looked around for somewhere to put it. The debris of the search was everywhere around him. Drawers were left open, boxes had been emptied. The clothes Lillian had abandoned in her hurry to leave were in a pile on the bed, where someone had sifted through them and left them as evidence. Patrick let the shirt fall back to the floor where he stood, defeated by the chaos around him. He moved into the kitchen. He checked the fridge. The bits of food left in there were slowly going off. He rummaged in the kitchen drawers for a carrier bag in which he could deposit the food and take it away. In the second drawer he tried he found Edward's spiral-bound notebook. On the front cover were the two circles Patrick had drawn for him.

Patrick took the notebook through into the lounge. He sat down and flicked through it. The pages were filled with Edward's entries in his curious, spidery handwriting. There were exercises Edward had practised each week in his literacy class, and the short diary pieces he had written as homework to be presented to the tutor. Each piece was dated and had a short comment underneath from the tutor in red pen as encouragement. Patrick stopped to read occasional sentences Edward had written, and the tutor's remarks. Halfway through the book the tutor's comments stopped. After that, Edward's entries became more disorganized. Patrick checked the dates that Edward had noted at the top of each page. The last comment in the book from the tutor was two days before Lillian had moved out of the flat and turned up at her sister's house. None of the increasingly rambling entries after that had been seen by the tutor. Patrick turned back to the beginning and read everything.

After they had moved into the flat, Edward and Lillian had caught the bus each morning from the stop on the main road cutting through the Gallowfield estate. It was there they had come to the boys' attention. For much of the three months they were there together, Jamie and Dwayne had been persuading the couple to hand over money to them. They had started by collecting 'membership subscriptions' for the local neighbourhood watch. They told Edward they could offer him a special service for an extra fiver for which the watch committee would arrange to patrol past the flat regularly each night to make sure the couple were safe from burglars who were everywhere on the estate. Jamie then explained that both he and Dwayne also worked for the community centre. They did meals on wheels, Dwayne said. They collected benefits and delivered stuff to people's doors. They took Edward's giro book and returned with handfuls of small change and a bag with Weetabix and Netto soup. Jamie showed Edward how to fix the meter in his hallway so the couple could get their electricity for free. When Jamie said they needed to have a front door key so he and Dwayne could get in to check things were okay, Edward said he would have to check with Patrick. Jamie wanted to know who Patrick was. When Edward told him, Jamie said that Edward wasn't allowed to tell anyone about the key. He said it needed to be a private arrangement between them because if anyone else found out about the special deal Edward had for the extra protection, Jamie and Dwayne could lose their jobs on the neighbourhood watch. The flat could easily get burgled if the protection was lost. Not only that, Edward could get sent to jail for defrauding the electricity board. Did he understand? *Comprende, asshole?*

The boys called in several times a week. They put their empties behind the sofa. They smoked spliffs while watching the telly. They exiled Edward and Lillian to their bedroom. They fired bits of pizza crust at them if either of them ventured into the lounge before the boys were ready to leave. When Dwayne got too high to find the bathroom one night, he crapped in the hallway. That was when Lillian had left.

*

She sat waiting for Tusa, picturing Katy. She sat waiting for Grace's blood test, remembering her own daughter. When they came, she would take them through to Paediatrics where the test would be done. She sat recalling the colour of the turquoise braids, the clematis that clouded Katy's window sill in the summer, the rag doll called Miss Lily who lived permanently on the pillow at the top of her bed. The jars of shells.

She didn't mind waiting. Like all non-clinic days, the department was comparatively quiet, and Friday afternoon meant it was even quieter. She was happy to sit in her office at the fag end of a day when she had booked leave and played hookey, when she had watched a whale swimming, or something close enough, and picnicked with Saul. She didn't mind that Tusa was late. She knew that Tusa was seeing the gynaecologist in Maternity first. She knew he would be talking to Tusa about her low CD4, the high viral load count, the details of the elective Caesarean they would perform some time next week. That was why Grace's test had been arranged for five o'clock, to follow on from her appointment in Maternity.

She was happy with the day she had had. She could sit in her office looking up at the picture of the whale in its ocean and wait for Tusa and Grace to walk over from Maternity, and think of her own daughter, and no one from the department would come in because she was on leave and no one except Tusa was expecting her to be there. She sat remembering Miss Tilly, Katy's shell collection, the way she sang to herself – small verses she made up and sang in a concentration of half-whispers around the house. At the age of four Katy demanded to be a vegetarian. She didn't want to eat animals. She had decided. Sarah was patient with her, recognizing it as a childish food fad, a ruse to give her licence to be picky. But it wasn't. Katy didn't eat meat again, and Sarah had been forced to learn about whatever the hell it was you did with pulses and with cannellini beans, and

Gary had slavered over lamb chops and sausages at her to demonstrate with relish what she was missing. She sat remembering the way that Katy ran, aggressively, like a butcher's boy, like a gun dog. All guns blazing. Her skin's smell of pears. The instant grubbiness on the soles of each new pair of ankle socks because Katy wouldn't wear shoes around the house and Sarah couldn't ever get them clean.

She looked at her watch. Tusa was late. The last time Sarah had seen Tusa she had given her the quilt. She had reached for it on the shelf and handed it to Tusa.

'It's nearly time for the baby,' Sarah had said. 'Take it with you now, in case I don't see you again before the delivery.'

'This is for me?' Tusa had said.

'Yes. For your baby.'

Tusa had been silent for several minutes, adrift, contemplating ways of refusing the unwarranted gift, but in the end yielding.

'I am very grateful,' Tusa had said.

'It's nothing.'

'It is *something*,' Tusa had corrected her.

Sometimes the loss of her child was not an absence but a presence. A needy creature secreted under the table that ate and ate at her. A thing that took up space and energy, and blocked the light. An eclipse. Strangely, when Sarah talked to her in the months after her death it wasn't to Katy as she was when she died but to an older version of the child at fifteen or sixteen, now grown out of rag dolls and of running like a gun dog. The two of them – Sarah and this older version of herself who Katy had not had time to grow into – looked back together at the little girl like confidantes. They remembered together the smell of pears, the girl's whirling, unfinished limbs, the singing, the way she and Miss Tilly sometimes arranged her seashell collection in lines like marching bands across the floor of her summer room framed with sunlight and clematis blooms.

At five thirty she rang the maternity unit. Someone went off to find out what was happening. It took a few minutes. The ward nurse came back on the phone to say that Tusa had been and gone. She had left an hour ago.

'She was supposed to meet me,' Sarah said. 'We were going to Paediatrics.'

'Sorry,' the ward nurse said, 'she's gone. Maybe she forgot?'

Sarah set off home to collect her kit bag and then drove to the leisure centre. The pool was empty. She sat on the edge of the swimmers' lane for a while, hands on the spread of her thighs, listening to the echoes of the reverberating noises of the pool under its high roof. A small fold of flesh sat across her stomach. She pulled on her ridiculous goggles, fastened her nose-clip, pushed in her earplugs, slipped into the water, hung in the blessed stillness for a moment, then started stroking forward, breathing firmly, not counting the strokes, not counting the lengths. No longer ridiculous. No longer part of the world. Separated from it by the goggles and the earplugs and the nose-clip, and the denseness of the water all around her.

Sarah knew that Tusa hadn't forgotten. Tusa never forgot anything. She filed away the smallest detail. It was something to do with the way that she survived. She couldn't afford to forget things. Sarah knew what it meant – that there would be no test for Grace. That Tusa had changed her mind at the last minute. That Grace was the thing that gave her hope. Not that Grace didn't have HIV, but that she hadn't been raped by the soldiers in the other room.

Sarah swam and swam, steadily, dreamily, and every stroke that she formed and carried through moved her further away from the clutter and bile of the world. She knew already what would happen when she went up to Maternity next week to see Tusa's new baby. She understood that Tusa would receive her politely, that a door would have closed, that their short time of intimacy had gone, that Tusa would have retreated behind a line. That her ability to dream of something better had gone, that her courage had dissipated. That she would leave the city shortly after the birth, take Grace and the baby with her. That Sarah would allow her to. That Tusa could not help herself. That she clung to the little things because the big things were out of reach.

Patrick was still reading the last of Edward's entries in the exercise book, piecing together the events from Edward's fractured entries, when he heard a key being fitted into the Yale lock on the flat's front door. A moment later two boys appeared. Patrick guessed them to be fourteen or fifteen. One was the same size as him and slightly built, the other was smaller, stockier. They stopped in the doorway when they saw Patrick. The taller boy, holding a carrier bag, turned and drifted away, back towards the door. The stockier boy held his ground. He stood there eyeing Patrick, weighing up the situation.

'Who the fuck are you?' the boy asked. He moved over towards the fireplace as if to demonstrate his claim on the property.

Patrick closed Edward's notebook. Suddenly, for the first time in weeks, he felt calm.

'Hey!' the youth said. 'I asked you what the fuck you're doing here.'

The world seemed simpler now. Its logic was narrower. The constraints were less obvious. It was a kind of white heat, a stillness.

'No you didn't,' Patrick said quietly. 'You asked me who the fuck I was. Am I talking to Jamie or to Dwayne?'

'You the filth?'

'You look like a Jamie to me.'

'Who are you?'

'I'm the man who's supposed to be here. What about you?'

The youth brandished the key. 'What's this, then – a frigging banana?'

'I think it's Edward's front door key.'

'And I think we're minding it for him while he's away, so why don't you clear off and leave us in peace to watch the telly?'

'They only wanted a quiet life,' Patrick said. 'Was that too much to ask? Was that too much, Jamie?'

'What you talking about? Fuck off.'

'They got married. They just wanted an ordinary life. They just wanted to be left alone.'

'Don't mess with me,' Jamie said. 'We did them some favours. Now fuck off. You're not the police, are you? There'd be two of you. Who are you?'

'Go now,' Patrick said. His voice had dropped to a whisper. 'Run, Jamie. Now.'

He stood up.

'Come on, Jamie,' Dwayne said from down the corridor. 'Let's go.'

'I'm not going nowhere,' Jamie said.

Patrick stepped forward.

'Fuck off,' Jamie said, but he hadn't expected Patrick's stride. He took half a step backwards and swung an arm towards Patrick, but the movement unbalanced him. Patrick took another step and Jamie tried to sweep his arm around to catch himself from falling but there was nothing to hold on to. His head struck the edge of the stone fireplace with a small, dense smack. He fell. In the instant that he heard the sound, Patrick's rage evaporated.

He rang for an ambulance and for the police on his mobile. He tried to stem the boy's bleeding with some tea towels. When the police arrived, he explained what he was doing there, how the first youth had run, how the second one had stood his ground. He told them there had been a short exchange. The boy had stepped back when Patrick had challenged him to leave. The boy had stumbled, Patrick said. He had caught his head on the edge of the brick fireplace and then the floor as he fell.

But the truth was that Patrick had wanted to hit him. He was going to hit him. He was stepping forward to hit him and the boy had stepped back. Patrick was going to wipe the smirk off the boy's cherub face. He was going to make him pay for what he had done to Edward and Lillian. He was going to hurt him for crushing their two lives so casually. It was only the boy falling backwards, and the sound of his head on the stone, that had halted Patrick's forward movement. If the boy hadn't fallen, Patrick had been ready to hit him over and over, and it was hard to know for sure when he would have stopped, but he didn't say these things.

From where Sarah drifted in the opaqueness, she could see the Earth far beyond her, its blueness, its swirl of life, its distant sirens and cries, the eddies and currents forever shifting people from their bearings, from knowing for sure where they were or how they got there. Only here, separated from everything by the movement of her clear, brave strokes and the diminution of her senses, was it possible to see things clearly, the big things and the little things, and to bring all of it to account.

It was on her way home, listening to the car radio as she drove, that she heard on the news that the body of the child who had been missing from the Gallowfield estate in the city for the last two weeks had been found.

8

THE THEORY OF EVERYTHING

Patrick's suspension came early on Saturday morning after a report reached HQ overnight that he might have hit the boy, and that the police were involved. The boy, it turned out, was fourteen. The hospital had operated to relieve a blood clot on his brain. Since he had come out of theatre the boy had been put on a life-support machine.

Human Resources said on the phone that the suspension was precautionary. Jeff Piggot, the operations manager, had been consulted. Everyone's feeling was that it was best to act quickly, before the thing spun out of control. They meant the press. They meant it was a sensitive time. There were bids in for some national tenders, and the Hobart Trust had started advertising for a new chief executive. The brief for the post said they wanted someone 'to steer one of the country's most rapidly expanding social care businesses into a new century in an environment in which the contract culture is set to dominate'.

Patrick asked what 'precautionary' meant.

Human Resources said there was the boy to consider; the family. There was the police investigation. There was the legal context. Patrick asked if he could speak to Jeff Piggot about what had happened. Human Resources said Mr

Piggot wasn't contactable until after the weekend. Patrick pointed out that Human Resources had managed to contact him. Human Resources said Mr Piggot didn't think it was appropriate to get involved personally at this stage. Patrick asked if Jeff Piggot and the people at head office knew what had been going on in Edward's flat for the last month. Human Resources said they didn't want to get drawn into details until the hearing. Patrick said what hearing – the boy *fell over*. Human Resources said it was important that the organization's profile was protected at this time. Patrick said it was Edward who should be being protected. Human Resources said things could easily get out of hand. What kind of things, Patrick wanted to know. Human Resources said that the data showed Edward had been progressed from outreach support and the final payment claimed a month ago. The case had been closed. Patrick shouldn't have been there, not on duty. He had no jurisdiction. Patrick said he had worked with Edward for more than a year, that Edward was being harassed, that social services said he no longer met their eligibility criteria for services, and who else was there to get involved? Human Resources said it was only conjecture about the harassment because Edward hadn't made a complaint to the police. Patrick said it wasn't bloody conjecture, it was because Edward was frightened. Human Resources said it might appear to some observers that Patrick had deliberately gone to the flat in order to lie in wait for the boy, to teach Jamie Chilton a lesson instead of using the proper channels, instead of doing what he was paid to do. Patrick asked why he would want to teach Jamie Chilton anything. He thought Jamie Chilton was past being taught anything. Human Resources said Jamie Chilton's family were alleging assault; they had spoken to the papers; they were already talking about suing the Hobart Trust. This was damage limitation. What for, Patrick repeated – the boy tripped and fell over. Would Piggot or somebody please listen to him? Human Resources wondered if perhaps it had been irresponsible of Patrick to put himself in that position. Patrick said it was the boy who was trespassing, not him. It was the boy who shouldn't have been there. Was that how things were going to be now? Two youths could terrorize a vulnerable man and break into his flat and then sue you for falling over? Didn't people understand? Patrick had stepped forward and Jamie Chilton had fallen and hit his head. What was there in all of this that Human Resources and Piggot and head office didn't understand? The boy just fell, that was all, and then Patrick had rung for an ambulance and for the police, and he'd given the police a statement, and he'd explained to the police as well that the boy had just fallen. Did they get it? Did they get any of it? For Christ's sake, what was there not to get?

Patrick could hear his own shallow breathing spilling into the mouthpiece of the phone. There was a silence that ran for several seconds.

Human Resources said it was best if the conversation ended there. A breathing space might be helpful for all concerned at this point. Patrick said quietly that he didn't want a breathing space, he wanted to get on with his job. Human Resources set out the terms of his suspension. He was to have no contact with any residents of the Limes, current or previous, for the duration of the suspension. Nor should he talk to the press. He would get notice in writing in accordance with the disciplinary code of conduct. Patrick asked about the residents. Human Resources said that someone from head office would be nominated to provide temporary cover from Monday. The usual emergency call-out procedure, effected whenever Patrick was off duty, would apply for the rest of the weekend. Patrick should collect any personal belongings. He should clear his desk by the end of the evening.

Patrick asked what he should say to the residents at the Limes. Human Resources said he should be discreet. He should not comment on the case, on the confrontation with the youth, on the youth's medical condition, on the fact that he might not survive. He should tell the residents he was taking leave. Anything beyond that would be considered a breach of his terms of employment.

Patrick put the items he was taking in a cardboard box. His diary. His address book. Two postcards from New York, bleached with age and taped previously to the side of his PC. Edward's ring-bound exercise book. A couple of sweaters he kept at the house. The two pictures, cut from magazines, of high-wire walkers – Philippe Petit walking between the Twin Towers of the World Trade Center in 1974, one hundred and ten storeys up; Karl Wallenda walking the seven-hundred-foot Tallulah Falls in Georgia. The photograph of Liam in the Brooklyn diner. Patrick's Brecon Beacons Jazz Festival coffee mug. A box of old tape cassettes from the former staff flat under the eaves: Billie Holiday, Benny Goodman, Charlie Parker. The fat-bottomed glass bequeathed to him by Benedict. He looked at the poster he had long ago stuck to the wall of the office from the 1968 Olympic Games – the now-iconic image of Tommie Smith and John Carlos, the two Americans, at the medal ceremony for the two hundred metres, each of them with an arm raised in a black power salute in the Mexico City stadium while whistles and boos of derision rained down on them from the stands. He decided he would leave the poster there on the wall, for whoever followed him.

There was something else. Patrick tried to think what was missing. He realized that the rosewood box was not on his desk. He looked around the office, but there was no sign of it. Occasionally he took it home with him if he wanted to spend the evening looking through Liam's old cards and messages. It occurred to him that this was probably another example of his head not being straight these days. A week ago he had mislaid the keys to his house, and then found them an hour later on a shelf he thought he'd already looked on. Later in the week he had sat at home with a clear sense he could pin on nothing at all that someone had been in the house.

He sat for a while at his desk, reviewing his collection of belongings. It struck him as the paltry inventory of a timid man. Surely, if he had been better, bolder, he would have made a bigger mark than this – a bigger impact than was suggested by the sum of these trinkets gathered from the day he had first turned up at the Limes to be interviewed by Benedict, and Benedict had said to him, 'Do you know what this place is? It is a place of safety. A refuge.'

When Benedict had said those things, Patrick had been a young man, knowing little, understanding even less. Now he was twenty years older. He had aged, but he had no great wisdom to show for it. To have wisdom, you had to have taken risks. That was how people like Benedict had grown wise. That was the difference between people like Benedict and himself.

'Life is being on the wire,' Karl Wallenda had said. 'Everything else is just waiting.'

The quote had been reported underneath the magazine photograph of Wallenda that, five minutes ago, Patrick had taken down from the notice-board where it had been pinned for years. Patrick was still waiting. All his life he had dreamed of flying above the rooftops with Liam, freed from the fear of things that kept him earthbound, but he had never risked anything. He was still waiting, and so he had never learned anything.

Sarah constructed her new life scene by scene. She was standing by the window in the woman's kitchen. On the small flagged patio outside was an irregular procession of pots in different sizes with begonias and honewort spilling from them. The biggest of the pots, glazed aquamarine and with a wide lip, had a cat curled and sleeping in the shadow it was casting. In the summer, Sarah would put simple bedding plants in there, and in the winter she would have heathers with flecks of pink and white in their beading. She would stand there on Saturday mornings like this looking at that aquamarine pot while the tea brewed and she considered what part of the garden to tend that day. She would buy a knitted cosy in garish colours from a charity shop for the teapot. She would leave the weekend papers spread across the hefty table in the centre of the kitchen and read bits idly as and when she pleased. She would have a cat – a stray, rescued from an animal sanctuary, with weak kidneys and one eye missing that no one else could love. She would have shelves in the alcoves of the middle room weighed down with books whose spines would be creased and whose pages would be dog-eared with reading marks. Once a week she would buy peasant flowers to stand in a milk bottle that would serve unselfconsciously as a vase on the dresser. She would make pots of coffee for friends. She would be brave. When she was forty she would buy herself something ridiculous – a stone sculpture for the garden, or a trip to Machu Picchu. She would stop talking to angels. She would stand in the hallway each evening when she returned from work and acknowledge each time how the right house, when you walked in, could seem to fit you like a good dress, and she would savour the sense of growing older in a house that loved her, with a wrecked cat that slept softly in the shadow of a glazed aquamarine-blue pot and watched her through one narrowed eye while she brewed tea unhurriedly.

The sound of another person's voice in the kitchen was surprising to her. She looked around, her face full of clouds.

'I'm sorry?' she said.

'Do you have children?' the woman repeated.

'No,' Sarah said.

'Is that your husband out there?'

Saul was standing outside in the garden. 'No,' she said, 'he's just a friend who came with me. He did the navigating, otherwise I'd never have found the place.'

'Is he all right?' the woman asked.

Sarah looked closely at Saul. He was staring thoughtfully down at the pair of white plimsolls she had stolen for him from Dr Vass a week ago. Everything Dr Vass wore, Sarah knew, was always immaculate. Vass wore cufflinks on all his shirt cuffs; his shoes were shone every day; his sports kit was always ironed and matching. A week ago the plimsolls had been spotless. After a week on Saul's feet, however, they had become old. They were scuffed around the toes; the fabric on both shoes was stained; the front of the right sole was starting to peel away from the upper. Their appearance seemed to reflect something about Saul himself. He was looking paler than Sarah remembered him being a week ago. His face was stubbled. He seemed suddenly tired.

'Do you live alone, then?' the woman asked.

Sarah glanced away, then around at the kitchen. 'Why are you selling?' she asked.

'I'm moving back to Yorkshire,' the woman said. 'Not real Yorkshire. Skipton – a half-hearted sort of place. My daughter lives there. I've just finished chemo, and she's bringing up Lewis on her own now. It's – what's the word – serendipitous.'

'I'm sorry,' Sarah said, 'I shouldn't have asked.'

The woman shrugged. 'It's easier to talk about it than not to talk.'

'What's your daughter like?' Sarah asked.

'My best friend,' the woman said. 'The worst bit about getting ready to die was the thought of leaving her and Lewis behind. The worst bit about surviving is that there's no one to talk about it with.'

'People don't talk to you?'

The woman smiled. 'People want to talk about the weather, or the Blue Cross sale. Who wants to hear about my adventures at death's door? It tends to make you feel a bit separate.'

They stood watching Saul watching the trees in the garden.

'I have a client,' Sarah said. 'She's expecting a baby. She watched her brother die. They said her brother was involved with the rebels when they took him. They said he had brought shame on the family. They gave him a machete and told him to kill her with it. He said no. They said they would cut off one of his fingers for every hour that he did not kill her. In the end they killed him. She thought she was going to die too. She knew they were both going to die. I speak to her and she tells me some things, but she is *separate*. I can't help her because she has been to a place I will never know.'

'She told you these things?' the woman said.

'Yes.'

'And you listened?'

Sarah nodded. They were both looking out through the window at Saul standing still in the garden.

'I made a quilt for the baby,' Sarah said. 'I don't know why. I think because whatever else I do for her isn't enough.'

'Yes it is,' the woman said. 'It's enough.'

'She called her daughter Grace. She said it was because, in this life, grace doesn't get handed down from above like money or power. She said it was gifted between people who have nothing else to give. She said that powerful men, strong men, can know everything in the world, but if they don't know this then they know nothing.'

The woman led her back through the house. Sarah noticed how the woman's hair was cut robustly short. It occurred to her that perhaps it was only now starting to grow back.

'Do you like the house?' the woman asked.

'Very much.'

'Good. Me too. You can tell a good house with a blindfold on. Women can. You can feel it. You don't need to see anything. Some houses you walk into and you wouldn't live there if they paid you to.'

'Thanks for showing me round.'

'My pleasure,' the woman said. 'Don't forget to collect your friend on the way out.'

'I'll go and get him.'

'You're looking at some more places?'

'I looked at one earlier. I've got one more to see this afternoon. It's one way of spending a Saturday.'

'Can I ask you something?' the woman said.

'Of course.'

'Your house-hunting, your looking round at places. I just wondered. There was a doctor in the hospital who used to say to me that most people are either running towards something or running away, but that it's not always easy to know the difference. I just wondered which one you were doing?'

Sarah pondered the question. 'Running away, I suppose,' she said. It seemed like the most honest answer for Sarah to give. It seemed at least to acknowledge that this was a game, that she had wasted half an hour of a good woman's time. It acknowledged that she hadn't the energy for running towards anything any more. She was simply playing a child's game. She was still playing hookey – with a broken man standing in the sunlight who might have been an angel if the world had been capable of organizing itself in such a way.

The woman nodded, then smiled privately. It was a small, secret expression born, Sarah reasoned, of facing the imminence of her own death and then somehow managing to slip past it quietly for now.

'At least you're running,' the woman said finally.

'Is that good?'

'I think so,' the woman said. 'That's the message I'd bring back from the land of the dead. It's better than giving up trying to get anywhere at all.'

There was a sweep of landscaped lawns above the cemetery with a view all the way down to the parkland below. A low stone wall separated the cemetery from the first of a dozen municipal football pitches. The open expanse of the lawns, and their elevation, offered a sense of separation from the city, of being above transient things. This was the place where Patrick had come to reflect on his brother's apparent death when the letter had arrived from New York. After that it was the location he had sought out whenever he wanted to rehearse or refine the speech he might have made at Liam's remembrance service in the light of his own gradual and gathering sense of failure. Ironic, now, that he was back here and it transpired that his brother was not dead at all. More than that – that *The King of Providence* was not his brother's, that his brother had criminal convictions, that Liam's life had not been Liam's at all but some perverse invention of some smaller man rescued from a Salford dosshouse and currently on Clozaril to combat the internal demons that had persuaded him that his name was Saul and that he had some divinely inspired mission to accomplish. Patrick had gone looking for him when he had finished gathering up his possessions at the Limes last night. He had knocked twice on the door of his brother's room and then gone in. The room had been empty.

Down on the recreation grounds, several Saturday morning schoolboy football games were under way. The boys themselves were nothing but ants, but the shouts of the games rose sharp and clear up the hillside, bubbles of noise riding on the breeze. Patrick could hear the voices of fathers and coaches on the touchline, scolding, encouraging, pleading. *Look up! Turn! See what's around you!* But boys in sudden possession, in their panic to please, in their crushing inability to see the bigger picture, habitually paddled the ball meekly upfield. Possession was batted back and forth. Up here, Patrick couldn't tell what agonies of effort the teams were going through, didn't know who was playing. Games ebbed and flowed beneath him in satisfying, random anonymity.

Sometimes at weekends, Benedict had invited Patrick to walk over to the recreation grounds from the Limes for exercise and they would spend an hour sauntering between the various matches in progress. Benedict loved the burgers sold by the café in the wooden pavilion that catered to the weekend hoards of amateur footballers. He would take a child's delight in drowning his shrivelled patty with mounds of charred onions and brown sauce from the squeezy bottle, munching on the damp bun contentedly as the two of them wandered around, switching allegiance from one game to another while Benedict offered sporadic commentary on whichever match they were electing to follow at that moment. It was the only time in the week when Benedict was, in any meaningful sense, off duty.

Benedict had played football professionally in Scotland. He had grown up in Paisley, been an apprentice at Partick Thistle, broken his ankle badly in a reserve team game at seventeen. It didn't set properly. Forty years later his foot still gave him occasional problems. Arthritis had long since settled into the ankle joint. One of the Partick coaching staff had encouraged him into a catering course at the local college. He had gone on to work in hotels and then to manage them. His drinking ('My real education,' he used to say) had started there. 'You don't know how far it's possible to go down,' he told Patrick, 'until you learn to drink.'

Benedict had already been with the Hobart Trust for twenty years when Patrick was introduced to him at his disconcertingly imprecise interview at the Limes. At that point, in his mid-fifties, Benedict still had a boxer's physique and the air of a champ who had seen off all comers. He was frightened of no one and nothing. He had beaten the drink – he still stared out that particular contender every night. He would stand up in conference seminars hosted by the trust and harangue anyone it pleased him to. He would castigate head office or board members at the annual meeting for whatever sins he presumed they had committed. Dick Baird wouldn't have done this, he would say. Dick would have called it like I'm calling it, Benedict would tell them, knowing with the certainty that only a pioneer could have what was necessary and right. Of course I fucking know, he would say to any one of the rising stars he took a dislike to, I was there while you were still sucking on your mother's titty in the home counties. He would let the last two words drip with casual disapprobation. He was, when Patrick arrived, still almost in his prime.

The problem was that Benedict was right. He *had* been there virtually from the start. He knew R.D. Laing when Ronnie was at the height of his power fomenting the anti-psychiatry movement. Benedict had come into the organization at Dick Baird's bidding when all Dick had was a new-found sobriety, a sense of mission about the potential for therapeutic communities in sixties Britain, and two mismanaged houses in violent crisis. Benedict had turned the houses around. He had instilled a sense of organization, but not at the expense of therapy. He had turned the fledgling Hobart Trust into a viable proposition.

As the organization had established itself and then started to expand, Benedict had spurned the offers to set up shop at the new head office. Instead, he had insisted on staying at the sharp end to work with clients; he was a strongman, a maverick, a founding father keeping the original flame alive at a time when a new breed of graduates – the psychology and sociology students who had never met Dick Baird and who couldn't even remember the sixties – started taking up post.

He could be short with people he didn't approve of or who he mistrusted. Jeff Piggot was amongst them. Piggot arrived as a young deputy of promise at the Limes and Benedict took a dislike to him within hours. The animosity continued for two months before Benedict summarily dispatched him to head office clutching a note demanding that they post Piggot somewhere else because there was nothing Benedict could do with him.

And yet with others, including Patrick, Benedict seemed to have unending patience. It was as if he saw something in Patrick that Patrick himself did not and was prepared to wait for it to emerge into the daylight. Benedict nurtured him, encouraged him, found him a tutor who finally made some inroads with his dyslexia. To Patrick himself, Benedict seemed to be immutable. He offered Patrick a new faith. In the vacuum within Patrick where once had been catechism and liturgy and the narrative of heaven and hell, Benedict's own narrower belief in resurrection took over. Lives could be turned around. People could be saved. Redemption was possible. It was all about honesty and truth. It was about bravery. It was about helping residents face up to who they were and who they wanted to be. It was about what we are, and what we think we are. It was about facing the glass of Scotch each night and telling yourself that you were choosing once more not to go down that road and accepting that the same choice would be lying there in wait tomorrow. It was about enabling people to find their own salvations. Everything was possible, Benedict preached. Nothing was out of reach. It was about having a faith in what people could be.

It was Jeff Piggot who brought him down.

There was a woman Benedict used to go and see. She was called Jeannie. She lived in Stretford. She kept cats. She had a thing about Maine Coons. They were the kind of cats that attached themselves to one person. When Benedict went round they didn't want much to do with him. Benedict didn't mind. He didn't like cats. He didn't like the hairs that showed up against the dark colours of his jackets. He'd sneeze for days after he'd been round, but he still went round. Not every day – it wasn't that kind of relationship – but whenever he needed company, or whenever she needed it. If Jeannie rang him at the Limes she would leave a message for him in code. She would say his suit was ready. That was the message, and when he read the message in the communications book in the office he would know to go round that night. Patrick knew, but he never said anything. He knew when Benedict had been because of the cat hairs. It was none of his business. It wasn't hurting anyone. Nobody was married. No one was being betrayed. It just seemed like every now and then there was a place that Benedict got to in his head, what with carrying all that weight on his shoulders, doing it year after year, having to be strong for everyone, standing up to the new boys and their classroom sociology, warding off the glass of Scotch each night, that only Jeannie could bring him back from.

Patrick knew that she had once been a resident. At the time of her breakdown she'd been a nursing sister at Trafford General. She couldn't leave a room without going back in a dozen times to check whether everything was okay, whether the windows were shut, the tap wasn't dripping, the gas wasn't on, the tea towel wasn't folded. After her discharge from the hospital, she was referred on to the Limes.

Jeannie had grown up in Govan. She had been to the same Glasgow dance halls as Benedict. She had married the brother of a Celtic football player who had been on the Partick staff when Benedict had been there. Their fathers had both drunk and worked in the shipyards. When she moved on from the Limes after almost a year, Benedict visited her himself rather than allocate the work to one of the other staff.

Even then there were people in the organization who were gunning for him. That was why he and Jeannie were discreet. That was why, ten years after they had slept together for the first time, she was still ringing up and saying that his suit was ready. That was why they lived apparently separate lives, the kind of lives that double agents lived, trusting no one, spreading misinformation, keeping each other afloat surreptitiously.

How Jeff Piggot came to find out was always unclear. Most likely it was from some temporary member of staff at the Limes, some chance remark. Maybe they had been seen together in some backwater country pub in the Pennines by some disaffected soul Benedict had once casually bruised. Jeff Piggot put his case together diligently over four months before presenting his file to Personnel. His paperwork recorded every meeting Benedict had had with Jeannie, each overnight stay. In the end he even impounded the communications book from the Limes and cracked the code.

'You must have the cleanest suits in Christendom,' he had said to Benedict at the disciplinary hearing. 'Do you even own a suit?'

'I don't recommend wearing a suit for this job,' Benedict had told him. 'There's too much shit flying around.'

In presenting his case to the tribunal, Jeff Piggot argued that a man who had slept with one resident could easily sleep with another. It shouldn't matter, he said, that the incident had occurred eleven years ago. It shouldn't matter that she'd left the Limes before the first recorded act of sexual intercourse took place. It shouldn't matter what people said or thought about his record of service before and after that time, about the man's alliance with Dick Baird. These things were immaterial. It wasn't appropriate, Jeff Piggot argued, for a man who had crossed such a fundamental ethical boundary to be trusted with the wellbeing of vulnerable people. He said these things in the over-cautious, clerical tones he had by now perfected. His bloodless face showed not a trace of excitement.

The question the panel kept returning to was whether Jeannie had still been receiving support from the organization when Benedict had first slept with her. There was some doubt about the precise date of the first sexual episode, which would have determined whether or not the offence should have been considered gross misconduct.

'Were the trust getting paid for it while you were screwing her?' was Jeff Piggot's take on it.

In the end it became clear that the only way for Benedict to escape outright dismissal was for Jeannie to be produced as a witness. It would involve her being cross-examined by Jeff Piggot. At that point Benedict took a pen and scrawled 'I quit' on the pad in front of him. He tore out the sheet and threw it in a ball into the middle of the table.

'You think I would have done things differently?' Benedict said. He was looking at Jeff Piggot. 'You think I would have had it any other way just to escape your adolescent prurience? You think I would have lived my life differently just to avoid you crawling on your belly through my garden, peering through my window, rummaging through Jeannie's dustbin looking for scraps of shit to throw at me? Is that what you'd like to think? That I regret what I have? What I did? Let me tell you, sonny. You do your worst. My life is my own and it's a fucking work of art.'

'I'm sorry it had to end like this,' the chairman of the tribunal had said.

Benedict shrugged. 'It had to end like this,' he said. 'It was always going to end like this. Isn't that right?' He was looking at the white face of Jeff Piggot, who was biting his lip to hold back the flush of imminent victory.

Apart from Patrick, no one from the Hobart Trust went to Benedict's funeral. Maybe they were happier to forget him. Maybe they thought suicide was contagious after all. The deaths of former employees were usually marked in the staff newsletter, but no mention was made of Benedict's passing. He had become a non-person. He had been gently lifted from the written history of the trust. What would they have written? Founding father? Maverick manager? Gross misconduct for fucking a resident? Jeannie sat on her own in the back row of the little chapel, still unable to sit centre stage in his life even when it was over, still pretending she was there to clean his suit. She had started to go back into rooms to check the taps were all turned off.

Sitting in the service, listening to some cleric summarizing the life of a man he'd never met, it occurred to Patrick that he was angry with Benedict. He had accepted everything Benedict had taught him. He had believed in the logic of redemption for people, in the possibility that salvation was at hand for anyone who needed it badly enough. Not in heaven, with harpists playing in a politely baroque final reckoning, but here on this grimy earth, part way through the whole damned thing, so that this wisdom, this grace, could become a kind of currency you could draw on for the rest of your days. He had swallowed it all, and then Benedict had gone and offed himself.

After the service for Benedict, Patrick had sat on a bench on the edge of the landscaped lawns, thinking not of Benedict himself but of Karl Wallenda. Wallenda had died in 1978, four years after Philippe Petit had made his own career-defining walk between the Twin Towers. Wallenda had fallen to his death in Puerto Rico. Someone had set a badly connected guy-rope. He was seventy-three. He couldn't give it up. Life was being on the wire. Everything else was just waiting.

'I'll probably be in the next Olympics,' Kipper announces.

'What you gonna do,' Liam says, 'carry the bags on to the bus for them?'

'I'm gonna box, you shitter,' Kipper yells back at him. 'I'm gonna fight at middleweight. That's what the trainer said at the YMCA. He said I'm gonna make a middleweight.'

Chris Finnegan won gold in the boxing ring at middleweight earlier in the week. The boys of Providence House watched it on the television sanctioned by the welfare committee and bought by the superintendent from the amenities fund. It has been set up in the big hall so that the boys can watch the Olympic Games being beamed back from Mexico City. Each evening they file in for the highlights programme put out by the BBC. The novelty of the TV means that they are happy to lap up anything – sailing, archery, gymnastics – although the most popular sports remain the boxing and the athletics. Last night they watched, curious and perplexed, as two American sprinters raised their black-gloved hands in one-arm salutes while 'The Star-Spangled Banner' played and the crowd in the vast Olympic stadium booed and bellowed at them.

Jacko has announced that Kipper will be captain of the boxing team in the impending match against the rat-catchers from Jubilee House. Every boy will either box or run as part of the match. As captain of the home team, it will be Kipper's job to shake hands with the opposing captain. He will hand over the Providence House pennant and receive one from Jubilee House that afterwards will hang on the wall of the basement gym and provide a focus for Jacko and the boys to recall tales of their victory – how they took their one chance at glory and sent the rat boys from south Manchester packing. Kipper's match-up against the Jubilee House skipper will be the last boxing bout of the match. If Providence House win – when they win – it will be Kipper who goes forward on to the stage to collect the trophy from the welfare committee chairman.

The buses containing their opponents from the far side of Manchester roll up on the morning of the event. Kipper, who is in fine physical shape, is scornful when a rumour spreads that the Moss Side boys box at a real gym each week. He is dismissive when the Jubilee House boys announce that Kipper's opponent broke the jaw of one previous opponent. He is quieter after the exchange of pennants at which his opponent is confirmed as taller than Kipper and eight or ten pounds heavier. But by mid-afternoon, when Jacko's team of boxers has been routed by swifter, sharper, hungrier boys, by the time Kipper's bout is the single remaining fight left on the card, the pains in his stomach have taken hold and Kipper is curled into a ball in the infirmary being dosed with Indian brandy.

The ring is set up in the big hall, with rows of chairs for the audience of boys and with the first two rows reserved for dignitaries from the welfare committee and the city council. The Jubilee House captain is jigging from foot to foot, tapping the inners of his gloves together as he waits for his opponent's arrival. Jacko, hoarse from bellowing instructions at his boys, whose losses in the ring have gradually mounted through the day, is facing the audience. He is holding a pair of boxing gloves and cotton inners, and the card with Kipper's competitor number written on it so he can attach it to Kipper's vest, but there is no sign of Kipper and the audience is growing restless. The superintendents of the two orphanages are seated either side of the welfare committee chairman in the middle of the front row. The Jubilee House superintendent taps his watch and leans across with the ghost of a smile on his face.

'Will you be wanting to forfeit this last bout to us, Mr Huddleston?' the man asks, confident already in the superiority of his own boys and happy to bestow one final humiliation on his rival.

'What is happening, Mr Jackson?' the superintendent asks, with irritation in his voice.

'One more minute,' Jacko pleads. 'He'll be coming, I'm sure. I'll go and find him.'

He hurries from the hall and goes down to the basement gymnasium, which is being used for the day as a changing room for the two teams. He pushes through a scattering of boys still milling around in the room. He sees Lloyd, one of the early losers to his Jubilee House opponent.

'Kipper?' he says. 'Where's Kipper?'

'He got sick, sir.'

'What d'you mean, boy?'

'Stomach ache, sir.'

'How can he be sick? He's supposed to be boxing. He can't be sick. He was fine this morning.'

Jacko looks around the room. The rules of the competition say that no boy can compete twice during the day, but every boy who has not boxed has run in the cross-country race. On the far side of the gymnasium, Liam and Patrick are sitting together. Liam was first home in the cross-country. At the end of the two-mile race, he was clear of the first Jubilee House boy by forty yards. The victory offered an early, tantalizing prospect of a Providence House victory. At the finish line, giddy with pleasure, the superintendent shook Liam by the hand and introduced him to the welfare committee chairman and the assistant director.

'You, Shepherd!'

Patrick and Liam both look up. Jacko's shout quietens the other voices in the gymnasium. Jacko strides across to them. He looks down at Patrick.

'Here's your chance at glory, boy.' He drops the pair of boxing inners he is carrying into Patrick's lap and holds out the gloves.

'He can't box,' Liam says.

'He has to box,' Jacko says. 'He's the only boy in the school still free to compete. I'm not having them claim a forfeit against our captain.'

Liam stands up. 'I'll box, then.'

'Don't be stupid, boy,' Jacko says, 'you've already run. You want us disqualified in front of half the welfare committee?'

'They won't know,' Liam says. 'Just say I'm Patrick Shepherd.' He picks up one of the cotton inners and pulls it on to his left hand.

'You won the bloody race, you idiot,' Jacko says. 'Every person in that hall knows what you look like.' He switches his attention back to Patrick. 'Put a vest on, boy, and pin this number to it. Somebody find this boy a vest to box in.'

Lloyd waves a vest in the air. 'Use mine,' he says.

'You can't make him box,' Liam says to Jacko.

'Are you telling me what I can't do?'

'He *can't* box. You can't make him. He'll get hurt.'

'I can do what I damned well like. Now get out of the way.' He thrusts the vest at Patrick. Liam grabs at it, trying to wrestle it off the coach.

Jacko pulls at the vest. Liam's hand, gripping it tightly, jerks up. His clenched fist involuntarily strikes Jacko a blow on the side of the face. Jacko flinches. He picks Liam up with both hands and lifts him clear of the bench. The group of boys near by scatters. Liam struggles to break free. His arms are pinned by the coach, but his legs are flailing. Jacko pushes him to the ground and drags him across the floor of the gymnasium and out into the corridor. As he reaches the boiler room, Jacko opens the door and bundles Liam inside. He lifts the chain of keys from his waistband and locks the door with one of them.

Liam bangs on the door. 'You can't make him fight,' he is shouting, 'you can't,' but by now Jacko is already hurrying back down the corridor.

Patrick is still sitting on the bench where Jacko left him. He is clutching a single inner. Lloyd's vest lies in his lap. The boxing gloves are on the floor.

'Put the inner on,' Jacko tells him. 'Never mind the other one. You'll be fine. Put it on and I'll lace the gloves. Just remember, keep moving around in the ring, keep watching his hands. Don't stand still and become a target. Two minutes, then a rest, then two minutes. That's all you've got to do to go the distance with this guy. Come on now – make yourself a hero.'

Jacko pushes the gloves on his hands one at a time and laces them up.

'Two minutes, boy,' he says, 'that's all it is in there. Two minutes. Now go and do me proud.'

The captain of the Jubilee House team has been made to stand around and wait in the ring for close on twenty minutes, and at the bell he launches an immediate flurry of blows. Patrick clings to the bigger boy. At one point he finds himself holding on to the ropes, then he is pushed away again into the middle of the ring. The impact of individual blows shifts him in time like film jumping between frames. Jacko yells at him to keep his gloves up in front of his face. Patrick again holds on to his opponent who tries to swing him loose. There is laughter coming from somewhere in the hall. Patrick is vaguely aware of the superintendent getting to his feet. A bigger strike comes in from beyond Patrick's peripheral vision and stuns him. There is a sense of floating in the dark. Then nothing.

When he comes round he is laid out on a bench at the back of the big hall being attended to by the nurse. The hall is crowded. The welfare committee chairman is making a speech. After that the prize-giving commences. Each winner of a bout in the boxing ring is called to the stage in turn to receive a handshake and a medal. There is applause for each boy. There is contentment in a satisfactory day. There is relief that things have run well in front of the welfare committee chairman and the other dignitaries. The final award before Jubilee House is scheduled to collect the team cup is for the winner of the cross-country event. Liam, now released from the boiler room, is called up to the stage. The chairman shakes his hand and hangs the winner's medal around his neck. He leads the audience in its applause. Liam glances at the medal, feels it through the cotton. He is still wearing the single inner he had pulled on to his left hand in his futile attempt to persuade Jacko to let him take Patrick's place in the ring. He looks out at the audience in front of him in the big hall. The applause continues. He lowers his head. Slowly he raises his left arm, his gloved hand, into the air above his head in protest. His head is bowed to the ground. The applause drips away to nothing. For three or four seconds after that there is silence in the hall.

Sarah realized it was the third time she had come to this roundabout. She took the main trunk road into town and found a car dealership to ask directions. She had been lost for about twenty minutes. The salesman said there was a nearer garage than the one she was asking for. She said no, she wanted the one with the car wash and the mini-market. He said it was about a mile away on the North Shore road. He drew her a map.

She had worked out that by driving north on the M61 and then taking the motorway from Preston she could reach the outskirts of Blackpool in under an hour, and that she could pick up the route to the garage after that. She thought that from there she would remember the way – it had seemed straightforward when Saul was navigating – but without him the line of the route seemed to drift away from her like smoke.

She had dropped Saul off in the city after she had viewed the house with the cat and the aquamarine pot on the patio. There was one more house to see on the list he had brought her. He said the estate agent would meet her there at four p.m. He had held up the envelope containing the directions to the house and put it in the glove compartment for her to use that afternoon. He said he wouldn't be there himself. He said there was something he needed to do. Besides, he said, she could do this thing on her own now.

'Playing hookey, you mean?' she asked him.

'That's right,' he had said. 'Playing hookey.'

'Will I see you again?' she had asked him when he was out of the car. His arm was resting on the sill of the passenger window that was wound down. The lights were about to change from red. There were cars behind her in the lane. There was a football match that afternoon and traffic was starting to build up.

'It's my last day,' he said.

'So that's a no?'

'Don't forget,' he said. 'Four o'clock. The estate agent will meet you at the house to show you round. There's a key in the envelope if she's late.'

The lights flicked to amber and then to green. The car beside her in the next lane pulled away.

'Do you know what it is you're going to do now?' she asked him. She wasn't sure whether she meant the thing he believed he had been sent here to do – his task – or what he would do after today; where he would go to; how he would manage.

The driver in the car behind her was revving tetchily.

'Saul?' she said.

There was the sound of a horn. She didn't care about the horn.

'Yes, I think I do,' he said.

She reached across and put her hand briefly on his forearm and then withdrew it back inside the car. His arm had been warm. It was flesh. A phrase flashed through her head. *The Word made flesh.*

'Four o'clock,' he said. He moved away from the car into the flow of pedestrians moving towards Oxford Street, and then he was gone, and a horn sounded behind her again, and she felt herself pulling away into the traffic.

In Blackpool, Sarah parked up on the opposite side of the road to the garage. She didn't know whether Findlay would be working today. She wasn't sure what she would say to him if he was. He was the only person on Saul's list she had actually met. She wanted to go back and talk to him. She wanted to find out more, but she wasn't sure how Findlay would react. She sat watching the cars coming and going on the forecourt for a while. She rang home on her mobile. There was no answer. Gary must have gone in to work. He liked working on Saturday. He got more done at the weekend, he said. He liked the idea that softer men were mowing their lawns and trailing around supermarkets behind their wives. He liked the idea that Saturday offered him a head start into the new week. Sarah climbed out of the car and walked across to the garage. The woman in the mini-market told her

Findlay was loading the day's new stock round the back. She told her where to go.

Behind the mini-market a small back door led into a breeze-block storeroom. Findlay was standing in the doorway smoking a cigarette. He was a big man. Like before, he was dressed in blue overalls. His left arm stayed by his side. He looked at her steadily and nodded. Then he seemed to remember who she was.

'You are the lady from yesterday? The lady with Saul?'

'Yes,' she said.

'You are out of petrol so soon?'

'No. I was just passing. I wanted to say hello. I was curious, really. I just wanted to talk to you. Is that okay? If you're busy, I can come back some other time.'

'You want to talk to me?' He seemed puzzled.

'It's just . . . I don't know. Saul has gone now, and . . . look, I really don't want to waste your time. I'm sorry. You look really busy.'

Findlay looked around him. 'This is my world,' he said. 'I think my boxes of baked beans will stay here while I talk. I don't think they will be going anywhere. Do you?'

'No,' she said, 'I suppose not.'

He took a long drag on the cigarette. 'What is it that you want to know?'

'I was curious about why Saul brought me here yesterday. I thought there might be a reason for it. I just wanted to know about you.'

'What you want to know about me? There is not much to know. I am nothing, really.'

'I wanted to know why you came here. What happened in Manchester to make you start again in another place?'

'There was some trouble in Manchester.'

'What kind of trouble?'

Findlay drew on the cigarette again.

'You are not police or anything?'

She laughed. 'I'm just a friend of Saul's.'

Findlay nodded. 'The firm I worked for – I did not like what they did. I did not think it was fair. They employed many people who should not work – people seeking asylum. I said they should pay a fair wage. The firm paid them little – less than the minimum wage – and took even most of that away, supposedly to pay rent for the house the men were living in. I told the supervisor that the firm should pay the same rate it paid the other workers, the real workers.'

'You mean the official workers? The ones on the books?'

'What is that?'

'The ones whose wages were going through the accounts?'

'That is right, yes. I said I did not want to take the matter further with the authorities who license the taxis.'

'What did they say?'

'They said it didn't matter what the illegals were given because they were not supposed to be working. Getting something, they said, was better than getting nothing. They said they were doing these people a favour. I did not agree. They told me I was in danger of spoiling things for myself, but I persisted. I said I would go to the authorities in two days if they did not pay the men fairly. That is when the supervisor agreed to pass on my concerns to the owner.'

'Did anything change?'

'I was told the owner had agreed to see me. A man collected me in his car so that I could meet him. I hoped to negotiate directly with him about what was being done, to say it wasn't fair. But when we arrived at the place the owner was not there. Instead, there were four other men. One of them had a bat, the others used their fists. They said there were things I needed to learn. They said if I spoke out afterwards then they would come for me and kill me. I resisted at first. I am a big man; I can defend myself. I tried to appeal to them but in the end I had to submit to my fate. I believed I was going to die. I believed I had died. I was told that I was found in an alley in the city centre. I told the police I had been set upon by a gang. I said I didn't know their faces. I was very sad. Broken-hearted. I had no spirit. After that I went to a place that made me better. Then I came here, to start again.'

'Findlay?'

'Yes?'

She had been watching him intently while he told her his story. 'What is that thing round your neck?'

'This?' Findlay said. He touched his throat. He shrugged. 'It is nothing. I just wear it.'

'Can I have a look?'

'It is just something to wear,' Findlay said. 'Something to help me, to remind me that I am strong enough to survive.'

Sarah took a step closer. The small pendant Findlay wore on a chain around his neck had a motif on it. It was a male figure with his arms and legs reaching out into a star shape.

'Did Saul give you this?'

Findlay shook his head. 'No. Another man.'

'Which man?'

'A man who helped me. A man who saved my life.'

'Have you not noticed?' Sarah said. 'The business card that Saul gave you yesterday – it had the same design on it. The same man. Leonardo's man.'

'I know that,' Findlay said. It seemed unimportant to him.

'Did you know Saul?' she asked. 'Before yesterday? Had you met him before?'

'No. That was the first time I met Saul.'

'What did he want with you? What did he tell you?'

'He told me I should go to Manchester tonight.'

'Where in Manchester?'

'To a hospital.'

'Why? Are you sick?'

'No, I am well now. I am to go there to meet Saul.'

'Do you know which hospital?'

'I have it written down.' He reached into his overall pocket and pulled out the business card Saul had given him yesterday. Saul had written the name of the hospital on it. It was Sarah's hospital.

'Why do you need to go to Manchester tonight?' Sarah asked him. 'Did Saul say why?'

'Something is going to happen tonight.'

'Do you know what, Findlay? What is going to happen tonight?'

'Something wonderful,' Findlay said.

Gary hadn't realized there was somebody else in the room. He didn't like people in his office. He liked it being his space. He didn't use it much for meetings. He liked doing business on the go. He liked the idea that he could spend his days in the car, moving from place to place. It made him feel superior to all those jackasses who turned up at factory gates every morning and spent nine hours doing what the boss told them to and asking permission to blow their noses. He liked it when the crappy English weather sometimes let him take back the roof on the Mazda and when he took calls on the move. He liked having meetings in restaurants. He'd had difficult enough times not to take the good things for granted when they came along. He liked knowing that the accountant would sort it all out.

He liked cars. He'd bought the MX-5 from Ray, who serviced his fleet of taxis. It was the V-Special Roadster with the flip-up headlights and the tan leather seats. It had speakers in the headrests. You couldn't buy it in Britain. It had been imported from Japan. Ray imported a bunch of cars at a time from Japan – Mazdas, Mitsubishi FTOs and GTOs. They were right-hand drives. They had fewer miles on the clock as a rule. They only needed mph clocks fitting and SVA tests to be road-ready. Gary fancied getting involved in it properly as a business sometime, bringing cars and bikes in from Japan and Cyprus and then selling them on. You could view them over the internet, ship them over in containers, pick them up at Dover. There was money to be made there, a grand a car, he was sure, although Ray never seemed to make much. Ray was too much in love with the cars, was Gary's reasoning. He was never out of his overalls. Fourteen years on and Ray was still dependent on the money Gary paid him to service the fleet.

When Gary was in the office he was almost always on his own. He was usually trying to iron out issues with the solicitors or the estate agents, or with the renovators. The property side of the business was where most of the problems were, but then that was where the money was. The taxi firm was no problem, but then no one ever got rich from shifting people around unless you were Richard Branson. The taxi business gave him a steady income, but who wanted a steady income? It gave him a place to push loose change through the books, but then that was another story.

The builder's merchant, where he had started with his father, had been a slog. His father was a stickler for doing things by the book. In all the years he'd been working with him, Gary had never seen his father manoeuvre a single penny away from the exchequer. His father was a straight-down-the-line man who dropped dead no wealthier than he'd been before the thirty years he'd invested in the business. When Gary took over, the first thing he did was look around for an operation that offered him a better return. How else could growth be encouraged? That was why he ended up selling the business and buying the taxi fleet. And he'd done all right, but only all right. Not as well as he'd expected. And then Bernie had mentioned one day about the money to be made in houses. So they'd made money, then lost a lot of it when the housing crash came at the end of the eighties, but for the last ten years they'd been making it again. That was how people were tested. That was life. Gary knew; he'd had his own share of tragedy, of being tested. He'd had his daughter die, for Christ's sake. It didn't get worse than that. You got knocked down, you had to build yourself back up again for yourself, for the people who depended on you. You sorted your problems. You let yourself drive around town with the soft top. You put safeguards in place. You showed courage when you needed to. You were careful who you trusted. You wore your lucky shirts when you needed to. You respected that the number eight was lucky. You only drove cars with an eight on the registration plate. You made sure your shirts had stripes on them. You tried to make sure they had eight stripes. You got dressed in a certain order in the mornings to keep the rhythm going. You put things in the right sequence. Katy hadn't made it to eight. She would have been safe if she'd made it to eight. The eight was lucky, but everything couldn't be tied to the eight. That was why he took precautions. He watched for trouble coming. He stayed on top of things. That was why it surprised him to find that someone else was in the room with him. He liked to be prepared for things. He didn't like surprises. He had been trying out expressions, talking to himself. They were things he did when something was bothering him, when he was alone in his office. He didn't like the idea that someone had been watching him in here. It unbalanced him. It made him feel like he did when his father caught him that time altering the cash ledger.

'Who the hell are you?' he said.

Saul had his hands in his coat pockets.

'Did Donna send you in?'

'No.'

'How did you get in, then? She didn't say there was anyone due.'

'I slipped in.'

'What do you mean, you slipped in?'

'Under the radar, so to speak.'

Gary moved around to his desk. 'So what do you want?'

'I want to talk to you.'

'About business?'

'Everything is business.'

'So what's your business?'

'You know my business, Mr Montague.'

'I do?'

'You knew it as soon as you saw me in here. You've been expecting me. You've been expecting somebody.'

'I have, have I?'

'I think so.'

'If you won't tell me who you are, maybe I should just get you thrown out. You think I should get you thrown out? You think I should press the panic button under the desk?'

'Is there a panic here, Mr Montague?'

'We've had break-ins. You think I should call the police so they can ask you if you're back here sussing the place out?'

'Sure, you can call them.'

'What are you? Inland Revenue? VAT?'

Saul shrugged. 'Take your pick.'

'You have ID, I take it?'

'Not until I'm ready to run with it. Just think of it as a social call.'

'Under the radar?'

'That's right.'

'If you've no ID you can leave now and I'm on the phone to my solicitor.'

'I have a story to tell you.'

'What if I don't want to hear a story?'

'I have a story, and then I'll go.'

'You're hacking me off now.'

'My story is about a man who made money out of doing houses up and selling them. But after he lost his first pile of money he thought he should be on the lookout for any small business advantages he could find. He didn't want to be like his father, you see. He didn't want to slog all his life and not get better off.'

'This is the story?'

'That's right. This is the story. This man, he thought his father was stupid for doing that and he didn't want to be as stupid as his father, so he talked to his accountant and they decided to avoid capital gains by making it look like some of the houses were being bought to live in. It was just a little step, it didn't make him a bad person, but it made him better off as a result and it showed him he wasn't as dumb as his father had been.

'Now and then he paid by cash rather than through the books for the gang who did the renovation work for him. It was just another little thing. On its own it was hardly anything. It was just small enough for him to fly under the radar, so to speak. So he made money. He lived well enough, you understand. He liked the odd awaydays down to London – business trips with his accountant friend Bernie when they'd hook up with a couple of nice young girls from the office and blow the odd grand over a weekend.

'Then someone put him on to a middleman who could supply cheaper labour to do the houses up. Guys whose paperwork wasn't through. Guys whose Home Office documents said they weren't allowed to work while their appeals were being considered. Guys whose appeals had been turned down. Guys who could drive taxis as well, even if they didn't have completely valid licences, but what the hell, they knew how to steer and they always turned up on time and they were grateful for the work, and they never made trouble even though the work didn't pay that well. Oh, and by the way, Findlay Olonge sends his regards.'

'Who?'

'You remember Findlay? Used to work for you?'

'Don't know him.'

'There was a falling out.'

'Black fella?'

'That's right. You do remember.'

'I remember he cleared off. Taxi driving wasn't his thing.'

'Yes he did. He sends you his regards. He wanted you to know that.'

'You need to know,' Gary said, suddenly wary of the line he was holding, 'I never meant for Findlay to get hurt. I only wanted him frightened off, but things got out of control.'

'Is that so?'

'Look – what is it that you want?'

'I want to offer you a deal, Mr Montague. I want to show you a way out.'

'It's just a story you told me, right. We can agree it's an interesting story, but it could be about anyone.'

'You've had two break-ins here in the last two months. Nothing broken. Nothing taken that you can see. You had one at your house six weeks ago, in the garage where you keep some stuff. Same thing. You didn't even tell your wife about it. Bernie, he's mislaid some papers from his offices. That's what he told you. Is that right?'

'What are you saying?'

'I'm saying it's just a story. It could be about anyone. I'm saying that with a story like that, a man leaves a trail. I'm saying there's a deal on the table. You want to know a funny thing?'

'What?'

'You know that funny feeling you get now and then, Gary, that you're being watched? I know you get it now and then. You do that thing where you slow down and you half look back over your left shoulder because you think there's someone been watching you. Wouldn't it be funny if you'd been right all along? Wouldn't it be . . . if nothing you'd done for years had been out of sight, wouldn't that be funny? Wouldn't it change the way you looked at the world if you knew there was nothing that hadn't been seen?'

'Have you been talking to Bernie? Is that it?'

'It's not about Bernie.'

'What's it about, then?'

'It's about you, Gary. It's about making a deal.'

'What do you want?'

'I want you to wait for something to happen.'

'What's going to happen?'

'Something's going to happen, Gary. I don't know when. Not for days, or months. Maybe longer. But one day something's going to happen.'

'So tell me, what's going to happen?'

'You're going to keep sending out your taxis. You're going to sell some more houses, make some more money. You're going to stop looking over your shoulder for me. You're going to hope that things have settled down again. Then one night you're going to go home and your wife's going to tell you that she's going to leave.'

'My wife? What's Sarah got to do with this?'

'That's what will happen. Your wife's going to tell you that she's leaving. That's the thing that's going to happen.'

'Says who?'

'And you know what you're going to do, Gary?'

'What?'

'You're going to let her pack a suitcase and leave.'

'Just like that?'

'Just like that.'

'Just let her walk away and try to clean me out?'

'And never go after her. Never threaten her. Never threaten violence. Never look for her again. You're just going to let her walk out and go. And do you know why, Gary?'

'Why?'

'Because you can't afford to do anything else.'

'You're not from the revenue, are you?'

'It doesn't matter where I'm from,' Saul said. 'It matters what I know.'

'Who put you up to this? Did she put you up to this?'

'Think of me as someone who's seen everything, Gary. Think of me as someone who's watched everything you ever did, every time you went some place, every time you made some move, every time you thought some bad thought. Just think of me as your guardian angel. See, I'll leave you my card. It'll help you to remember.'

Saul reached into the breast pocket of his coat and took out a card. It was a playing card. He put it down on the table and walked out of the room. Gary turned the card over. It was an eight.

9

SWITZERLAND

It was only when Sarah arrived at the final house that the arrangement struck her as unusual. As Saul had promised, there was a key in the envelope he had left with her along with the directions to get to the house. But why would an estate agent trust her on her own with the keys to a property they were selling? Now that she was here, she could see that there was no 'For Sale' sign up on the property, and there was no sign of the estate agent.

She sat in the car outside the house for a while, waiting for the estate agent to arrive. She had already decided it wasn't the kind of house she would be interested in. Even if she had the money. Even if she was buying. She knew that she could flee from here – drive home – or she could have one last small adventure and go in using the key Saul had given her. What was the worst that could happen? She could set an alarm off. She could get arrested for breaking in. She could stumble across someone living in the house, or across someone lying in wait for her in the house. But for that to happen Saul would have needed to plan for something bad to happen. In the new house I will be brave, she reminded herself. I will put flowers in a milk bottle on the kitchen table once a week. I will love a rescued cat with one eye.

She picked up the envelope with the key in it and climbed out of the car.

Sarah opened up the house and took a single step inside the hallway.

'Hello?' she said out loud. 'Is anyone at home?'

There was no answer. Her breathing had become a little shallower. She pushed open the door to the lounge. There was still no sign of life. She edged in, wandered tentatively around. The room was open plan, knocked through from the original front parlour and living room when the terrace had been built. The décor was practical. Nothing matched. The sofa and separate armchair were old and comfortable. The pine unit had three bookshelves with only the top shelf being used to hold books. The vacuum cleaner stood ready in one corner of the room. There was a rack of drying clothes under the window. The place was vacuumed and tidy and undusted. Sarah imagined someone living here alone, neatly, functionally, but with no desire or ability to put their stamp on the place as their own.

She went through into the small kitchen, separated from the rest of the lounge by a breakfast bar. On the wall was a chalkboard for messages or shopping lists. Across it was written, *Pass here, you princes of hope.*

Pinned underneath the message board was a gas bill for the property. She read the name on the bill. She went back into the lounge. She stood there for a while looking around, not understanding what it was she had been brought here to see. Then she went upstairs.

Saul was sitting on one of the chairs in the waiting room of the GUM department when Tusa appeared. Her daughter was close behind her. The room was empty. The department was not open at weekends. Tusa was moving slowly. She was heavy with child, clearly in her last days of pregnancy. It wasn't clear whether Saul was expecting anyone. He was quietly shelling peanuts, dropping the nut each time into his coat pocket, letting each shell fall to the floor by his feet.

'What are you doing?' the child asked, appearing from around the folds of her mother's big skirt.

'I'm glad you asked me that, Grace,' Saul said. 'They're for my cat. Have you seen him?'

'You have a cat?'

'Yes I do. Have you seen him?'

'Yes,' she said. 'I saw him.'

'Good,' Saul said. 'I'm glad someone's seen him. I was starting to get worried.'

Tusa held up a supermarket carrier bag. 'I have something for Sarah,' she said.

'She's not here right now,' Saul said.

'I know. I was going to leave it here for her. Will you give it to her?'

'What is it?'

'It is a baby's quilt.'

'Is it a present?'

'She gave it to me.'

'You don't want it?' Saul asked.

'It is not that. She made it for me. For my baby. It was a kindness. But I think it is better that she has it. I think she made it for herself. She gave me enough.'

'What do you want me to say?'

'You will give it to her? The quilt?'

Saul nodded.

'Tell her she will need it,' Tusa said. 'Tell her the quilt is for her. Tell her – not yet, for when she will have the child. You know in the end I believe she will have a child?'

'I know,' he said.

Tusa led her daughter towards the door. She turned as she pushed at the handle and looked around at him.

'You're not from this place,' she said. It wasn't clear if she meant the hospital, or the city or something else. It wasn't clear if it was a question or a statement.

'No,' he said.

'So what are you doing here? You are just passing through? That's what? Just visiting?'

The little girl looked at her mother who was looking at Saul.

Saul nodded. 'That's what,' he said. 'Just visiting.'

Several times during the day Patrick had rung the residents' phone at the Limes. He wanted to speak to his brother, but no one had answered. By late afternoon he decided to drive over. If his brother still wasn't there, Patrick would leave him a note to explain what had happened, to provide details of how he could be contacted.

He could see the graffiti from the road as he approached the Limes. The word KILLER was sprayed in luminous red capital letters across the front door and the brickwork of the porch. Underneath it was scrawled *Fuck Off Peedos*. The door had been forced, presumably by whoever had turned up with the aerosol can. There was no sign of any of the residents. Patrick hoped they had been out when the callers had arrived. He had always encouraged them to go out on a Saturday, to do what other people did as a small way of rejoining the world they had sought temporary sanctuary from. The fish tank had been pulled to the floor, the contents spread across the hallway, the fish lying lifeless on the carpet. In the big front lounge, where the house meetings were held, several of the chairs had been slashed. The TV had been upended. The red aerosol paint was sprayed on the walls of most of the ground-floor rooms. In the office, the red line circled the room at head height until it came to the edge of the poster Patrick had left pinned up on the wall, the one of the 1968 Olympics medal ceremony, the one of the black power salute. Whoever had brandished the aerosol can had seemed to pause in his tracks at this point because there was a thick circular scum of paint as if the sprayer had been drawn to stand and look at the image of Tommie Smith and John Carlos, the two American athletes, for several seconds while his finger, perhaps without him realizing, had stayed pressed to the nozzle. Then he had inscribed the word SHIT across the poster and moved on.

Patrick pulled the poster down from the wall. After all these years, Patrick knew the details of the image intimately – the three tracksuited sprinters (the Australian Peter Norman had come second in the race); the green ribbons around their necks; the black Mexican night; the tracksuit sleeves of the two Americans rolled above the elbow; the two Americans shoeless; Carlos's string of beads around his neck as a symbol of two centuries of lynchings; Smith's gloved right hand, Carlos's left, raised; their two heads bowed. Tommie Smith, higher than the other two on the podium as Olympic champion, looked resolute, focused. John Carlos, standing behind him, had always seemed to Patrick to be more casual, or subdued, in his stance; as if, able to witness the gesture of his compatriot directly in front of him, a part of him was already distancing himself from the event; as if he were already armed with foresight; as if he were watching things unfold from outside himself. As if he already knew what was coming.

'If I do something good then I am an American,' Tommie Smith had once said, 'but if I do something bad then I am a negro.'

Patrick folded the poster in half, then half again, and pushed it into the waste-paper bin. He decided that he would wash the graffiti off the front of the building as his final act before leaving. He went through to the kitchen to get the turpentine and warm water. As he stood at the sink running the hot tap he heard music playing outside. He looked through the window into the back garden. There was someone on the lawn. He couldn't make out who it was. He went outside. There was a portable radio propped on the path. Music was coming from it. Lillian was standing in the middle of the lawn. She looked at Patrick but did not acknowledge him. He walked over to her.

'Are you all right?'

Lillian looked at him.

'I know what happened,' Patrick said. 'At the flat. The two boys. I know what happened.'

She didn't reply. She was concentrating on the music. She was wearing her purple dress. Patrick had never seen her wearing the dress before.

'What made you come back?' he asked.

'I have a message from Saul,' she said. 'He says it's nearly time. He says first you should dance with me, then it'll be time.'

'Time for what? Is he in trouble, Lillian?'

'He's not in trouble,' Lillian said, unperturbed. 'It's just that there's something he has to do before he goes.'

So they danced on the soft grass to the music coming from the radio, Lillian feeling so slight to him it was as if she were hardly there at all. Above their heads a pair of wood pigeons *clap clap clapped* out of the tall trees and swept low.

'Did you come back for Edward?' Patrick said.

'Saul said I should come back,' she told him.

'Did he say why?'

'He said everything's going to be all right.'

Patrick nodded. He did not believe her. He knew that Edward had been charged and that his stay at the Limes had been reported in the papers, but he could think of nothing else to say, and so he danced with her, and the music played on from the radio in the garden, behind the smashed rooms of the empty house.

The first door off the landing led to a bedroom. Sarah held the handle and peered in without stepping into the room, then closed the door again. The next door was the bathroom. The final door led into what the estate agent would no doubt have described as the second bedroom, but there was no bed in it. There was a desk and a chair over by the window, three or four boxes, an ironing board. Looking out of the window Sarah could see a line of other roofs. The wall opposite the window was covered by a series of small pieces of paper. Each one was attached to the wall by a single drawing pin so that when Sarah had opened the door the draught had made them all flap briefly against their spikes as if they were alive and straining to be free.

She moved closer to them. She realized that something was written on each of the pieces of paper in blue biro. She read one. It was a woman's name – *Lillian Shaw*, and a year, *2005*. Underneath it was a single phrase. It said, *Dancing with someone to music*.

She looked at another, and another. Each one had a name written on it, and a year: 1999, 2002, 1986. Each one had something different written underneath the year. Some of them had clearly been there for a long time. Some of the pieces of paper were turning slowly into the texture of leaves. She kept on reading the names. She came to one that said *Findlay Olonge*.

She remembered finally where she had come across the name on the gas bill. It was Patrick – the man who ran Saul's hostel. She stepped back and looked at the pattern on the wall in its entirety, working out in simple stages that these were the residents he had worked with over the years. These were the wishes they had arrived with at the hostel he ran. These were the small things they had wished for.

I will be brave. I will put fresh flowers in a milk bottle. I will love a rescued cat.

She stood in silence looking at the pieces of paper, understanding them to be acts of hope, and stubbornness, and salvage. She imagined Patrick Shepherd – the man she had not yet met – carrying their weight around with him privately for the last twenty years like some solitary Atlas hauling the weight of the world in such a way that no one else had noticed or paid attention.

Eventually she would come to see that it might be possible for someone to rescue a man like that, to love him, to make that long, slow, elegant, trusting fall. Standing in front of all those pieces of paper butterflying in the draught in an almost empty room in a terraced house in Salford was the beginning of it.

Kipper says, 'Have you got it?'

Patrick holds out an oil-stained cloth. He places it down on the table.

They are in the basement gymnasium. Kipper has a key. It is cool and dark.

'Is that it?' Lloyd says.

Kipper touches the cloth cautiously, then lifts up one corner to reveal the gun. He wants to shoot rabbits. The frustration that he couldn't fight last week against Jubilee House has built and built. He has a sense of being diminished. He senses there is an answer here, a way of rebalancing himself and the world. Shooting the rabbits that colonize the woods on the edge of the orphanage grounds – who knows, maybe even skinning one – will help the rebalancing. That was the dare for Patrick. To get the gun so that Kipper can shoot the rabbits. Patrick has carried it across the grounds up his jumper. He has completed the dare. He has passed the test Kipper has given him. Last week he survived for almost a round against the Jubilee House skipper in the ring when Kipper was taken sick, and now he has completed the dare Kipper had set for him. Kipper says this is his initiation. Everyone in Kipper's crew has taken one. Patrick became eligible when he almost survived a full round in the ring against Jubilee House. Now he is one of them. Now he will get invited to the card games Kipper runs down here, and Kipper will shoot rabbits, and then Patrick will get the gun back to the coach house before Joe sees that it is missing.

'Bloody hell,' Kipper says, grinning, pleased with himself. 'Bloody hell. Brilliant.'

'I thought it'd be bigger,' Lloyd says.

'What sort is it?' Kipper asks.

Patrick picks the notepad from his shorts pocket and writes down 'Colt' with his stubby pencil.

'It doesn't *say* Colt,' Lloyd says suspiciously. Indented on the barrel of the gun are the words *Ithaca Gun Co. Inc, Ithaca NY*.

'NY,' Kipper says. 'New York. It is. It's bloody American. It's a Yank gun. It's probably shot people in the war, has this. Germans and stuff.' His face is beaming. He picks up the gun and inspects it. The handle and the barrel are shaped like two rectangles jammed awkwardly together. Kipper rubs his thumb against the brown diamond-patterned grip on the handle. He holds the gun at arm's length. He makes a machine-gun noise as he aims it at the wall.

'*Ka-ka-ka-ka.*'

'There's no bullets in it, is there?' he asks.

Patrick shakes his head. He rummages deeper in the cloth and pulls out a small cardboard box the size of a cigarette packet. He shakes it. Something rattles inside.

'How many bullets did you get?' Kipper asks.

Patrick holds up three fingers. It is the most he dared take without risking that Joe would notice them gone from the locked drawer where he keeps them.

Kipper puts the gun down on the table. He prises open the top of the box to look at the bullets. Lloyd takes his chance to examine the gun. He picks it up and feels its weight. He presses on the trigger but there is no give. Patrick leans over to show him how the safety catch works.

'I can do it,' Lloyd says, brushing Patrick's hand away. He lifts the catch. He looks around the gym, aiming the gun first at the door, then at the big cupboard where Jacko keeps the boxing gloves, and finally at Patrick, sighting him through the two notches at either end of the short barrel.

'We could play Russian roulette,' Lloyd says, grinning.

'Don't be a pillock,' Kipper tells him. Kipper is rolling one of the bullets between his thumb and forefinger, absorbed in its shape and texture.

'Baggsy me first,' Lloyd says. The gun is still aimed at Patrick's head. Patrick watches him. Lloyd presses the trigger.

There is a dull, metallic click.

Lloyd laughs out loud. 'Ha ha, you're dead,' he says to Patrick.

They hear a second click. A latch. Their heads swivel round. A door is pushed open. Lloyd puts the gun on to the table, pushes it away from him.

Liam stands in the doorway.

'What do *you* want?' Kipper says. 'Clear off.'

Liam ignores him. 'Patrick,' he says, 'what are you doing here?'

'He's with us,' Kipper says. 'He's doing us a favour.'

Patrick has picked up the gun. He knows how to use it – Joe has shown him – but he has never fired it. He is curious about how it would feel to hold a gun. Somehow he has the right to pick it up. The boxing, the being hit, the standing in for Kipper, the almost staying upright for the length of the first round, completing the dare for Kipper – these things give him the right to pick it up. He wants to know what it feels like, even without ammunition, to hold the gun.

'What is that?' Liam says.

Patrick lines up the sights on top of the gun towards Lloyd.

Liam moves towards him.

'I told you to bugger off,' Kipper says. He stands up.

Patrick feels the curl of the trigger on his finger. He is curious – no more than this.

'Is that a real gun?' Liam says.

Patrick knows what it feels like for the gun to be aimed at him. Is it different to aim it back, or just the same? The same blank click? The same nothing? Does it feel different if you are the one pulling the trigger?

'Patrick, come on out of here,' Liam says.

Patrick is looking into Lloyd's face.

'Patrick?'

He pulls the trigger.

There is a small kick against Patrick's shoulder. What occurs to him in the split second after the squeezing of the trigger is how easy it is, how there is no mystery in the thing after all, how all Joe's wearisome routines and caveats when it comes to guns have been shown to be a smokescreen for something that in reality is unremarkable. It is a simple thing. It isn't like the priest saying mass, turning water and wine into the body and blood of Christ, performing tricks of that magnitude. It is ordinary. It is nothing.

The basement room explodes in noise. Lloyd is slammed backwards off his chair.

Kipper's face is the colour of butter. It has a fluid shape to it, as if the bones have been stripped from it.

The single, sudden sound has faded now. It has died into the old walls and is replaced inexplicably by silence once again. It is all over so soon, Patrick thinks. It's all back to where we were before the trigger was pulled with such a casual amount of force.

On the floor, Lloyd has the glassy eyes of a shot rabbit.

The main hospital car park was less than a quarter full in its weekend lull. Patrick parked up and helped Lillian out of the passenger side door. They stood together looking across at the line of the new wing being pieced together behind geometrical lines of scaffolding. The construction site itself and the builders' compound in front of it was fenced off to hospital staff and visitors by a perimeter of mesh fencing wedged into breezeblock feet. Patrick looked around and saw that there were several other people dotted around the car park. They were looking upwards, watching something.

There was a figure on the top of the new building. Patrick heard someone say that a man had been walking around up there. It couldn't be a workman, they knew, because it was Saturday and construction work had been halted for the weekend.

Patrick turned to Lillian. 'Is that him?'

Lillian, in her purple dress, was looking up towards where the man was.

'What am I supposed to do?' Patrick said. 'What does he want? Is he going to jump, Lillian? Did he say he might jump?'

'He said something's going to happen,' Lillian said.

'Did he say what?'

'He said it was going to be something wonderful.'

'He said . . . there's . . . is there somebody else up there with him? Are there people up there with him? Jesus, Lillian, what the hell does he think he's playing at up there?'

'What will you do?' Lillian asked.

'I'm going to get the stupid bugger down.'

Patrick walked up to the perimeter fence looking for a way in. He looked around, then began to edge his way towards the secured entrance to the builders' compound. There were notices fixed to the gates saying *No Unauthorized Personnel* and *Hard Hat Area*. There was also a piece of paper fixed to the wire mesh of the gate, flapping in the breeze. Patrick unfurled it. It was one of Liam's notes that Patrick had kept safe in the rosewood jewellery box. It said: '*Tasks are called superhuman when men take a long time to complete them*' – Albert Camus.

He reached for the padlock on the gate. The clasp swung free in his hand. He lifted it off and pushed open the gate. The compound was littered with piles of aggregate, tin drums, coils of yellow plastic piping. Bulldozers were parked up, stilled for the night. Skips were lidded and locked. Patrick moved forward cautiously, looking for a navigable route through the compound. Ahead of him he saw another note pinned to a length of piping. There was another one beyond that wedged on the lid of a metal drum, and another one beyond that on a skip. Each of the notes had been taken from the rosewood box. All of them were Liam's notes sent long ago to Patrick himself. They were marking the way.

When he reached the foot of the new wing itself he saw there was another note nailed to a door. There was another hard-hat symbol on the door. A sign said 'No Entry'. Patrick craned his neck up towards the roof five storeys above him.

'Liam! *Liam*! It's me. Can you hear me?'

His shouts were washed away by the distance and by the sounds of the passing traffic on the road running past the hospital.

Patrick pulled open the door and stepped inside. The cavernous shell of the new building's interior was cool and dark. Across the concrete floor the series of notes and cards continued, each of them held in place by pieces of breezeblock. Patrick followed them, occasionally stopping to fold back one of the pieces of paper to see which one it was. The path led him to the far end of the building and up a flight of bare concrete steps. He worked his way gradually up through four more flights until there were no more steps to climb. The partially completed flat roof was still above him.

'Liam! Where are you?'

There was no answer. There was another note pinned to the safety ring of a vertical steel ladder rising to the roof. Patrick read the note.

Pass here, you princes of hope.

'Liam?'

There was no answer. Patrick felt his shout fade and melt into the big space around him. He squeezed inside the frame of the ladder and started to climb. He could see out into daylight above the partially breezeblocked sides of the building. He could feel his palms begin to dampen with sweat. He told himself not to look down. He felt his pulse quickening in his chest. There was a line of what seemed at this height to be miniature cars on the road running past the hospital. His mouth was dry. There was a metal hatch above him over the top of the ladder. He had to push it open before he could climb out.

The final platform covered the two ends of the flat roof. The incomplete middle section of thirty feet was straddled by a series of evenly spaced horizontal steel girders running from one end of the new wing to the other. Patrick could see his brother standing on the edge of the other platform looking across at him. His brother was still wearing his long black coat and his preposterous white plimsolls. Patrick could see that there were other people standing behind his brother.

Through the gap between the platform where Patrick stood and the one on which his brother and the others stood he could see the ground ninety feet below. He moved a few feet closer to the edge and stopped. He looked across to his brother again. He looked at the others. Why were so many people standing behind his brother on top of a half-constructed building? Who were they? What were they doing here? One by one, as he adjusted to the situation, he began to recognize them. He saw Kenny, then Brenda. He saw Findlay Olonge. They were his residents. They were people who had been at the Limes. There were twenty or thirty of them. They did not seem panicked or distressed. They did not seem to have been brought up here against their will. They were passive, or perhaps they were merely quiet. They were waiting to see what would happen next. They were waiting for something wonderful.

'What the hell are you doing with all these people?' Patrick shouted. 'We need to get them all down. It's not safe up here.'

Saul shook his head. 'Can't do that.'

'Why not?'

'Something's going to happen,' Saul said.

'What's going to happen?'

'Something.'

'What are they doing here?'

'I asked them all to come. They wanted to come.'

'What for?'

'I told you, something's going to happen.'

'For God's sake, Liam, let's get them all down on the ground. Whatever it is you're planning to do, it shouldn't concern them.'

'You have to come across,' Saul said.

'You want me to come across to your side?'

'Yes.'

'If I come over there, will you let me take them down?'

'You can take them down, yes.'

'How do I get across? Is there another way up?'

Saul shook his head. 'You need to come across the girder.'

Patrick glanced at the pattern of girders connecting the two platforms.

'How did everyone else get up there?'

'They came up the ladder on this side, but the hatch is locked.'

'What do you mean, "locked"? Who locked it?'

'I did.'

Saul indicated behind him where the metal safety hatch had been dropped in place and wedged with breezeblocks to prevent it from being opened from below.

'What have you done that for?'

'Because something's going to happen.'

'This is crazy. You have to let me come over there before there's an accident. There are no walls up here. It's a sheer drop. Someone's going to go over the edge.'

'All you have to do is walk across,' Saul said calmly.

*

'All you have to do is say what happened,' the woman from the welfare office keeps saying.

Patrick is sitting alone in the reception room in the Big House. It is the room where boys wait before going in to see the superintendent. It is where welfare officials and prospective adopters wait. The walls of the room are yellow. There are magazines on the table for people to read while they wait. In a corner of the room is a compendium of wooden games to distract young orphans waiting to be received into Providence House. There is a single large painting hung in the room to relieve the monotony of the plain yellow walls. It is hung above the fireplace. In the painting, a boy is rowing a boat on a lake against a background of mountains in Switzerland with snow on their peaks. The sky in the painting is bruised purple, as if a storm might be due.

'Liam told us what happened,' the welfare officer has said. 'He told us that he shot Lloyd with the gun. When the superintendent and the policeman come in, we want you to tell us what you saw. We think you were there, too, but you're not the one in trouble. You're not the one who will be sent away. If you were thinking of covering up for your brother, it's too late now because he's already told us what happened. When they come in, you need to tell them the truth and then it will all be over for you.'

And Patrick waits. He looks at the painting over the fireplace. He doesn't know what has compelled the boy to row out alone on to the lake. He wonders if the boy can swim, and what will happen if the wind picks up, if the storm comes, if the boat is turned over into the water.

Patrick stood a stride away from the edge of the gap separating him from his brother and the others. The silver stubble was rooted on his brother's face. His cheekbones seemed more pronounced. His eyes looked bigger.

'I'm not walking across there. No way. Someone'd have to be mad to walk across there.'

Saul shrugged. 'I did it.'

Patrick hesitated. 'I didn't mean that.'

Saul suddenly walked out two steps on to the girder. He stood there, unmoving. In the gradually draining light it was as if he were hovering unsupported in the air. He was ninety feet above the ground.

'Oh, God,' Patrick said. He saw the space open up below his brother's feet. He felt the blood drain from his face. Saul himself seemed unconcerned. He took two steps backwards to the safety of his own platform.

Patrick understood that he needed to talk to his brother, to find some way of connecting with him, to bring him away from the precipice over which, perhaps, his mind was poised.

'I need to ask you something,' Patrick said. 'There's something I don't understand.'

'What's that?'

'I don't understand why you didn't ever come and see me.'

'I'm here now.'

'Why did you let me think you were dead all that time? Do you think I give a damn about the book? You think I care about a criminal record? Screw that. Screw all of that. Why did you let me think you were dead?'

Saul was watching the central girder closely, as if he expected it to do something.

'Because I am dead,' he said. 'You'll understand. One day you'll understand. I came back to save someone. That's all.'

'You're on a bloody building site five storeys up. What are you telling me, that you've brought the residents up here so you can save them?'

'No, not that. They're just here to watch. They have a stake in this.'

And he stepped out again on to the girder.

Patrick, unable to bear it, closed his eyes. When he opened them again his brother was back on the platform, grinning, but there was no joy in his smile.

It was then that Patrick understood. Eventually, tonight, his brother was going to step off, or fall off, and maybe even take some of the residents with him. Patrick had to get across. There was no other way of reaching him – of reaching them. At some point the police would arrive, alerted by one of the observers down on the car park, but that would be too late. That might even be the signal for some final lunatic gesture of his brother's.

Patrick looked at the girder. He tried to estimate its size. It was twice the width of his foot. It was doable. On the ground it would be doable. On the ground, he could walk across the girder nine times out of ten without overbalancing. He could do this on the ground. The gap between the two concrete platforms was thirty feet. There was no other way over there. The only way to get to his brother and the residents was to walk across the girder.

He stood on the edge. The drop to the ground was ninety feet. A minute passed. Then two. He felt the wind picking up around him and then suddenly falling away. The evening lights were starting to go on all around the city. Saul wandered away towards the edge of the roof, looking curiously down at the car park. He took out a handful of peanuts from a pocket and started to shell them.

'Come away from there,' Patrick pleaded.

'I'm fine. I wouldn't jump – honestly. Who'd feed the cat if I did? Besides, you can only die once and I've already died.'

Patrick stood facing the thirty feet between them across the girder. Another minute passed, and then another. Images locomotived through his head, one after another – of Karl Wallenda and Philippe Petit walking the wires; of Switzerland and dominoes and yellow walls; of Edward in his cell; of Little Lucy's body; of residents who, broken, lived the same repeated lives over and over; of Benedict, who'd killed himself; of Liam, who was not the King of Providence, who'd been in prison, who lived in dosshouses and thought he was an angel and had two dozen residents lined up with him while he shelled peanuts for an imaginary cat and dropped the shells casually over the edge of the precipice.

Patrick took off his jacket and let it fall to the ground without taking his eyes off the length of the girder.

'Look at me,' he shouted into the void. '*Look* at me!'

Saul glanced up from his handful of peanuts.

'You're Liam Shepherd,' Patrick shouted. 'You understand me. You're Liam.'

His brother shook his head sadly. 'Liam's dead,' he said.

'Listen to me. Liam! Listen! All you did was not become a writer. That's all. All you did was not write a book. You were still the fastest, the cleverest, the bravest. You were, you were . . . You could *fly*. I thought you could fly. You could do anything. You got away. You did things. Look at me. I'm still here – I got nowhere. I failed you and I got nowhere and I carried on failing and you didn't. You survived. You got away and you've seen places and it doesn't have to be like this. It doesn't, Liam. You can start again. Anyone can start again. You don't have to be like me.'

'You didn't fail anyone,' Saul said.

'They made me sit in the room. There were yellow walls. I wouldn't tell them what happened and they took you away in the van.'

'It doesn't matter, Patrick.'

'I wanted them to send me with you, but I didn't say it.'

Saul shook his head. 'You were better off where you were.'

'I wanted to be with you. I should have been with you. It was my fault.'

His brother's face filled out into a wide, uncorrupted smile. 'You know what saved him?' Saul said. 'It was you, turning up when they let you visit, when they drove you up there once a year from Providence House on Whit Sunday. You saved him. *You* saved him. You came up and he sat there on the other side of that Formica table and made up stories of what it was like, what a big adventure it was, of how they let him keep a cat.'

'I can't walk across there, Liam.'

'Yes you can.'

'I can't.'

'Besides, there isn't any other way to end this thing.'

Patrick was staring at the girder. He was breathing quickly. He was trying to forget about the line of ex-residents watching him in silence behind Liam. He was trying to find the space in his head to work out what to do.

'You're a madman, Liam Shepherd,' he said. 'A fucking madman.' And he moved forward, placed one tentative foot on the girder. As if he were checking that it was real, that it would take his weight. He rested it there. He looked down at the ground and his belly ripped and rose. The drop to the ground below was ninety feet. He had a sudden blinding impulse to run across it. He could be on the other side in a dozen strides that way, the same way Liam used to run across the rooftops of the world to collect the stories he brought back for Patrick. All of this could be over in a handful of seconds. He let the ball of his front foot on the girder take some part of his weight. He could feel the air running up in the gap between the two completed sections of the platform and jostling him. He was trying to think of nothing but his head was filled with Switzerland, and the boat was sinking and the boy was drowning. The walls were yellow. The walls are always yellow. He keeps looking at the walls and they are yellow and he is waiting for the superintendent to interview him but the superintendent is still in with the police, or with Liam. Patrick has been kept on his own in the waiting room in the Big House on his own for most of the day and he keeps looking at the yellow walls while he waits, and when his eyes move they fall on the domino bricks left out on the table by someone, because the only other thing to see apart from the dominoes and the yellow walls is the painting above the fireplace of the boy who is rowing across the lake. Mrs Joyce from the welfare office says it is Switzerland. She is being nice to him. It is Mrs Joyce who comes to see him and Liam once a year now that Mr Briffet has been promoted. Each time she comes into the room to check on him she says that the superintendent and the policeman aren't ready to see him yet. She says the mountains are the Swiss Alps. She says the boy isn't going to drown, he is just rowing across the lake. Each time the door opens and she comes in she says that Patrick should think about what he is going to say. She tells him that Liam has admitted what he has done. She says he has told them there was only Liam and Patrick in the room with Lloyd, that it was Liam's idea to get the gun, that it was Liam who fired the gun, that Patrick picked it up after that. Liam is probably going to be sent to a Borstal in Cumberland for what he has done. She says all the doors there are locked like in a prison. She says only bad boys go there. She says there is nothing Patrick can do now to save Liam. She says Patrick can only help himself now by telling the truth – that Liam had taken the gun and fired the shot. Each time she comes into the room to check on him, the turn of the handle pulls his eyes away from the yellow walls and the domino bricks, and he knows she is lying because the storm is going to come and the boat is going to capsize, and the boy is going to drown.

'Oh, fuck,' he says out loud. 'Oh fuck.'

His brain flashes with white light. He steps away from the girder back on to the concrete platform. He releases his caught breath. He tries to compose himself again. He stands there on the edge for another minute. Two minutes. Three minutes. He puts one foot out again on to the girder, lets it rest, then presses his weight slowly on to it. The evening breeze gusts and the drop to the ground is ninety feet.

Nothing else happens.

He looks over at his brother, at the silent chorus of faces beyond him. He is going to look at Liam all the way across.

He will look at Liam and walk across and then it will be done. He gazes steadily at Liam and swings his trailing leg out in front of him on the girder. The world rises up from the ground like a monster and rocks and shakes the narrow steel beam on which he is now balanced. He feels his body sway first one way and then the other as he overcompensates. Instinctively he holds his arms out to steady himself, to search for a balance, a middling point, a resting place, and he knows he is trapped in the moment and that the only way to end it is to reach the other side, and the only way through is to let everything else go, to cast all other baggage, all extraneous things, all thoughts, all histories aside, to make it step by step, beat by beat, towards the platform at the far end where his brother and the others wait for him.

He lifts his back foot slightly off the bar. He finds a balance, holds it, brings the back leg through, past the pivot of his standing leg, reaches with his foot for a plant on the bar just ahead of him. He rests it down. Three steps. He cannot allow himself to think ahead. He is a man with no future and no history. He is lost in the act, in its simplicity, its innocence. He must do this simple, possible, remarkable, human thing for ever, step by step, in this universal present in which he is cast free. He glances down. The drop to the ground beneath him is ninety feet. A million volts of panicked electricity surge in his chest, and the past and the future come crashing in at him like waves and suddenly he wants to go back but he doesn't know *how* to get back. One misplaced foot, one sway and he will die four storeys below after the fall. He clenches his fists on his held-out arms. He is frozen in fear. He is waiting for the fall. There is a kind of benediction here – this being found out, this cowardice on the wire, in front of people he was meant to save. Soon the fall will come and that will be the end. All he can do is wait for it, and so he waits.

'I can't do it,' he says. It is not a shout. Not a protest. It is a simple observation. He is not shouting because shouting will topple him. Shouting will be the start of the fall. He whispers it and he knows that, even though it is whispered, his brother – out there somewhere in the universe beyond the single living moment that exists for him on the wire – will hear him.

'You can do it,' his brother whispers back.

'No,' he whispers. 'No, I can't.' And his head is full of yellow and dominoes and Switzerland, and he is running after the van that is taking Liam as it moves down the path. He opens his mouth and howls. A bubble caught deep in his throat is dislodged, and the cry that he makes volleys out across the grounds. The sound becomes louder and more desperate – he is screaming now, but it is too late. The van reaches the junction beyond Joe Swift's cottage and turns into the road and pulls away with a grind of gears, and Patrick is banging on Joe's cottage for help. He knows that Joe is in because he can see the smoke from the log fire seeping patiently from the chimney, but Joe will not answer the door to him any more, will not respond to any more of the notes that Patrick thrusts at him or posts under his door pleading with him to explain that it wasn't Liam who fired the gun because now they have reached this stage they won't believe his changed story.

'Don't you get it, boy?' Joe has yelled at him. 'I don't *want* to be involved. It was *my* gun. *My* bullet. My job on a knife-edge. Who else is going to employ an epileptic?'

And then, somehow, Patrick is in the clearing. He is looking at the Jeep. Perhaps minutes have gone by, or hours, since the van left with Liam. He stands there for a long time. He keeps thinking of the boy rowing, of the storm in the mountains. Patrick picks up a stone and throws it in the direction of the tarpaulin sheet covering the Jeep. It misses. He throws another. This time it strikes the Jeep with a sudden, crisp *clack*.

He is crying silently now. He walks over to the Jeep and heaves the tarpaulin off. He scavenges for stones and throws them one by one. Sometimes they hit a door, a wheel arch, a tyre. He finds a pile of larger bricks in the undergrowth. He hurls them one at a time. They smack against the Jeep's side and ricochet off. He goes over to investigate the scarred bodywork. On the driver's seat is the box of spanners Joe has been using on the engine. Patrick picks out the longest one. Using both hands, he crashes it against the bonnet. It punches a shallow indent into the metal. He swings a second time, then a third. The metal bonnet sighs and cracks. He walks around the Jeep slowly, picking spots at which to aim his blows. He swings the head of the spanner into the bodywork for several minutes, breathing hard with the physical effort of destruction, when something causes him to glance up. Through the trees he sees Joe. He does not know how long Joe has been standing there watching him. Patrick looks down at the spanner in his hands. He drops it to the ground. He looks across again towards the trees. Joe does not say anything, does not signal, does not move. He stays there a moment longer, looking at the boy, then turns and walks away along the path in the direction of the coach house, and then Patrick cannot see him any more.

'You know how many times in our lives we are alive?' his brother whispers to him from somewhere. Patrick cannot see him, though he knows that he is there. He can only see the wire and how it stretches there ahead of him. There is only the wire, without a future or a past, but somewhere, somehow, there is Liam's voice.

'You know how many times, Patrick? Once? Twice? Three times, maybe. No more than that. We sleepwalk through our lives, most of us. We hide. We're not real people. We're not alive, except for the first moment when we suddenly realize we are in love, when our children are born, when the airplane hits turbulence and drops. All of us. Never on the wire. Never risking anything. But you, Patrick, you're on the wire every day. You've been on it all your life. You don't believe me? What are you thinking now? I know what you're thinking. You're thinking this is not so strange after all. You're thinking there's something familiar about trying to cross this wire. You know why? Because you've been crossing it your whole fucking life. Patrick, it's not your fault. It was an accident. What happened wasn't your fault. What happened to Benedict. To Edward. They weren't your fault. You think it's your fault what happened to Edward and Lillian? You think *she* thinks that? Come in off the fucking wire, Patrick. You've been out there long enough. Come home. We all failed, Patrick. We're all forgiven.'

Patrick isn't sure where the voice is coming from. He knows it is somewhere in his head but he can't locate it. He sees that his brother has produced the rosewood box. He sees him take out a clutch of papers – small squares, the kind he wrote things down on when each of the residents arrived at the Limes and told him what they wished for. Small talismans promising a normal life. IOUs from Patrick to the world. Saul moves amongst the people standing with him on the platform, passing out the pieces of paper, one for each person, until everybody is holding one. He leads them to the edge of the roof. They lean over. Patrick wants to cry out to them, to persuade them away from the edge, but he cannot because to cry out is to fall the ninety feet.

Saul offers some kind of signal. He is the first to release his piece of paper. The others follow, one by one at first, and then in clusters. A flock of small white silent birds takes flight – pieces of paper riding on the breeze, scattering, sweeping, dropping into the cathedral of space beneath. Patrick sees them fall and blow, sees them roll out on the wind. The names of all his residents; the wishes each of them had named; the measure of his failure. They fly like doves released over the city.

He breathes. There is him and the wire. There is this single moment. He clears himself. The drop to the ground is ninety feet. He feels for a middle point. He sacrifices it in lifting his back foot, readjusts, draws the leg forward and beyond him, adjusting, looking for the midpoint all the time. He moves in and out of equilibrium: planting his feet, steadying, resting, drawing, separate from the world, not knowing whether he is still alive, forgetful of the past, not knowing what has brought him here, not knowing what might lie ahead, knowing only this single moment, looking for the midpoint, finding an equilibrium in a line between his belly and his head, between the earth and the sky. Holding a peace inside himself.

He does this for ever, for an immeasurable period of time. He sits in the room for an immeasurable period of time. He sits amid the yellow and the dominoes and the Alps of Switzerland, and when the superintendent and the policeman and Mrs Joyce are there in the room with him, and he is holding the pencil Mrs Joyce has given him, Patrick stares at the painting over the fireplace of the boy about to drown in the lake and he says nothing, writes nothing, indicates nothing. Just watches the boy about to drown.

He has done this for all of his life. He has been crossing this wire for the whole of his life. He takes another measured step. He feels for the midpoint, holds it. And another. And another. And one final step. He stumbles, falls off on to the platform, somehow into his brother's embrace.

He wants to say something but when he speaks, instead of words, ghosts fly out of his mouth.

And so they clasp each other in silence.

They lay on their backs on top of the unfinished building facing the sky, surrounded by the gathering gloom of evening and a million sodium flares lighting the lines of the city streets below them.

'It was you,' Patrick said finally.

'What was me?'

'Halfway across, I understood why I could never find the quotation. *Pass here, you princes of hope*. It was you. The graffiti on the bridge all that time ago. When I quit selling the buffer pads. It was you.'

Saul said nothing.

'And those other times? When I thought someone was watching me. That sense I had?'

'You think you're alone with that? What d'you think Edward is thinking right now in his cell? What would you tell him if you could? That he's not as alone as he feared he was. We all fail, Patrick. We're all forgiven.'

'Do you remember teaching me how to star-float?' Patrick said.

'You think I should teach you again?'

They lay facing the sky on the concrete platform, star-floating on their backs, their arms outstretched, their legs relaxed, remembering the first time they had done it.

'The King of Providence.' Patrick laughed.

He looked across. His brother was smiling.

'It would have been a good book,' Saul said.

'Come back with me,' Patrick said. 'Stay at my house for a while. Get yourself settled. You never know, maybe you could have a go at writing something.'

'That's us,' Saul said. 'That's what we were.'

'What?'

'Kings of Providence.'

'Both of us?'

'Yes.'

'Kings of Providence.'

'And Princes of Hope.'

Patrick could feel his breathing growing steadier, slower, deeper. He could feel the companionship of his brother beside him, as if for once in his life he was in the right place. He felt as a man might feel if he had truly flown across the sky and somehow landed safely. And only later, as he led the residents down through the flights of steps and emerged back on to the building site, when he saw the crowd of people on the other side of the fence who had been drawn to watch the spectacle from the car park, when he was starting to guess at what came next, thinking what to say to people when they asked him, as they would, what had taken place up there on the roof, calculating for himself what those things meant, wondering whether Lillian was still waiting steadfastly in her purple dress at the car, only then when he looked back did he realize that his brother was not there.

Sarah was standing on the top level. She had traced a route across the compound and up through the building by following the line of markers – the pieces of paper, the postcards weighted down by pieces of breezeblock. She had stopped to read each one as she had climbed up through the five floors. She had emerged on to the open roof to find herself alone. The only sign that someone else had been there was a pair of battered plimsolls abandoned in the middle of the platform. She walked over to them and picked them up. They were Dr Vass's white size tens. They were the ones Saul had been wearing for the past eight days. She watched a man emerge on to the far section of the flat roof separated from hers by a line of girders. She watched him look around, across the space between the two platforms, and then notice her there standing alone, holding the plimsolls, one in each hand.

They faced each other.

'You're Patrick,' she said.

He nodded.

'I'm Sarah.'

She held out the plimsolls in her two hands as if she might be offering them to him – as if this was all that was left of the man they were both searching for. They stood there watching each other, working out what it was that had brought each of them to this place and this moment so high above the lit city.

10

ONE QUIET NIGHT

Patrick never saw him again.

There were moments, coming down again in twilight from the roof of the half-finished building, when Patrick expected him to emerge from the swell of people on the car park. There were times in the days after that when he thought he had glimpsed him in the city in a crowd of bobbing heads. There were weeks when he waited for Liam to call, when the phone would ring and Patrick was sure that this time it was him, or a call about him, but it never was. He could only wonder what it was that had drawn his brother back only for him to slip away again so soon. For Patrick, still landlocked, still tied to the place he had grown up in, he found it hard to see answers, and after a while he stopped looking for them.

In the years that followed, Patrick found a kind of accommodation with the world. He worked at achieving a settledness. He remained a private man, never truly at the heart of things. He was not assimilated. Now and then he would try to explain it to his wife. He was never very good at speaking out loud about these things. The necessary distance he needed to traverse from his inner life to the surface was almost too much, but she had a listener's art and understood his exile, and he came to feel this – almost physically – as a kind of blessing. It allowed him to fashion for himself the incomplete endings to the stories he had once wrestled to form, and the meanings they represented: the possible fates of his former residents, their lives flowering and falling, flowering and falling once more; the stepfather's arrest for Little Lucy's death, the incriminating DNA that trapped him and the confession that he had dumped the girl's coat in a park to throw the police off the scent; the realization that Edward must have found the bag and taken it home and, days later, out searching for Lucy with her coat in the bag in case she was cold when he found her, walked into the dipped beam of a cruising patrol car. Here were simple lessons to be learned, that redemption was never a finishing line but an acceptance of the incompleteness of things. Beyond that, it seemed, the narratives people built for themselves inevitably frayed and fell apart, and so men made and remade them in their heads like ants building towers from scraps of sand and dirt.

Little things and big things.

Every now and then Patrick mentioned his brother to someone, told them the tale. Eventually he came across a man who had worked on the *Evening News*, who explained about microfiche archives and who went back through them for him until at last he came across a reference to Liam Shepherd in Manchester more than a decade before. The article reported the conclusion of a court case.

A children's game of tag ended in tragedy when a seven-year-old girl was killed by a car in a hit-and-run accident. Katy Montague was playing outside her house with friends when, at 5.40 p.m., she was struck by a stolen Rover which had mounted the pavement at speed. The impact left Katy with multiple injuries while her eight-year-old friend suffered chest injuries and a broken wrist. The emergency services, who were called out by neighbours, found Katy being attended by her mother, 29-year-old Sarah Montague, who was said by one eyewitness to be inconsolable. Katy died despite treatment from staff at the local hospital where her mother works and where Katy underwent emergency surgery. She was pronounced dead four hours later. A neighbour giving evidence in court said, 'I heard a noise outside on the road. When I went out it was just carnage.'

The court heard that when Liam Shepherd handed himself in to police three days later he still had a significant level of alcohol in his bloodstream. Shepherd was reported as being of no fixed abode and had previously been deported from the United States following a series of minor drug offences after living there for a number of years. Katy's parents, who have stayed away from court throughout the trial, elected to be absent once more on the final day when Shepherd was found guilty of manslaughter. Following the verdict he was sentenced to eight years in prison and was banned from driving for life.

The night he knocked down the girl who was playing on the pavement was the night that he died. He went to prison, was released, eventually turned up at the hospital's GUM department, reappeared briefly in his brother's life, but by then he was already dead.

I'm not Liam. Liam's dead. My name is Saul.

The parcel that was eventually found on top of the wardrobe in the room at the Limes had the words 'For Patrick' written on it. Someone remembered that the place had formerly been run by a Patrick Shepherd and took the time to track him down. The manuscript ran to barely thirty pages. It was entitled *The King of Providence*. It was the story of a man who had wanted to be a writer but who was haunted by demons; how the only story he was truly successful in creating was the one he composed over thirty years for his distanced brother in a series of posted notes. There was no ending; there was merely a last paragraph consisting of a single word imprinted in the middle of the page, seeming to hang there in the space of the otherwise blank sheet – *Sarah*. It had been banged out on a manual typewriter. The strike of the characters had bruised the surface of the paper. The 'a's were slightly twisted and sunken just below the horizontal line formed by the other letters.

Until one quiet night when Patrick woke up and shook his wife.

'You're crying,' she said.

'I smelled violets,' he told her. 'Liam's dead.'

Sarah held him while he sobbed.

'How do you know he's dead?' she asked.

'I told you,' Patrick said insistently. 'I smelled them. That means he died.'

Eventually, Sarah put on her dressing gown and went downstairs to put the kettle on. Patrick stood at the darkened window looking out into the garden. After a while he moved across to the wardrobe and from the back of the shelf reached for an envelope. He pulled out the photograph from inside and stood looking at the young man snapped long ago in the Brooklyn diner. It would always lie between the two of them, this knowledge, this uncleansable stain, that it was Liam who was at the wheel of the car that night. But men and women since the birth of time have carried unbearable sorrows on their backs, and somehow the act of carrying such burdens across the landscape from one day to the next can sometimes make them bearable. Patrick turned over the photograph. On the back, written in pencil, was the definition of providence. It was the one that Benedict had long ago looked up for him at his interview at the Limes. Benedict had scrawled it down for him at the time on the back of the menu from the Brooklyn diner on which Liam had written the name of his book. When the picture of his brother had arrived in the post from America in the apparent aftermath of his death, Patrick had been moved to write the definition out on the back of the photograph. He read it again now. 'The foreseeing protection offered by God or by some other force. From the Latin *providentia* – to have foresight.'

He put the photograph back in the envelope and pushed it back on the high shelf in the wardrobe. Downstairs, he could hear the simple sounds of his wife in the kitchen making tea. Outside, the garden was so faint it seemed barely to be there. He stood looking out at the trees made insubstantial as ghosts by the night, waiting for Sarah to come back upstairs, and with the smell of violets still clear in his head he recognized at last the narrative his brother had constructed. Standing at the window, he understood that everything Liam had done on his return had been in the cause of the story he was forming, the strands he was drawing together. Patrick saw that he himself had calculated nothing, discovered nothing, that Liam had not intended him to. After the hit and run, it was Liam who had confirmed his own death in the days before he had surrendered himself to the police – perhaps even sending the letter to America and having someone forward the envelope on to Patrick along with the rosewood box. In the months after his release, he had entwined himself in Patrick's life and in Sarah's. He had rescued them both, and he had, in the end, seen the possibility of a shared life for the two of them. He had brought them together finally on the scaffolding – deliberately, inevitably – with Sarah clutching a pair of Vass's battered plimsolls and Patrick scouring the building site for his vanished brother. He had composed his own *King of Providence* across the streets and spaces of the city he had briefly returned to, and then walked quietly away as any author, in the end, walks away.

For all of his life, when Patrick had thought of his brother he had pictured him writing stories on creamy paper in an apartment in a tall New York building with long windows looking out on the East River with the sun flashing brilliant and clean on the water. He had imagined Liam in half-empty diners dreamily plotting lines in his head as waitresses, oblivious and forgiving, served lunches and bagged take-outs at the counter. He had seen Liam somehow perched, mid-afternoon, on top of the Brooklyn Bridge tower – as photographers sometimes did to capture Manhattan's bulk from the Brooklyn shore three hundred feet up, seeing the bridge striking out across the water half a mile away; the Woolworth Building, the US Courthouse, the Empire State in the distance, the Staten Island ferry terminal down at the bottom of the island. But in the months and years after his brief reappearance as Saul, this remembrance of his brother became something different. Patrick would still imagine Liam with the gift of flight, still moving between skyscrapers, standing lookout on tall harbour bridges as ocean ships slipped heart-stoppingly by, but his flight now seemed to signal not a strength but a form of brokenness. It was the curse of someone seeking a refuge he could not find. It was the image of a man condemned to wander these places alone and separate.

He thought he heard a sound. He looked around. He moved away from the window and went to look. He stood in the doorway of the bedroom across the landing. He watched his son shifting restlessly, asleep, oblivious to the darkness. He went over to him and leaned down. He pressed the palm of his hand slightly against the exquisite, simple line of the boy's back, feeling his warmth through the cotton pyjamas of his thin, tough body.

Sarah brought tea. They drank it propped up in bed in the shadows of the night. He explained again about the violets. The clocks made no sound and did not move.

'I love being with you,' he said. There was no reply. When he looked around he saw that her eyes had closed. Gently, Patrick lifted the half-filled cup of tea that was balanced in her lap and put it aside.

He lay in the darkness afterwards with his body spooned against hers, with his hand on the flesh of her full thigh, feeling the rise and fall of her body in settled sleep. All her life she has wanted to dance with a man at night to Sinatra ballads in her kitchen, and one day soon he will do this – walk in from work with wine and a Sinatra CD and a look of hopelessness on his face that signals an invitation to dance amid the fixtures and fittings of their ordinary evening. When they drive somewhere he navigates for her; in return she names the stars in the sky for him. And sometimes he will go to watch her swim. He is not comfortable in the water himself but, sitting high in the rafters of some anonymous municipal pool, with the light bouncing off the walls of polished tile and his son nestled beside him, he is happy to worship her diligence, the steady strokes, the accrual of lengths, the way she smiles unselfconsciously at nothing in particular when she climbs fresh from the water, and the beauty in her face that she has won, that this unexpected life has bequeathed to her.

Acknowledgements

My thanks go to a number of people who were generous with their time in talking both on and off the record about their work in health, social work, policing and immigration.

I am particularly grateful to Terry Mortiboy, whose experiences as a boy provided much of the background for the fictional Providence House.

About the Author

Photo: Steven Greenwood

Paul Wilson lives in Lancashire. He has worked in a range of social care settings and is Vice Chair of the British Association for Supported Employment. In 1997 he won the Portico Prize for Literature for *Do White Whales Sing at the Edge of the World?* His other novels include *Noah, Noah* and *Someone to Watch Over Me.*